"One-night stands are meant to be *un*complicated."

"What we had—*have*—is not a one-night stand. It's not a two-night stand, or even a three. What we have is different...I don't know how it is, or why. But I suspected it when I first laid eyes on you, and the more time we spend together, the more I know...it just *is*."

She tilted her head away from his touch. "It's because I'm your job."

"No. It's *you*. It's because I've never met anyone like *you* before and I'm pretty sure that I'm not going to again. And it's because I can't get you out of my head, and a huge part of me doesn't want to."

Elle let her eyes drift closed, hoping the break in eye contact would dampen the effect of his words, but she had no such luck.

"Look at me." Trey softly coaxed them open again. One second, she worked to fight the pull, and the next, she was on his lap. "The ship *Uncomplicated* has already sailed, sweetheart. It is so damn far out to sea, Poseidon himself can't track it. Get complicated with me, Elle. What do we have to lose?"

Everything.

ACCLAIM FOR
APRIL HUNT'S NOVELS

HEATED PURSUIT

"Smartly balances slow-burning passion and explosive high-stakes danger. This book kicks off an adventure-packed romance series, and readers will eagerly anticipate the next installment."

—Publishers Weekly

"4 stars! Fast paced and intriguing."

—RT Book Reviews

"Fun and sexy."

—SmexyBooks.com

"April Hunt creates a sexy, thrilling, action-packed story with *Heated Pursuit*. I could not put this book down."

— JoJoTheBookaholic.blogspot.com

"A fantastic, fast-paced, and well-developed debut! A hot alpha saving a feisty woman...what's not to love?"

—Sidney Halston, *USA Today* bestselling author

"Heat, humor, and heart-pounding action! I couldn't turn the pages fast enough!"

—Annie Rains, *USA Today* bestselling author

HOLDING
FIRE

ALSO BY APRIL HUNT

Heated Pursuit

HOLDING
FIRE

APRIL HUNT

FOREVER

NEW YORK   BOSTON

Copyright © 2017 by April Schwartz
Cover photography by Claudio Marinesco
Cover design by Elizabeth Turner
Cover copyright © 2017 by Hachette Book Group, Inc.

Forever
Hachette Book Group
1290 Avenue of the Americas, New York, NY 10104
forever-romance.com
twitter.com/foreverromance

First Mass Market Edition: March 2017

Forever is an imprint of Grand Central Publishing. The Forever name and logo are trademarks of Hachette Book Group, Inc.

The publisher is not responsible for websites (or their content) that are not owned by the publisher.

The Hachette Speakers Bureau provides a wide range of authors for speaking events. To find out more, go to www.hachettespeakersbureau.com or call (866) 376-6591.

ISBNs: 978-1-4555-3948-2 (mass market), 978-1-4555-3949-9 (ebook), 978-1-4789-4117-0 (audiobook, downloadable)

Printed in the United States of America

OPM

10 9 8 7 6 5 4 3 2 1

To Mom—the reason that I've become the strong,
independent woman that I am today

ACKNOWLEDGMENTS

So many people go into the process of writing a book, and it starts at home. My children remind me every day that there isn't a limit on what you can do—and that when faced with a challenge, you should only try that much harder. To my family, who've supported me and showered me with encouragement from the time I said, "I want to write a book": Thank you for believing in me!

Sarah E. Younger, my southern-belle agent with a spine of steel. You're my champion, my listening ear, my dream-maker, and sometimes, my therapist. There's no way I could navigate all this without you. I'm so glad that I have you in my corner every step of the way! Go #TeamSarah!

Madeleine, my patient, soothing editor—you have a habit of reading my mind even though we're hundreds of miles apart, and I'm so glad that I have you on my side, loving my characters as much as I do. Thank you to *everyone* at Forever. You're all amazing, from the beautiful covers you design to the support you give through social media.

ACKNOWLEDGMENTS

Ever since I picked up my "pen," I've met so many wonderful, supportive people. People whom I've met online have become real, truly amazing friends—like my #girlswritenight crew—Tif Marcelo, Rachel Lacey, Sidney Halston, and Annie Rains. Our late night nudges are the best. You ladies rock!

To my beta readers for *Holding Fire*, Leslie and Nicole—thank you so much for taking time out of your own busy writing schedules to help me mold Elle and Trey into who they are today.

And thank you to my readers...for Alpha-ing Up and joining me—and my characters—on this wild ride.

HOLDING
FIRE

CHAPTER ONE

A quick tinge of panic held Elle Monroe's breath hostage. Her gaze shifted from the masculine, tattooed arm draped over her waist to the door on the other side of the dimly lit room—a ten-foot distance. Maybe fifteen.

It might as well have been a mile-long obstacle course complete with rotating floorboards and mud pits when it came to crossing the distance without detection. And that was exactly what needed to be done—and sooner rather than later. Once she got back to her own hotel room, she could figure out why it had taken her nearly thirty years to experience the best sex of her life.

With a ridiculously sexy stranger.

In a rural Thailand bar.

To be more accurate, the sex happened in Trey's room *above* the bar, repeatedly and with such vigor that her face flushed with each mental replay of the last six hours. Mouths. Hands. Naked, sweaty bodies. He'd worn her out to the point that she'd passed out cold—and woken up feeling way too trapped for comfort.

"Trying to plot the best escape route?" a deep voice rumbled behind Elle's shoulder, low and husky with the perfect amount of gravel thrown into the mix. Trey With-No-Last-Name drew her deeper into his embrace until her back met his massive wall of a chest. "I heard your breathing change so I know you're awake. Are you going to answer my question or keep pretending you're sleeping?"

"No. Yes. I mean...*crap*." Elle's heart climbed higher into her throat. *This is what happens when you develop a rebellious streak seventeen years past puberty*.

"No, you're not escaping; yes, to feigning sleep; and crap to answering questions? Is that what you're saying or am I not following at all?" His mouth brushed against the curve of her neck, conjuring a trail of goose bumps.

Between his spicy musk filling her head and the brush of his morning wood against her left butt cheek, Elle didn't know what she was saying anymore. It was as if her mouth wasn't attached to her brain.

Trey skated his wide-palmed hand over her hip and gently guided her onto her back.

Don't look. Don't look.

She looked.

Propped up on one forearm and staring down at her, Trey granted her the prime opportunity to ogle every hill and valley of his impressive body. And it was definitely impressive. His chest, broad and covered with just the right amount of hair, couldn't have been sculpted more perfectly if done by an artist. Covering his right shoulder and arm, a colorful sleeve of tattoos contrasted his bed-rumpled short blonde hair in a sexy, bad-boy-meets-golden-boy combination.

Wicked intent gleamed from the emerald depths of his

eyes, and when his attention momentarily dropped to her mouth? Forget it. The man could cause an epidemic of wet panties with a five-second glance. Not even her ex-fiancé had affected her on such a primal level. Of course, James Worth didn't do *a lot* of things, including travel anywhere that didn't have a five-star hotel with a masseuse on speed dial. That, along with an arm's length of other reasons, was why they never would've worked.

"Look...Trey." Elle winced at the movie-script cliché about to come out of her mouth. "Last night was nice. Really, it was, but—"

"Nice?" Trey's lips twitched with a forming grin. "Damn. You really know how to inflate a man's ego, don't you?"

"Somehow I don't think you need help in that department."

He traced the ridge of her collarbone. "Maybe not, but last night was a hell of a lot more than *nice*. It was fan-fucking-tastic."

Well, that was a different way to say incredible. And he was right. It *was* a lot more. She supposed if a woman was going to have sex with a stranger, it should at least be memorable, and Trey definitely ensured that. But in the light of a new day, she needed to get back to her regularly scheduled life—or as much of it as she was willing to resurrect.

"Look, I get it," he said first, stopping her upcoming platitude by palming her cheek. "When I came to Thailand, I sure as fuck didn't expect to meet—much less take to bed— a gorgeous blonde, but I did, and it was—"

"Fan-fucking-tastic?" Elle repeated his earlier sentiment.

His intense green eyes flashed. "Exactly. So why do I get the feeling that you're itching to make a break for the door?"

Because she was.

Ever since she'd wiped her hands of the nonsense back

home—specifically, with James and her father—she'd vowed not to get invested in any one man or relationship. That meant no planning romantic futures. No dating. And no falling asleep after fan-fucking-tastic sex—except she'd already broken that rule, and the consequence was literally staring her in the face.

Elle gripped the starchy bedsheet to her chest like a flotation device and slid out of the bed. "I've got to go."

Trey's blonde eyebrows shot up. "Wait. Seriously?"

"Seriously. I have a best friend to assure that I'm not lying dead in a ditch somewhere and a plane to catch." She expertly avoided direct eye contact with the man, who was watching her every move as she tucked a found shoe beneath her arm. "I'm sure you know how this kind of thing goes."

"Yeah, I do," Trey agreed in a slow drawl, "but I never thought *I'd* be the recipient of the morning dodge."

"I guess there's a first time for everything."

Trey slowly rose from the bed, as naked and proud as when they'd fallen into it hours ago. The man really was gorgeous from top to bottom. Elle's gaze strolled lazily up from his muscled legs and over his perfectly chiseled abs. Before him, she'd lumped men with countable abs right up there with flying purple unicorns.

Trey caught her admiring glance. His mouth slid into a naughty grin as he reached for his pants and pulled them on—sans boxers. "I'm sure it happens to some guys, but not to me."

Elle rolled her eyes despite the fact that it was probably true, and resumed her clothing search. "I'll consider it an honor to be your first because as soon as I find my panties, I'm going to be on my way."

"You mean these?" Her polka-dot bikini briefs hung from the end of his finger.

"Yes, those." She grabbed the dangling panties, but before she stepped back, his tattooed arm slinked around her waist and brought her flush against his sweat-dampened body.

"What do you think you're doing?" she asked, her voice going breathy. *Dammit*...why did this man make her feel like she was walking a high-wire? "Seriously, Trey. I need to get out of here."

"Why?"

His question took her by surprise. Following her breakup with James, Elle had had exactly two brief flings— one during a crazy, best-friend-sponsored beach vacation nearly immediately post-breakup; the other a temporary benefits arrangement with one of the clinic doctors. They had enjoyed each other's company and then parted ways. No sleeping. No cuddling. No overdrawn conversations. And neither of them had ever asked *why*.

"Why what?" she asked carefully.

"Why are you running out of here like the building's on fire?" Trey clarified.

"Why is knowing so important to you? Or are you just upset that I beat you to the punch?"

Trey's mouth tightened into a thin line. Sore spot touched. "Yeah, I've had sex. A lot it. And I'm not going to deny that I've participated in my fair share of morning dodges. Actually, it used to be pretty fucking routine."

"You don't need to explain anything to me. Honest."

"I really think I do—because I'm trying to tell you that I haven't been that man for a while now. I'm fucking routine-less."

Elle gave his chest a reassuring pat and prayed her forced smile didn't broadcast the nerves flipping her stomach upside down. "It's sweet of you to try to paint what happened here as something more than it was, but I came upstairs with you without any kind of expectations."

"Then I guess that makes one of us."

His stern tone took Elle by surprise. Most men would've sunk to their knees in relieved gratitude that their latest one-night stand wasn't going to turn into a clingy stalker, but Trey almost looked...pissed.

She shimmied from his hold and nearly tripped over her feet in a world-record rush to collect the rest of her belongings. Then, finally dressed and more than ready to get back to reality, she turned and nearly came nose-to-chest with Trey.

"Jesus. What are you, a freaking ninja?" Elle asked, startled.

He'd gotten closer without her realizing, his laser-beam stare drilling into her from inches away. When he took a step closer, she reflexively took one back, and they repeated the dance until her back hit the wall.

Her heart pounded in her chest, but not in fear. Even after only twelve hours together, she knew he wouldn't hurt her. He leaned into her space until his muscled arms caged her in. Heat radiated off him in waves, and her body soaked it up, wanting to fall back into bed with him in the worst way. That intensity was what had drawn her to him in the first place; ironically, it was also what fueled her need to escape.

Trey brushed his lips down the curve of her neck as he spoke, the sensation making her work to fight off a whimper. "If your plan is to walk away and not look back, why not stick around and enjoy it a little longer?"

Because of her sanity. After hours in his company, she didn't know the difference between left and right, and probably wouldn't even if she held both hands out in front of her to look for the magic "L."

"Because I really do have a plane to catch." She plied him with the half-truth.

Her first six-month assignment as head nurse for the medical relief outfit Caring Hands had come to an end, and it was time to figure out what came next. Most likely it would be another community in need, but until the orders came across her desk, it was girl-time with her best friend.

"Elle." Trey's soft murmur was interrupted by the inward burst of the room's lone window.

Shards of glass and wood chunks rained down on their heads. Shouts echoed from the busy street outside. More things crashed. And then a Mack truck knocked Elle to the ground.

Breathless and dazed, it took a second to realize the Mack truck was Trey's half-naked body... and to recognize the rolling *tap-tap*s coming from the busy street below.

"Is that—" she started to ask.

"Gunfire," Trey grumbled. "Stay here."

He returned to his feet, moving with a speed that shouldn't have been possible for a man his size. Back against the wall, he skirted the room's perimeter until he neared the broken window.

Her eyes nearly bugged out of her head. "What the hell are you doing? Are you freaking *crazy*? Stay down!"

"*You* stay down, Elle. I mean it. Don't fucking move." He looked out to the street and cursed under his breath before producing a cell phone from his pants pocket. After one press of a button, he was talking to someone on the other end, but thanks to a new series of gunshots, only every fourth word or so reached her ears. When he finished the call, she was just climbing to her feet.

He picked up her dropped purse and tucked it back into her arms. "We're going to get you out of here. Do you have your passport with you or is it back at your hotel?"

"It's with me, but—"

"Good. Then we'll get you on the next bus out of town."

Leaving sounded better by the minute, but Elle didn't take directives well, probably because she'd lived her whole life being subjected to them. "I don't know how you were raised, but I'm not leaving my best friend to deal with whatever's happening out there by herself. Besides, who died and made you my travel agent?"

Agitation flashed in his green eyes. This time when her back hit the wall, she wasn't so sure what he'd do.

The rigid angle of his jaw flexed with tension. "I appointed myself your travel agent when trigger-happy yahoos drove into town and started shooting the place up. Are you seriously going to fight me on this, sweetness?"

"Are *you* seriously going caveman on me, *sweetness*?"

"If that's what it's going to take to make sure you're safe, then yes. I'll pull my club out of the fucking closet and throw your sweet ass over my shoulder—whatever it takes."

The door to the room burst open, nearly cracking in half. Trey was in front of her in an instant, blocking her from the giant man standing in the doorway. Head-shaven and mountainous with tattoos decorating both arms, he looked mean, lethal—and armed.

Only when the stranger registered Trey's presence did he lower his gun, and just barely. "What the fuck, man? You in here napping while shit's going down?"

"What exactly *is* going down?" Trey asked.

"Hell if I know." The two men's familiar banter did little to comfort Elle when Trey's friend slipped his attention her way. He scanned her from head to toe and back, taking in her very bed-rumbled appearance, and gave the barest of headshakes. "It's a fucking epidemic."

"Shut it, Vince," Trey growled. He shifted his stance, the move showcasing the gun clenched in his hand.

Well, crap.

While both men were distracted, she shimmied past the walking mountain. "I've obviously stumbled into something here, and you two look like you need time alone to talk, so I'm going to make myself scarce."

"Elle, wait," Trey barked.

"Thanks for everything. It was fun."

"Elle!" Something thudded to the floor, making Trey curse, "Damn it, stop!"

"Bye!"

"Stop!"

No way in hell was she stopping. She moved faster, flying down the stairs as if wings were attached to the heels of her sneakers. Hitting the deserted bar below, she navigated her way through the empty tables and out the back door. The echoing gunshots sounded farther away than they had a few minutes ago, but she stayed watchful as she hustled down the street toward the marketplace.

No one seemed concerned about the happenings a few blocks down. Crowds converged on busy vendors, some people stopping to haggle over the price of produce and handmade jewelry while others briskly walked as if on a special mission. Elle politely slipped away from an overzealous man attempting to unload his recently caught octopus, and wove through the throng of people toward the first empty alley—except it wasn't really empty.

Her gaze landed on the wide-eyed, frightened face of the old Thai merchant first—and then she saw the gun pointed mere inches from his head. Elle skidded to a stop. Her foot smacked into a discarded tin can and the gun-owner snapped to attention. His sharp blue eyes immediately locked in on her, giving her her first glimpse at the puckered scar bisecting his left brow and cheek.

"Elle! You need to wait!" Trey's voice shouted from down the street.

She glanced over her shoulder to see Trey and his friend winding their oversized bodies through the crowd of shoppers—run up toward her. Alley Man or Trey. Neither option gave her the warm fuzzies, but she'd pick a one-night stand reunion over an armed gunman any day.

"Don't you fucking move," Alley Man growled as if sensing her decision.

He swung his gun in her direction just as a local driving a bicycle cart pedaled in front of her. Elle didn't need an engraved invitation to move her rear end. She turned and half-ran, half-walked back through the market and toward the other side of the village.

Ten minutes and limp-noodle legs later, she finally slipped into her hotel room—with no Alley Man and no Trey on her heels.

Shay stepped out from the small corner kitchenette, relief written all over her face. "There you are! I was about five minutes away from calling the Thai police! You were supposed to text me every hour so I knew that Hunkalicious didn't throw you into a trunk or somehow convince you to be his drug mule."

Shay braced her hands on her ample hips and waited for a response that Elle couldn't seem to conjure. Since college, Shay Whitney had been single-handedly responsible for every drunken, free-spirited decision Elle had ever made—except she hadn't been drunk last night. Hell, she'd barely finished her single beer before brazenly propositioning Trey back at the bar.

Misreading Elle's silence, Shay's full lips broke into a sly grin. "Please tell me you can't talk because your throat's raw from some astronomical number of orgasms. And even if that isn't the case, lie to me and tell me it is."

It wouldn't be a lie. Elle had definitely lost count. But instead of rehashing the evening with her friend as she would normally do, she shook her head. "Sorry. I should've just come back here with you."

Shay's shoulders slumped, her face crestfallen. "Well, damn. He had that look, you know? I guess just because a man has hands the size of dinner plates doesn't mean he knows how to use them for the good of womankind."

"Definitely," Elle agreed, knowing that Trey could no way be lumped into a group with the sexually clueless. Not only had he thrown her off guard, but he'd been the only man who'd ever made her lose her orgasm count.

And she didn't understand why her first instinct was to keep that information to herself.

CHAPTER TWO

Trigger-happy kids with toy guns. That was the reason the locals gave for the chaos two hours ago that had left an entire neighborhood in a blind panic. Trey Hanson, former Delta and current Alpha operative, knew it for the unlikely story it was.

Toy guns didn't shake the ground or break glass windows, and they sure as fuck didn't peg bullet holes into brick-and-mortar buildings. As quick as the chaos had erupted, it disappeared, leaving no trail to the responsible party—or to a petite blonde who'd been in his bed minutes before the hail and brimstone broke out around them.

He and Vince had scoured the area for Elle for close to an hour before lighting up the bat signal that brought the rest of the team. Then they'd combined their efforts and searched for another goddamned hour with nothing to show for it.

No trail. No Elle. And no clue how he'd been given the slip by one lone woman.

A civilian.

A nurse.

And according to the file open in front of him, the woman he and his team had been sent to Thailand to protect.

Trey stared down at the photograph in his hand, barely suppressing a long list of expletives that would've had his mother reaching for Paddington the Paddle. He blinked, rubbed his eyes, and stared down at the image again. Nope. Didn't fucking change.

Despite the double-stranded pearls and sophisticated updo, the woman peering up at him from the eight-by-ten glossy photo was most definitely the one whose ass he'd watched run away from him a short time ago. The only difference was that the woman in the picture looked like she belonged on the red carpet while *his* Elle wore cotton from head to toe and pulled her hair into one of those sexily messy ponytails he loved sinking his fingers into.

Two different images, the same damn woman.

Elle Monroe—the daughter of the man who hired them.

His boss, Sean Stone, didn't have a formal rule about mixing business and pleasure, but that didn't mean there wasn't an unspoken one. And then Trey had his own. Blurring the fucking boundaries was a shit-storm waiting to swallow you whole and spit you back out onto a dung heap. He didn't do it—except that he had last night. And this morning. Hell, he wished he was upstairs *still* doing it.

Trey transferred his scowl toward the head-shaven former SEAL who'd given Elle a mode of escape.

Vince Franklin's mouth twitched, the small move practically an earsplitting smile for the Man of Brood. "Don't look at me like I killed your fucking poodle, man."

"How the hell do you want me to look at you?" Trey demanded.

"Like I was the only one who came to check on your sorry ass."

Trey tossed Elle's photo back onto the personnel file and grunted. "Why the hell are we only getting the assignment details now, when we've been in this godforsaken town for three damn days?"

Vince shrugged. "You want to tear someone a new asshole, start clawing away at Ortega's. Rafe was the one who sent us down here before the ink was even dry on the assignment papers."

"I already did, and he claimed the operation was time sensitive. They couldn't chance us being in travel-limbo. They needed our boots firmly on the ground."

"Then there you go. Besides, it's not like anyone could've expected your gut instincts seeking out our care package before we even got the full details—and by 'gut instincts,' I mean your dick."

Trey's displeased snort made both Vince and Logan, Alpha's resident sniper and all-around good ol' Southern boy, chuckle. *Assholes*, the both of them. Charlie Sparks, the fourth man—*er*, woman—on their operational team sat tucked between them, her nose buried in her laptop as she attempted to find the whereabouts of Elle Monroe. Without warning, she took both hands off the keyboard and biffed Vince and Logan on the back of their heads.

"What the hell was that for, English?" Rubbing his head, Vince shot her a glare.

"For making fun of Trey while he's obviously having a bloody moment. It's not his fault that the male species have two brains, and it's the smaller one that usually wins out. It's like embedded genetic code."

"I'm not having a moment," Trey grumbled in his own defense. "And I take offense to you implying that I make decisions with my dick."

Charlie smirked. "I never said anything about your goods, Hanson."

No, but it had been implied. And once upon a time, he *did* let his dick lead him around like he was a show-pony in a parade. Hell, it had been fun—in his twenties. Now, at thirty-four, going home alone—or with a different woman each weekend—had lost its appeal. And seeing his best friend and pseudo-sister's happiness confirmed what he'd already started realizing himself—that he wanted what Rafe and Penny had.

He wanted lazy mornings in bed—with the same woman. He wanted secret smiles and shared jokes. He wanted someone in his life that he'd lay down his life for—besides his family and the bastards he called brothers.

Maybe that made him the caveman Elle had called him; he wasn't sure. What he *did* know was that the second he and Elle had locked gazes, he'd experienced that protective tug in his gut that had him searching behind her sultry smile and come-hither stare. His need to get her into his bed had come later, albeit not by much.

And now, not only was he not buried balls-deep inside her sweet little body, but he sure as hell wasn't protecting her either. She was roaming Thailand without any fucking protective detail…because of *him*.

"Where the fuck would she have gone?" Trey had no one to blame but himself, but it didn't mean he couldn't be pissed about it.

Logan covered a chuckle with a cough. "You know what would make finding her easier? If you'd taken the time to ask where she's staying."

"That didn't really come up in conversation."

Charlie cocked up a single blonde eyebrow and paused in her typing to shoot him a glare. "You're bloody lucky you're sitting across the table right now or you'd be getting clobbered in the head too."

Trey didn't doubt it. The British analyst held her own in their all-male outfit, showing them every day that she was a lot more than a smart brain, pink-tinged hair, and a few half-hidden tattoos. Though not a full-fledged operative yet, it was only a matter of time before she wore Stone down enough to give her a true shot.

He nodded toward the laptop. "Find her now. Maim me later. The medical clinic director said Elle and her friend headed into town for a little R&R before heading back to the States, and it's not like this place is tourist central. There's only so many places they could be."

Heads swiveled as the outer bar door squeaked open and four men walked into the building. All large, all menacing, they scanned the room, their alert awareness labeling them as some kind of military, despite their civilian dress. And then there were the unsightly bulges where they'd made a poor attempt to conceal their weapons.

Ten to nil odds they weren't toy fucking guns.

Charlie pulled her hat low over her brow, and Vince leaned on his elbows to block the better side of her face. They settled into the relatively dark corner of the bar. And waited.

The front man of the small group beckoned to the bar owner behind the counter. The Thai man rushed over and the two had a quiet conversation that looked pretty peaceful until the new arrival yanked the old man up to the tips of his toes.

Charlie went stiff in her seat.

"Easy," Trey murmured.

"Aren't we going to *do something*?" she hissed.

"Not unless we have to." Having a public tango with these four definitely wasn't on the day's list of things to do. They had enough wrinkles in this op to iron out; they didn't need to blow a big-ass hole in it too.

As suddenly as he'd lifted the old man onto his toes, the gang leader released his hold. For the first time, Trey got a good look at the wicked, three-inch scar on the left side of his face.

The bastard didn't look right. His nose was a bit too broad, a slight indentation on the bridge indicating it had been broken a time or two. Smaller, more subtle scars marred the rest of his face and the left side of his neck.

Trey tried to pin down the sense of déjà vu playing tug-of-war with his gut, but before he could find the reason for it, the four men walked out of the building as efficiently as they'd walked in.

Ignoring Vince's curse, Trey approached the old bar owner. Going for laid-back and nonthreatening, he gifted the nervous man with a smile.

"Those men looking for someone special?" he asked in broken Thai.

The bartender gave the entrance an uneasy glance before nodding and replying in English, "The American nurse. The one here last night—with you. I did not tell him anything. She was here helping our neighbors. I did not tell them a thing. I swear."

Trey's gut somersaulted. "Did he say why he was looking for her?"

"No. But he said he would be back if he did not find her."

From across the room, Charlie let out a whoop. She jumped up, laptop in hand, and hustled to the counter, followed by Vince and Logan.

"I found her," Charlie announced. "Or more accurately, where she's going to be. She and her friend have an evening flight booked back to the States. To JFK."

Logan glanced at his watch. "Tally up the three-hour drive to the city airport, security screening, and an evening commercial departure with twenty hours of flight time, and she could be in New York late tomorrow or early the next day."

"We need to beat her back," Trey stated adamantly. If they didn't, she'd be easy pickings. "Charlie?"

Charlie already had the satellite phone in her hand. "That private jet was the best bloody acquisition I ever convinced Stone to make. It'll be fueled and ready to go by the time we hit the airfield."

Vince looked physically pained as he smacked his unfinished beer down on the counter. "First goddamned beer in a week and I can't even finish it."

"I'll buy you one when we get stateside," Trey offered. "But we need to move. I don't know who the hell those guys were, but I know enough that we can't let them get to Elle first."

Logan scoffed. "Looks like the Senator wasn't talking out of his ass this time. Go figure."

"We're not doing this for the fucking Senator."

Vince snorted and Charlie smirked knowingly. Yeah, Trey knew how it sounded, but damn if he didn't care. It was the truth. Alpha might have been hired to keep Elle Monroe safe, but it now meant a lot more to him than a job.

* * *

Elle stared, transfixed by the clock behind the airport's claims counter. Each snap of the second-hand took about five years off her life. Being a few weeks shy of her thirtieth birthday, she estimated she had roughly ten-and-a-half seconds until the coroner needed to be called. Twelve, max, with a little bit of luck, but her luck seemed to be in short supply.

Her normal patience was at an all-time low, sucked into a black hole right along with her personal hygiene and her luggage. Twenty total hours in a plane, plus an unscheduled six-hour stop for mechanical repairs, was to blame for the first. The latter two were entirely the fault of the airline.

Behind the counter, the gray-haired hospitality worker never bothered looking up as she called for the next traveler in line. One more person. One more step. The closer Elle got to the cracked, yellow Formica counter of the claims department, the more that surface looked like a goose-feather pillow. *To leave or not to leave.*

Jeans. Shorts. Granny panties. All cotton, no sexiness. Everything in her suitcase could be easily replaced by her modest paycheck and the nearest discount store. She could call it a loss, go home with Shay, and pass out on her couch for a week.

With a deep sigh, Elle looked around the large, open space. People milled through the airport, bulky suitcases bouncing behind them as they scrambled to their destinations, while others procured blankets and pillows and looked to be settling in for the duration of the night.

On her left, two children tackled the legs of a tall, slender soldier dressed in desert fatigues. Laughing, the woman bent, spreading kisses over every surface of their little cheeks. A smile ghosted over Elle's lips at the sweet sight.

She'd once wanted that. Not only the children, although she couldn't deny being a mother had been high up on her to-do list. But to be missed—to have someone care about you so much that they nearly threw you to the ground because they couldn't wait to have you in their arms.

That's what Elle had dreamed of since she was a little girl...and it was that crushed dream that had sent her thousands of miles away. To say she felt uneasy being back was an understatement.

Elle ignored the faint ache in her chest and watched the happy family walk away. As they disappeared around the corner, a new sensation whittled its way in—a *tingle*; the one she'd felt the instant she and Shay unloaded from the gate— the one that came with the ardent focus of someone's attention. It took root in the pit of her stomach and didn't let go.

When she'd sensed it earlier, she blamed the paranoia on lack of sleep and inhumane travel hours. But the prickle of awareness came back tenfold, turning her head until she noticed the man leaning against the far wall, reading a newspaper.

Elle did a double take. It wasn't Trey. It couldn't be. She'd left him back in Thailand without so much as her last name, much less her travel itinerary, yet the longer she stared at the stranger across the room, the faster her heart galloped.

Worn blue jeans encased his thighs perfectly. Not tight. Not baggy. No doubt if he turned around, the rear would look as impressive as the front. Both his face and his hair were disappointedly half-hidden by a baseball cap and sunglasses, but he had the same strongly chiseled jaw and sexy blonde scruff that made her want to throw every razor known to man straight into the garbage.

Though he never looked away from his paper, the wall lounger's lips twitched, almost as if sensing her visual appraisal. That smirk. Those lips. The stretch of a long-sleeved T over a chest wide enough to land an airplane on. Elle nearly collapsed into an X-rated memory of how lips nearly identical to those of this stranger had pleasurably ripped away all her sensibilities only a scant few days ago.

Standing in the middle of a busy airport definitely wasn't the time to relive her night with Trey. When her turn came up at the counter, she gave herself a mental slap and focused on giving the attendant the information the airline needed to reconnect her with her suitcase. And then with a *Have a nice day* and her single carry-on, Elle shuffled away to wait for Shay to finish in the bathroom.

She searched her purse for her cell phone and bounced off the chest of another traveler.

"Oh, my God. I'm *so* sorry." She reflexively reached out to steady her victim.

"*Shut* it," a low voice snarled.

Oh, hell no. Exhaustion mixed with an insane need to shower off the last day and a half made her head swivel to Mr. Attitude. She looked up. And up. *Whoa.* He was ridiculously tall.

If she'd had a little bit more sleep she'd probably be able to talk herself out of confronting someone so freaking huge, but she'd had a middle seat, and both Shay and the man to her left had been armrest hogs. Elle was eight hours past polite.

She narrowed her eyes, wishing her glare would make him squirm. "It was an accident. I said I was sorry. There's no need to be a jerk about it."

"Actually, there is." Mr. Attitude clamped a hand around her upper arm and squeezed.

"*Ow.* Hey, watch it!" She tugged, and he tightened his hold.

He leaned his large body way past her personal boundaries. That was when she saw the scar, half-hidden behind his sunglasses. It looked angrier up close, the skin around his eye socket puckered straight up to his hairline. Cold dread licked up Elle's spine.

It was Alley Man.

"I told you to shut. The fuck. Up." He emphasized each word and punctuated it with a sharp jab to her ribs. When she attempted to twist away, the poke came again—this time with the cool sensation of metal.

A gun.

Alley Man stepped closer, careful to keep it hidden from view. "If you so much as twitch, sputter, or look at anyone cross-eyed, I won't hesitate to make this very bad for you. Do you fucking understand me?"

Elle re-swallowed the bile that had risen to her throat. "I should probably warn you that I don't have any money. Well, I have about ten dollars' worth of Thai baht, but that's about it. And maybe a fuzzy breath mint."

Tightening his grip, he steered them away from anyone who would remotely care what was happening. And let's face it: This was one of the busiest airports in the country. No one was going to notice one travel-ravaged blonde, even if she stripped down to her cotton undies and streaked half naked through the terminal.

Alley Man kept the gun pressed firmly between her ribs as he directed them to the exit. "I don't want your money, Miss Monroe."

Elle's heart went from a steady thunder to an apocalyptic roar. *He knew her name*. He knew she'd be at *this* airport. On *this* day. On *this* flight.

The only thing Elle knew was that she was really—and completely—screwed.

CHAPTER THREE

Elle whipped her head from side to side, hoping to catch someone's eye, but everyone was too involved with their own travels. Even the station cop across the room looked busy, standing between two passengers about to come to blows.

"So I'm your meal ticket, huh?" Elle kept talking, willing any of the nearby travelers to catch on to her dilemma. "You obviously need me alive or you wouldn't be going to all this trouble to get me out of here. What's stopping me from screaming bloody murder at the top of my lungs?"

"This." He drilled the gun into her ribs as a not-so-subtle reminder. "Not only could you get hurt in the process, but just look at this crowd of innocent people. You wouldn't want to be responsible for any of them getting hurt, would you? Then there's your friend in the women's bathroom—and just in case you think I'm bluffing, Miss Whitney happens to be in the one directly across from the newspaper stand...the one with one working stall and a dripping faucet."

Shay. Panic seized Elle's throat, making it difficult to breathe. Jeopardizing her best friend's safety or that of any other innocent bystander wasn't an option, and the evil smirk distorting Alley Man's face said without words that he knew it too.

She needed to think. She needed her own plan. She needed—

Elle snapped her gaze to the far wall where she'd last seen Mr. Tall, Ripped, and I-Can-Flick-Off-a-Man-with-My-Fingers-and-Send-Him-Across-the-Room. Her baseball-cap-wearing stranger remained in the same spot, but he wasn't leaning against the wall. He stood upright, newspaper tossed to the side, looking straight at her.

"Keep up." Elle's captor tugged her closer to the exit.

In front of them, the doors slid open. A gust of frigid air spurred Elle to move—to do *something*. She stiffened her legs and forced both herself and her captor into a stumble. That small bit of space was all she needed to plow-drive a fist straight into his man-goods.

Thank God for hospital-sponsored self-defense classes— even if it was the only move she remembered.

As she hoped, Alley Man released her arm to deflect the blow—and then he was gone. A whir of black zipped by her shoulder, followed by the sounds of flesh on flesh. Much to the horrified fascination of nearby travelers, her wall-lounger and would-be abductor exchanged punch after punch.

Curious bystanders stopped and stared, some even pulling cell phones from pockets and pointing them toward the action. Across the lobby, the uniformed cop finally looked their way. Then with one final blow, her stranger sprawled Alley Man flat out on the ground.

"With me." He palmed her lower back and hustled her into New York's fresh-as-can-be air. She opened her mouth to object, but he cut her off. "Save the questions for when we're not about to become target practice, and walk faster."

Elle followed the direction of his attention and immediately locked eyes with her almost-abductor. He was back on his feet as if nothing had happened, his gun clenched tightly at his side. And he was pissed as he produced a cell from his back pocket.

"Get in the car." Her stranger nodded toward the SUV half-parked on the drop-off zone's sidewalk.

Elle's feet screeched to a stop. "Yeah, I may be blonde, but I'm not stupid. What makes you think I'd get into a car with you any more than I would with him? Thanks for helping me because I've obviously landed in the Twilight Zone instead of New York, but if you want me to get in there"— she gestured to the door he held open—"then you're going to have to physically toss me in and sit on me."

"If you think that would be a deterrent for me, you're mistaken. And as for manhandling you into position, I'd be more than happy to cover your body with mine, but I sure as hell wouldn't be sitting *on* you. Get in the car. *Now*."

Elle folded her arms across her chest, purposefully not moving. That tone of voice and the familiarity with which he spoke to her tugged at her memory vault.

"Have it your way." He bent. His muscled arm took her legs out from under her and hoisted her into the back of the SUV.

"What the hell do you think you're doing?" she howled.

"Saving your stubborn ass. You can thank me later, sweetness."

A sucker punch would've stunned Elle less. That voice. His smell. That damn term of endearment which never failed to rub her the wrong way. Recognition tightened her nipples and sent a zap of warmth straight between her legs.

She didn't know how it was possible. Or why.

But she suddenly knew that she didn't need to imagine what her wall-lounger looked like beneath his clothes. She'd already had a private viewing. She knew how his body felt against hers, knew that each touch felt like she'd brushed against an exposed electrical wire. Those large hands, especially, gave her a treasure trove of pleasurable memories.

Lying sprawled on her back in the rear seat of an SUV, Elle Monroe: nurse, reformed yes-girl, and daughter of a United States senator, pulled her stranger's sunglasses from his face and stared into the piercing green eyes of her forty-eight-hours-recent one-night stand.

* * *

Rafe Ortega, Trey's best friend and teammate, pulled the SUV away from the curb a split second before three men stepped through the airport doors, one of them the asshat from the lobby. *Fucking bastard.*

Trey knew control. He lived it. Breathed it. Hell, control ran through his veins along with red blood cells and a genetic disposition toward high cholesterol. But it had taken every ounce he possessed not to snap that mercenary's neck for putting his hands on Elle, control be fucking damned.

Once Trey could unclench his jaw, he corralled his focus back to the woman sitting next to him. Elle glared, her eyes packed with questions—and anger. The latter he could try to handle now, but the answers weren't his to give. Not yet. And not until they put more distance between them and the hired guns who were seconds from riding hard on their asses.

"Elle…" He searched for something—anything—to help her understand.

"Shay," she cut him off. "She's back at the airport and that man threatened to—"

"She's with one of my guys. She's safe. I promise." Though Trey couldn't say the same for Chase. Odds were high that the former SEAL medic would have to give himself some kind of first aid, thanks to the ornery brunette doctor.

Silence hung so goddamn heavy in the SUV that Trey waited for the vehicle's undercarriage to start dragging down the Belt Parkway. In the two days since Trey had last laid eyes on Elle, she seemed different. She *held* herself differently. The woman in that Thai bar—and in his bed—had been relaxed and open. The one next to him looked like a statue—a beautiful, golden-haired, and very pissed off statue.

She shivered, and Trey realized that in a thin T-shirt and stretchy yoga pants, she wasn't dressed for February above the Mason-Dixon Line.

He holstered his gun and shrugged out of his leather jacket. "You're going to need this when we get out of the car."

Her scrutiny rested on him like an anvil. "Am I going to be allowed to use my own two feet or am I going to be thrown over another shoulder and treated like a sack of potatoes?"

Trey ground his back molars. He didn't like her mistrust, despite the fact it was deserved. "That's going to depend on whether you can listen to directions."

He was starting to wonder if that capability was even within a mile radius of her wheelhouse.

"Can you tell me where you're taking me?" she asked, her tone frigid.

"Not right now."

"Then how about what you want...or what that *other* guy wanted with me? Because something tells me it wasn't to offer himself as escort back to the States."

Trey snapped to attention. "What do you mean, escort you back to the States? This wasn't the first time you've seen him?"

Elle bit her bottom lip, deep in thought and no doubt wondering whether to share anything with him.

"Look, Elle"—he treaded carefully—"I know I can't share much right now, but I can tell you that I'm here to make sure you stay safe. I can't do that if you hold back on me. Now, did you see that man from the airport before?"

Finally, she offered him a faint nod. "The morning after we...I mean, when I—"

"Ran like a track star." From *him*.

"He'd been in an alley a few blocks down from the bar. He didn't seem very polite then either, but I didn't stick around long because some guy and his friend came barreling down the street."

Trey scrubbed a palm over his face. "Goddamn, that was fucking close."

"Do you know who he is?" Elle asked again. "Or why he's so eager to get his hands on me?"

"He's not going to put his hands on you," Trey growled, "I can fucking swear to that." Rafe's cough pulled Trey back into the moment. "And no, we don't know who is he, but that's all I can tell you right now. You're safe with us."

"But you can't tell me who your collective '*us*' is. Am I right?" With her cheeks flaring far past crimson, she tossed his jacket back into his face. "Fine. Keep this. Keep your secrets. And you better keep your hands and all other appendages to yourself...*Trey*."

When it came down to Elle Monroe's body, there wasn't

much he didn't know. He knew how she trembled when he nibbled her neck in the right spot, and how she sighed when he ran his tongue through her wetness. He knew how her body went soft and pliant right before it gripped his cock like a fucking vise.

But he didn't know how to make her fucking listen.

"Do me a favor and try not to pass judgment until you know what we're dealing with. Okay, sweetness? Things will be a lot clearer soon," Trey heard himself promise.

"You do *not* get to call me that." Anger flashed in her eyes, making her baby blues look cobalt. "It's not 'Elle' or 'sweetness' or 'baby.' It's '*Miss Monroe*,' or you don't address me at all, got it? But you probably already know my last name, right? Along with my credit score and bra size."

From the driver's seat, Rafe cleared his throat. "Well, we did have to pick up a few things for you…figured you'd need some odds and ends."

Trey growled at his friend. "Dude, not fucking helping."

"Didn't claim to be." Rafe chuckled.

Best friend or not, if the bastard wasn't driving, he'd have kicked him in the balls. As it was, the look on Elle's face made Trey worry about his own reproductive health once she had a clear shot—and dammit, his mother would filet him alive if he put future grandchildren on the line.

"I already know what I'm dealing with…or at least *who*, because this entire screwed-up mess reeks of my father," Elle said. "What remains to be addressed is your role in all of this. You're not Secret Service. I suppose you could be an off-duty cop, but knowing my father's love of the military, I'm going to say that you're an ex-something. Navy? Army? You don't strike me as a Marine, but I've been wrong before."

"I was Delta Force before jumping into private security."

"Ah. Army elite. Tell me, *Trey*, was sleeping with me one of your operational goals or did you give that to my father as a freebie?"

When they'd first climbed into the SUV, Trey figured the hole he was in was around dick level, but the more he tried digging himself out of it, the deeper it got. Right now, it was probably hitting his fucking chin.

Rafe navigated the busy New York streets, going deeper into Manhattan. The city meant people. People meant traffic. And New York City traffic made quick getaways impossible unless you had a satchel of fucking pixie dust. If Trey had his way, they'd be heading north until they hit the fucking Canadian border. But orders were fucking orders. He might not agree with them, but he needed to follow them.

"Stone and the others have already cleared everything south of the hotel lobby," Rafe said, catching Trey's attention in the rearview mirror. "Logan's going to meet us at the loading dock, and then we're going to take her up from there."

Trey nodded grimly. His team was always on point. As long as she was by their side, Elle was safe, but that didn't mean this entire plan wasn't horseshit. Rafe turned the corner that took them to the rear entrance of one of the swankiest hotels in the city. Trey noted Elle didn't show the least bit of surprise.

"There's Logan." Rafe nodded toward the loading dock where Logan, dressed in baggy shirt and pants to hide the fact he was heavily armed, waited.

He pushed off the wall he'd been leaning against, and before the SUV even crawled to a complete stop, he tugged the door open. "About damn time you lazy shits showed up."

"Rafe drives like your gran." Trey got out of the backseat

and turned to help Elle, but Logan was already extending a hand in her direction.

"It's a pleasure to meet you, Miss Monroe. Logan Callahan," the Texan drawled, putting a bit of extra weight on his twang. "Don't listen to these guys about my gran. She drives like a bat out of hell. Keeps the sheriff busy when she goes speeding through town."

Trey scowled at his friend. Goddamn Rico Suave. "I think she's been getting in and out of cars on her own for a while now, Callahan."

The bastard gave him a shit-eating grin. "Oh, I'm sure she's more than capable of a lot of things."

Elle slid her hand into Logan's and let him guide her out of the car.

"You'll have to pardon my friend, darlin'," Logan started saying. "There's a difference between South country and North country, and he had the misfortune of being raised in the wrong one."

Fuck it all if Elle didn't give him a small smile. "But you were raised in the right one?"

"Abso-freaking-lutely. Texas boy through and through. If you need anything, you just look my way, and I'll be more than happy to get it for you."

"I'll be happy to give you a few things, Callahan," Trey muttered under his breath.

Logan barely suppressed a chuckle. "I don't want what you're offering, man. No offense, but you're just not my type."

Despite the seemingly light mood, no one lowered their guard. They formed a triangle around Elle, with Rafe taking the front point, Trey and Logan behind, and continued through the underbelly of the hotel until they reached the staff service elevator.

It was a quiet ride up to the twelfth floor. The bell chimed, and the doors opened. Two people stood dead center in the corridor of what should've been a locked-down floor. Reflexes had Trey reaching for his gun a split second before he fully registered that the two intruders probably had a good few years on Logan's gran.

"Ladies," Logan intervened before anyone could move. Arguing softly between themselves, the two women didn't notice him approaching until he was practically on top of them.

"Oh, my." The taller of the two gave the Marine a boot-to-eyeball scan.

"I'm afraid this floor is closed off to guests." Flashing his signature smile, Logan gently—and without their even realizing—corralled the two women toward the main guest elevator on the other end of the hall.

"What floor is this?" the shorter woman asked.

"Twelve."

"See, Rose," the eye-roaming older friend clucked. "I told you we got off on the wrong level. I may have cataracts, but I'm not completely blind."

"Absolutely nothing to worry about, darlin'," Logan could be heard soothing them. "Y'all just tell me where it is you're trying to get to, and I'll get you there right quick."

Trey, Elle, and Rafe watched him lead the women away.

"Am I the only one who can't wait for him to meet a woman who isn't so taken with that damn accent?" asked Rafe.

"Definitely not," Trey replied.

Elle let out a soft snort. "Maybe it's not so much the accent as it is his manners...as in the fact that he *has* them."

She tossed a scowl his way, making her meaning clear. Rafe smothered a chuckle before leading the way to suite 1202 and performing a series of elaborate knocks.

"Seriously?" Trey arched a brow. "We have the entire floor on video feed."

Rafe lifted his broad shoulders in a noncommittal shrug. "Boredom."

Vince opened the door. "What's with the fucking musical routine?"

"What's with leaving two little grannies roaming the floor?" Rafe retorted.

"I am *not* fucking with someone's grandma. They would've given up eventually." Vince stepped aside and led them into the small foyer. "Any problems leaving the airport?"

Trey shook his head. "They had men inside, but not on the perimeter. We were probably already on the Parkway by the time they pulled their thumbs out of their asses and brought their car around."

Vince gestured for Elle to follow him into the next room. She took a hesitant step, then looked toward Trey. Her seeking his reassurance made him feel damn good.

He nodded his encouragement. "You're okay. I'll be along in a bit."

"You, my friend, are an idiot," Rafe said the moment Vince and Elle disappeared into the living area.

"Don't hold back, Ortega," Trey said dryly. "Tell me what you really think."

Rafe pounded him on the shoulder and smirked. "That you're a *huge* fucking idiot. You know that, right?"

"Things wouldn't be this fucked up if someone would've sent the goddamned file on time."

"And if you would've gotten it a week before, would that have stopped you?"

Before Elle, Trey would've answered a swift yes. But she'd blown up his work ethics and made it damn difficult to think of anything but the time they'd spent together—and the fact that she found it so easy to dismiss.

A year ago, he would've thanked the heavens for her view on mornings after. Now? Not so fucking much.

Rafe, the fuck-wit, grinned like a damn lunatic and punched him on the shoulder. "This is going to be fucking fun."

CHAPTER FOUR

Elle knew her father was somehow behind everything that had happened since stepping off the plane, and quite possibly before. That didn't mean she expected to find him sitting at an elaborately adorned dining room table with a piping hot cappuccino—and her ex-fiancé.

She blatantly ignored the condescending smirk James sent her way and focused on the once robust and domineering Senator Samuel Monroe. Her father looked . . . aged. During the six months she'd been in Thailand, gray hair had declared a war on his dark brown locks, and an entire family of wrinkles lined his mouth, a wonder since the man rarely smiled.

Elle stopped a few feet shy of the table, making sure to keep a physical barrier between the two of them as she mentally summoned an emotional one. Going face-to-face with her father while metaphorically naked was never a good idea.

One of his bodyguards stepped forward. "I'll need you to put your hands on the table, ma'am, and spread out your arms and legs."

Sprawl facedown on the table and let herself be touched—for the third time today?

She opened her mouth to tell him what he could do with his body search, but Trey stepped forward, blocking the agent's advance. "Hands to yourself or *you're* going to be the one spread-eagle on that table."

The guard puffed out his chest like a peacock. "No one gets near the Senator without being thoroughly checked. His safety's my responsibility."

Trey didn't look the least bit impressed. "And her safety's mine."

Trey glared at the bodyguard. The bodyguard glowered back at Trey. The suite door clicked open, and Logan rejoined them. The Marine's gaze slid around the room. "Jesus, I was gone for, like, five seconds. What the hell happened?"

"Nothing's going to happen," Trey retorted, not backing down. "Unless Big Shot here doesn't back the hell off—then a whole lot of shit's going down."

Rafe and Vince—the heavily tattooed man who'd opened the door—stepped closer. It was a good thing Elle wasn't claustrophobic because being surrounded by all these oversized men was starting to get out of hand.

"We can forgo the search, Tom." Elle's father stood, reigning in his guard dog. "The only thing my daughter's capable of hurting is my heart."

Zing. A direct shot straight through the chest in less than a minute. Time apart hadn't affected his aim in the least.

"I would've thought you'd look refreshed after six months away from all your responsibilities." Samuel Monroe frowned. He looked her up and down with the Monroe blue eyes. Each visual pass tightened his lips a little more until he looked like he'd swallowed a lemon. "Did *none* of your mother's lessons stick?"

A few: Always carry Band-Aids in your purse. Nylons were a sadistic male invention. And never let him—meaning Elle's father—see you sweat. The last Linda Monroe bit of wisdom had been passed her way when Elle was twelve, right before her mother lost her battle with cancer.

"I was providing medical care to tsunami victims in Thailand," Elle corrected him, despite the fact that he'd known exactly where she'd been and what she'd been doing. "I wasn't lounging on the beach working on my tan. And it's wonderful to see you, too, Dad. I'm doing okay, considering that I've been roughed up twice in as many hours. Thank you for asking."

"I already received the report that you were uninjured, Elle," her father said curtly. He walked casually to the wet bar and poured himself a few fingers of whiskey. "If you would've returned calls or answered emails, you would've known to be careful upon your return from your little trip."

Do not show weakness. Be strong. Stand your ground.

Elle fought the tremble of her hands and clenched them into tight fists at her sides. "Nowhere in any of those emails did it mention that I should expect men with guns to be waiting for me near the luggage carousel."

"Your father's been worried about you, Elle," James interjected. "We've *both* been worried. There's no need to get defensive or be so flippant about our concerns."

Laying eyes on the jerk again unleashed the flood of emotions that had sent her away from New York in the first place. But instead of backing down like the old Elle, she lifted her chin and gave her ex a hard look. "Concerned? The two of you? Did you take up stand-up comedy while I've been gone? If either one of you have felt any kind of concern, it was for how my absence would affect your careers."

James's stark shock at her remark gave Elle a jolt of confidence and encouraged her to continue searching for the real reason she'd been brought to one of her father's known stomping grounds for schmoozing and hobnobbing.

She turned her attention to her father. "Why am I here?"

"For your safety." His twitching left eye said otherwise.

"Why am I *really* here?"

A vein bulged at his temple, and his previously pale face went red. Six and a half months ago, she wouldn't have questioned. She would've folded and made the peace like she'd done for nearly thirty years. Post-Thailand-Elle wasn't so flexible.

"You're here to make an appearance at the charity gala tonight," her father finally admitted. "And it's non-negotiable. Many of my supporters will be there, and I can't afford to show anything less than the full support of my family—not with us heading into an election year. You *will* attend—on James's arm—and you will smile and play the doting fiancée and dutiful daughter."

There was so much wrong with his little speech that she didn't know where to start. Oh, yeah. She did. "I'm not going anywhere on James's arm."

"Stop acting ridiculous!" Samuel hissed. Spittle collected at the corners of his mouth and his face went from red to purple. "This little spat between the two of you ends now. I refuse to let you ruin a young man's life because of a simple, insignificant misunderstanding."

"I agree that it was insignificant—as in, I don't care. But it's a little difficult to misunderstand seeing your fiancé with his pants around his knees. It wasn't like he was at the doctor's office getting a medical exam."

Someone behind Elle chuckled.

Trey cleared his throat. "Sir, in light of what happened at the airport, we're going to suggest that you rethink your plan to have your daughter at the gala. It's not safe."

Samuel knocked back his drink and filled his tumbler again. "Keeping her safe is why I hired your outfit a few days ago, is it not? Your boss led me to believe that your firm could handle *anything*. Are you saying that you're incapable of a simple protective detail at an upscale, private event?"

"We're capable of handling *any* task we take on, sir. My problem is with you putting your daughter's safety in jeopardy for a few photo ops," Trey snapped roughly.

Elle held her breath.

Thirty years and she couldn't remember a single time where someone had raised his voice to her father. She was shocked, awed, and more than a little impressed. And dammit, she was thankful. *No one* had ever stood up for her when faced with the wrath of Senator Monroe, and that tally sadly included her late mother.

"I'm paying your company to perform a job, not spew lectures." Her father attempted to skewer Trey with his stare before returning his attention to her.

"Who did you offend this time?" Elle asked. If there was ever a point in time when her father hadn't offended a group or organization and received some kind of threat, she'd be shocked.

"It isn't relative."

"Their guns looked pretty fucking relative to me," Trey muttered, touching her arm. Her skin warmed from the contact, and her first instinct was to get closer. Those intense green eyes lasered in on hers, making her feel like she and Trey were the only two people standing in the room. "You don't have to go to the gala, Elle. You *shouldn't* be going."

"The hell she doesn't have to go!" the Senator howled. That vein at his temple began pulsing.

"Enough." Elle stepped between her father and Trey. "I'll do it," she said aloud, "but there is no way on this earth that I'm stepping into that room with James—absolutely no chance in hell. So you can get that delusion out of your head right now."

"But James—"

"Isn't going to happen in a million years and a low male census." She waited—and expected—her father to continue to argue. When he didn't, she nodded. "Good. Then Logan's going to be my escort."

"Say what now?" Trey asked at the same time her father bellowed a roaring, "Like hell."

Logan's low chuckle slipped through the chaos. "I'd be honored."

Trey's attention snapped to his friend. "Like fucking hell. *I'm* the lead on this assignment. *I* take point with the asset."

"The asset?" A red haze clouded over Elle's vision. She narrowed her eyes and drilled him with a pointed glare. "If there's anyone who's being an ass in this situation, it sure as hell isn't me."

"You can call me any name you want, sweetness, but if we're going through with this fucked-up idea, then I'm going to be the one at your side. There is no other option."

Control over her and her life was all anyone seemed to want from her. She longed to make her own demands, to raise her chin and tell them all what they could do with their *only* options. Instead, she heard herself agreeing.

She wasn't caving, Elle told herself. She was doing what needed to be done so she could get her life back where it belonged—in her own hands.

At least, that's what she kept telling herself.

* * *

After a much-needed shower and a tense phone call to Shay, where Elle spent nearly a half hour convincing her best friend to stay holed up in her parents' vacation home, Elle adjusted the strapless, powder-blue gown that had been brought to the hotel room by her father's stylist and looked in the full-length mirror.

Less than a few hours ago, she was being jostled into the backseat of an SUV, and now she was prepping to be manhandled in an entirely different way—and *she'd agreed to it*. "What the hell was I thinking?" Elle murmured. "This was a bad idea."

"Sometimes the worst ideas are the most entertaining," teased a melodic English accent.

Elle smiled and turned just as Charlie, the petite blonde security operative, stepped into the room. "Then maybe we should be selling tickets. I'm sure we'd make a fortune on tonight."

"Love, *this* kind of entertainment is priceless." Charlie tugged on the bust-line of her own show-stopping black gown and grimaced. "Bloody hell. If I have to run, the girls are going to make an appearance, and then I'm never going to hear the end of it from the guys. How the bloody hell do you move in these things?"

Elle chuckled. "Carefully. I wasn't joking when I said I missed my mosquito-repellent jammies."

Charlie gave her dress another yank. "And I miss my

camo and boots. And what I wouldn't do for a good, supportive sports bra right about now."

The two women looked at each other and laughed.

"It's about time." Charlie gestured toward the door and led the way into the suite's living room where Trey, Vince, and Logan waited.

"Hot damn." The flirty blonde cowboy belted out a whistle. "Lookin' good, ladies."

"Lasso your eyes back in your head, Callahan," Charlie warned sternly, but Logan didn't appear the least bit deterred as he continued eyeing the gorgeous operative.

Elle chuckled at how uncomfortable the other woman looked, and she understood all too well. If given by the right person, an appreciative gaze or sincere compliment could mean a lot. Given by the wrong one, it got old quick, a lot like these functions her father has been dragging her to for years. The magic of slipping into a beautiful down dissipated when it came along with expectations of perfection.

"Do you remember the rules?" The question, asked from across the room, sent Elle's attention toward the overstuffed chair.

Trey stood when their gazes clashed. She nearly forgot how to walk. *Double-O-yowza*. Talk about perfection. A sleek black tux that did nothing to hide the broad width of his shoulders had replaced the battered jeans and long-sleeved T. And the scruff…

Elle nearly shivered from the memory of those raspy stubbles rubbing against the sensitive skin of her neck… and her inner thighs.

The room had gone quiet. Elle took a quick look around her and, thankfully, all eyes were on Trey in varying forms of disapproval—except for those of Trey himself, who was still waiting for an answer.

"Rules," Elle repeated. "Smile. Flirt. And play dumb. Oh, wait, you didn't mean Sam Monroe's Rules of Butt-Kissing."

Charlie laughed and then rolled her eyes when she was the only one. "Sometimes I think the high loads of testosterone prevent them from having a sense of humor."

"I grew up in a house without any humor, so it's not a new experience for me."

Trey shifted his glare between the two of them. "Are the two of you done treating this like some kind of fucking game? Because I'd love nothing more than to scrap this entire ridiculous idea and get Elle to a safe house."

"I'd love to get out of here. Shall I drive or you?" Elle snapped.

"I gave you a way out earlier, sweetheart. You're the one who decided to cave."

His words smarted—because he was right. Even with her own terms thrown into the mix, she'd still backed down, but no way would she admit the embarrassing truth that it was an improvement from six months ago. Pre-Thailand, Elle would've caved to the Senator's demand without a second thought, even the one that included James as an escort.

Funny how, when it came to Trey, she didn't budge even an inch. "Stay close. Stay alert. And stay put," Elle repeated Trey's *rules*. "I suppose it's a good thing I went to obedience school."

"Okay, kids. I've been told it's time for us to make an appearance," Logan interrupted. He placed a small plastic earbud into her left ear. "Trey's going to be at your side through the entire event, and Charlie and Vince are going to be inside the room, blending in with the other guests."

Logan snuck a look at the former SEAL. Vince's tux covered his tattoos, but the man still managed to exude a don't-mess-with-me vibe. "Okay, so *Charlie's* going to blend in. Franklin's going to stick out like an awkward thumb. Stone, the big boss-man, is going to be canoodling with the rest of us with event security. Rafe's on getaway duty. We'll all be close by, but no matter the distance, we'll be linked by these mics. If you see someone who makes your internal alarm blare, say something, and we'll come running."

"This sounds like a ridiculous amount of manpower." Nerves made Elle's stomach somersault, and she fought not to nibble on her lower lip. "Are you sure this isn't overkill?"

"I think it's not-enough-kill," Trey muttered beneath his breath.

Charlie gave her a gentle pat on the arm. "We take our job seriously, and right now, that job happens to be you."

That's what she was—and what she'd been—to Trey. *A job*. It shouldn't rankle her. A fun, memorable twelve or more hours without strings or attachments had been exactly what she wanted…which was why she didn't understand why those two little words—"*a job*"—left a bad taste in her mouth.

CHAPTER FIVE

Trey studied the sleek curve of Elle's neck; the way her golden hair slipped from it artsy updo to caress the satiny skin of her bare shoulders. She looked soft, warm, and oh-so-touchable—which was funny, since he hadn't so much as laid a hand on her since they'd reached the ballroom.

Others had, though. Elle returned smiles and hugs, making nice with everyone who stopped to say hello—which was nearly everyone in the damn room. Hell, she even amped up her manners and introduced him as her date. Anyone on the outside looking in would think her a social butterfly, content to flutter around the room and bask in the attention.

Not Trey.

He'd seen it in the field, soldiers gone immobile but still prepped to go on the offensive. That was Elle. She smiled, but when the other person looked away, it cracked. She hugged, but when they first stepped up, she tensed—and stayed tense—until they walked away. And then the cycle started all over again with the next person. It was fucking exhausting to watch.

When an older couple finished their good-byes and stepped away, Trey couldn't take another second of Elle's silence.

"Are we ever going to talk things out?" He stepped up next to her, fully aware of the warm *zing* that traveled up from where their arms brushed.

"About what?" Elle returned the wave of an older gentleman across the room and avoided looking in Trey's direction. "Your caveman tendencies, the fact you're on my father's payroll, or that you took the phrase *bring your work home with you* a bit too literally?"

Trey ground his back molars. "Thailand."

"Then the answer is no, we're not going to talk *things* out." Elle returned the wave of another couple.

Trey had been fucking the hell up ever since he'd let her slip from his bed. Not only had she evaded him back in Thailand, but he'd let the Senator get his way about the gala appearance and then acted like a jealous ass upstairs when she'd tried replacing him with Logan.

She would've been just as safe standing next to the former Marine, but something in his gut revolted at the idea of her spending quality time with the country boy Casanova.

"Not talking about it isn't going to make it go away," Trey reminded her.

"No, but it's a coping mechanism that's worked well for me in the past, so why fix it if it's not broke. I swear to God," Elle muttered, sounding more like she was talking to herself, "the next time Shay tells me to let loose and walk on the wild side, I'm going to gag her. She gets a vacation in her parent's Catskill home and I get *this*."

"Elle Monroe," a voice interrupted Trey's retort. "I thought that was you."

A tall, willowy brunette sashayed toward them a lot quicker than should be possible on her mile-high heels. Bright lips matched her fire-engine-red dress, the kind a woman wore to say to everyone, "Look at me!" The brunette's attention bounced from Elle to Trey and back, as she closed the distance.

Next to him, Elle groaned. "And it keeps getting better."

Trey couldn't help but wrap his arm around her waist and give her hip a little squeeze. She gifted him a quick glare before slapping on a smile and turning to the incoming brunette. "Stephanie! How nice to see you. It's been a while."

Damn, she was good at the fake politeness, too.

"It seems like forever!" Stephanie leaned in and the two women exchanged a hug. "I didn't know you were going to be here. Daddy said that, as far as he knew, you were still out of the country. I wish I could vacation like that—just drop everything and go see the world. That must have been so exhilarating."

"I'm sure it would be, but I wasn't on a vacation. I was establishing a medical clinic that was helping tsunami victims."

The other woman looked baffled for a minute, then another. "A tsunami is the wave thing? So if there was an ocean, you must have been able to get in *some* beach time…right?"

Trey waited for Elle to break the sudden silence. And waited. She stared at the brunette, and if he didn't know any better, looked to be counting silently in her head.

"After the tsunami, there really wasn't much of a beach— or anything else—nearby," Elle finally said.

The brunette didn't even register her underlying annoyance. She waved her hand, as if brushing away a fly. "Oh, never mind. I guess it's not really important because you've obviously been *very* busy." Stephanie blatantly ogled Trey. "Hello, there...and you are?"

"Trey." He purposely shifted his body closer to Elle, the move drawing attention to his arm, still snugly hooked around her waist.

The woman's look of surprise, then confusion was almost comical. "What happened with James? The two of you—"

"Are ancient history," Elle finished.

"Really? I haven't heard a word about the cancellation! Oh, my God. I'm *so* sorry," Stephanie said, sounding horrified. "You poor thing. You must be devastated."

"Not in the least." Elle sounded sincere, her voice steady as she curled herself into Trey's side and looked up at him through her long lashes. "This incredible man right here reminds me on a daily basis that I definitely made the right decision."

Stephanie eyed him again, with, if possible, even more renewed interest. "And what is it that you do again, Trey?"

Trey forced a polite smile. "I didn't say...but I happen to own a bar with some of my military buddies."

Elle's attention had yet to waver from his face, but Stephanie's was already gone as she made an excuse to leave and joined a larger group of women. Heads bowed, the group of whisperers threw an occasional glance their way.

"You know you're now going to be the talk of the gala, right?" Trey pointed out.

"A bar?" Elle ignored his comment.

Yeah, she knew about Alpha Security, but it was only part of him. The rest: Alpha—the bar—his hometown of Frederick, his family...they were as far from this kind of life as a person could get, her metaphorical caviar to his beer nuts and trail mix. As a punk teen looking for an adventure of a lifetime, plain ol' beer nuts hadn't been enough. He'd left—

his hometown *and* his family—and he'd stayed away for a damn long time.

Now beer nuts was what he lived for—and why he continued to work for Alpha Security.

To keep those he cared about safe.

Trey forced himself to meet Elle's gaze, half-expecting to find some kind of disappointment lurking on her face. Instead, she looked…curious. "Are you going to answer me?"

"About what?" Because he honest-to-fuck couldn't remember. The second he looked into her eyes, everything had flown out of head like it had been catapulted.

"You own a bar?" she asked again.

Trey shrugged. "It's home."

"So it's a real place?"

"Real enough, with its scuffed bar top, ornery regulars, and malfunctioning jukebox."

Elle's mouth pulled up into a small smile. "It sounds like a place that I'd like."

"You probably would." But Trey wondered if that would be the case. To a woman who grew up going to parties like this gala, where you could turn around and come face-to-face with a dozen or more Hollywood actors, Nacho Night Friday wouldn't be a big draw. The only thing close to a celebrity that Frederick had was Old Man Johnson, who'd been on the local fishing show for about five minutes.

"Elle Monroe, what the hell do you think you're doing?" someone hissed.

Trey snapped to attention and shifted toward the owner of the irate voice. James. The ex. Red-faced and livid, steam practically poured out of the man's ears as he stalked closer. Trey barely resisted the urge to pull Elle back.

James pointed toward Trey and snarled, "*Him*? Are you for real? It's bad enough you're attempting to go through with this ridiculousness of ending our engagement, but now you're going to embarrass me even further by insinuating that you're with this...*barbarian*?"

Trey opened his mouth to retort, but Elle beat him to it. She pushed her shoulders back and stared the asshole dead in the eye. Good ol' James looked a little surprised at her open defiance.

"Let's get one thing straight, because you were obviously not listening six months ago or in every email and phone call since. I am not *attempting* to end the engagement. I ended it. It's done. I'm not marrying you now or anytime in the future, and if I wanted to embarrass you, I wouldn't dangle a military veteran—a man who's actually done good in his life—in front of you. What I *would* do, is tell every available woman in this room that you're a narcissistic, cheating piece of horse dung who wouldn't know loyalty if it bit you on the ass."

"And where was your loyalty to me, Elle?" James growled low. "You completely checked out on me and at the worst possible time. You left me alone to deal with all those potential investors to your father's campaign. They wanted to know where you were, and it was embarrassing trying to explain."

"Embarrassing?" Elle asked through gritted teeth. "I was in the fucking hospital, you idiot."

This was the first Trey had heard about a hospital. Witnessing Elle's face transform from a heated rosy glow to a pale gray, he guessed her visit wasn't to put in volunteer hours. Trey stepped closer, ready to do whatever was needed to keep this asshole at a distance.

"You want to talk about checking out, James?" Elle scoffed. "You want to talk about being left alone? Where were you after the accident? Or during the doctor's appointments that came afterward? Oh, that's right—you were screwing your secretary. You want to know what's *really* embarrassing? Admitting that I, for even one second, ever contemplated marrying you."

James's mouth dropped open and closed, making him look like a goddamned fish. Trey would've chuckled if a severe need to put his fist through the bastard's face hadn't flooded through him.

"This isn't over, Elle," James warned. "I mean it."

"And so do I," Elle stated firmly.

James glared a little longer and then he turned, muttering under his breath.

After a few tense seconds of silence, Charlie's voice came over the comm-link, "Bloody hell, love. Thank God you ditched that wanker."

A speck of color blossomed on Elle's cheeks. Her eyes went wide as she looked to Trey. "They can hear *everything*?"

"Every little thing," Logan chimed via his own mic. "And can I just say that I second Charlie's sentiments. That man is a new, lower class of pond scum. Count your blessings that you walked away when you did."

"Oh, I do," Elle admitted. "Every day."

"We've got a fucking problem, kids," Stone, heading the detail along the hotel perimeter, interrupted. "Event security found one of their guys unconscious on the north end of the grounds, and we just found another two on the east who were sleeping on the job, thanks to tranq darts in their asses. Looks like someone's come to play."

"Fuck," Trey cursed.

"Play it cool, boys and girls," Logan reminded them. "We got famous people out the ass in that room. Doesn't mean whoever's about to crash is after our girl."

"Yeah, well, I'm not taking any chances," Trey announced. "I want to start the evac now. She's been at this party long enough. Can we get Route A cleared?"

"Already on it," Stone affirmed. "Ortega will be waiting with the car."

Trey cupped Elle's elbow, ready to disappear through the rear entrance that would take them toward a pair of service elevators, when a large body stepped through it. Trey registered the assault rifle in the masked man's hands a split second before someone fired off a string of rounds into the ceiling.

* * *

For the second time in less than a week, Elle found herself facedown on the floor, Trey's body covering hers. Any hope that it had been because of a hypersensitive reflex had died the moment the loud taps of gunfire ripped into the room.

People around them screamed, some running, others frantically pulling out cell phones. Elle peeked to the left, where one masked man roughly stepped on the hand of a movie producer. The sound of crunching bones and the producer's screams turned Elle's stomach.

"Don't bother trying to send out a mayday," one of the men announced to the room. "We're jamming all cell signals, and all you'll do in the meantime is piss us the fuck off. Cooperate, and this will be quick and painless. Resist, and there are no fucking guarantees."

"Everyone lay the fuck down on your stomachs, hands on your heads," another of the men ordered.

Above her, Trey shifted, but he wasn't following orders. He was watching the men—at least ten of them—as they walked through the crowd of prone bodies. They ignored the men in formal wear, barely glanced at the older women, and then bypassed the younger brunettes completely.

They were scoping out the blondes. Elle's eyes widened in realization.

"Trey," she whispered.

"Fuck me," Trey cursed. He'd noticed it too. "Charlie. Vince."

"Here," Charlie's voice came on the comm-link. "Bloody hell, I'm glad our mics don't use cell frequencies."

"Forget Route A. I need another way out." Trey slowly scanned their side of the room and stopped on a swinging corner door a bare ten feet away. "I got eyes on the kitchen, but we're not going to make it there without getting spotted."

Stone muttered a curse before barking an order to someone on his end. "We're not going to be able to take over the room—not with that many civilians inside."

"I just need a distraction," Trey murmured.

"Leave it to me, love," Charlie drawled. "Wait for my count and then run like bloody hell for the kitchen. There should be a separate service elevator in the back."

Time slowed to a near standstill, and with each tick of Elle's heartbeat, two of the masked men got closer and closer, lifting the heads of the blonde women scattered over the room.

"Three," Charlie's voice counted down. "Two...one."

A commotion broke out near the champagne fountain. A petite blonde in black satin scrambled to her feet, nearly lurching into the arms of the nearest armed man.

"Don't shoot me," Charlie pleaded, fisting the masked man's shirt in her hands. And then she turned on the water-works, sobbing hysterically. "Please, I'm too young and beautiful to die!"

It worked. All attention was diverted to the crazy little blonde's theatrics.

Trey slithered off Elle's body and urged her to her feet. "Let's go."

"But the others?"

"No time right now, sweetheart. It's not the others that they're here for."

A few people nearby watched them, wide-eyed, as they ran to the swinging door. From behind, someone shouted, and Trey urged her faster. The door crashed open as they hit it, slamming hard against the wall behind. Apparently already evacuated by hotel security, the kitchen was an empty void of metal prep tables and abandoned plates.

"Over there." Elle pointed to the back corner, where the staff elevator allowed for easy delivery of food from floor to floor.

Trey linked his fingers through hers and practically tugged her through the maze of the kitchen. Behind them, the swinging door crashed open again. Elle had barely glanced over her shoulder when a strong arm wrapped around her neck from behind. The solid hold and Trey's forward momentum ripped their hands apart.

"What the fuck?" Trey spun, gun already raised and aimed—at *her*.

No, at the man over her shoulder.

"Let her go before I put a bullet in your head," Trey demanded.

"Neither of those things are going to happen," her captor promised.

Alley Man. Elle would have recognized that raspy voice anywhere. Her heart skipped a beat and then continued to thump wildly.

Her pursuer pushed his masked face against her cheek, the contact making her skin crawl. "Why are you making this so difficult, Miss Monroe? This was supposed to be a quick job. Easy money. I'm starting to think I'm going to have to up my price."

"You won't be able to enjoy money from six feet below," Trey growled.

He kept his gun steady, not once taking his eyes off the armed man behind her. And he *was* armed. Elle felt the cool press of a gun against her lower jaw.

"I'm not the one who's going to take a dirt nap, my friend," Alley Man threatened. His hold around Elle's neck tightened, and suddenly breathing became an issue. She wheezed, her hands flying up to the arm banded around her throat.

Trey's entire body tensed, the first time she'd seen him react.

Alley Man chuckled. "Maybe I should offer my services free of charge since I'm being given a gift. Making you pay would be worth the loss of income."

Elle caught movement on the edge of her periphery, a spot of black toward the left. Trey side-stepped right, and it was then Elle realized that their ear mics had been suspiciously quiet. The cavalry. That's why Trey hadn't made a move.

Trey issued another warning. "I don't know what you think I need to pay for, but it's you who's going to be hurting if you don't let her go. Last chance before things get ugly." He took another step right, making Alley Man's attention move with him. "If you don't, I can promise that this isn't going to end well for you."

"Things already haven't ended well for me," Alley Man howled, "and all thanks to you!"

Both his gaze and his gun snapped to the left side of the room where Vince and Charlie stood, advancing with their own weapons drawn and pointed their way. Alley Man threw a glare back at Trey, who was slowly stalking forward. For every step the team took in their direction, her captor took one back toward the swinging door.

"You have nowhere to go," Trey stated firmly. "My friends are here, and more are on their way. Do you know where yours are?"

Vince snorted. "Fuck, I'll answer that for him. They're on the run. At the first sign of our backup, they scrambled all over the place like newbie fighter pilots. Left his ass here to rot."

"See!" Trey glowered. "I have a surplus of friends. You have jack shit."

"This isn't going to be the end of it," Alley Man growled. "No way in hell am I just going to walk away now."

He released his hold on Elle's neck and flung her forward. Her balance lost, she tumbled headfirst into something hard and unforgiving. Pain erupted on the side of her head, followed by a gorgeous display of stars. Around her, voices shouted. People moved.

Gentle hands brushed the hair off of her face. The ground. She was lying on a cold, hard ground.

"I think she's okay," Charlie's voice drifted in on a fog. "Bloody hell. We have to get her out of here. Trey! Leave him. We have to get her out of here. Now."

"Give her to me."

Elle barely registered the fact that she was moving when she felt a warm, thundering wall beneath her cheek. She burrowed her nose into the familiar musky scent and felt the hovering dark cloud close in around her.

"Sweetness, you can sniff me later. Right now I need you to stay awake." Trey's voice was weighted heavily with concern.

Elle tried to listen . . . but the dark cloud swept right in and took the stars with it.

CHAPTER SIX

Nursing a slight headache, Elle inconspicuously pinched herself on the thigh and hoped she'd wake up to realize that everything that'd happened in the last few hours was nothing more than an extremely high-adrenaline dream—the airport, the father-daughter chat, the gala. Everything.

But nothing happened.

She either needed a large-bore needle to the ass, or to accept that at some point, her life had taken a drastic turn, morphing into a real-life action movie; or maybe a romantic comedy, considering her one-night stand and the man responsible for her protection were one and the same—and sitting next to her in the back of an SUV.

Elle fought the urge to glance at Trey and instead, stared out the window. They'd left the city two and a half hours ago, and in the last thirty minutes, there hadn't been much around in the way of scenery. Behind them, the headlights of the SUV carrying the rest of Alpha Security occasionally lit up a lone tree or, like now, a handful of glowing eyes from resident deer.

Civilization had long since disappeared.

Eventually, she'd start demanding answers to the questions loitering in her head, but every bit of energy currently in her possession went to avoiding Trey. And it was difficult, almost impossible, when the heat of his gaze shifted—and stayed—on her.

God, the things he'd heard at the gala—about James, the accident. The only good to come out of that conversation, other than that it eventually ended, was that James hadn't taken her hospital slip-up and elaborated for all to hear. It wasn't others knowing about her condition that bothered her. It was what had come after; how naive and trusting she'd been in thinking that people who were supposed to care would actually be there for support.

Instead, they'd torn her down—and Elle wasn't going to put herself in that position again.

Ever.

Unable to resist Trey completely, she performed the side-eye glimpse she'd perfected while working in a pediatric unit. An unapologetic intensity radiated from his body. That had been fine in Thailand, when she'd thought she could enjoy his strength and then walk away, but it was beginning to unnerve her in her uncertain future.

"One step closer to home-sweet-home." Rafe's announcement veered Elle's attention away from Trey to the open field in front of them.

An airplane hangar loomed in the distance, the only building—or anything—in the immediate area except for the jet sitting atop a macadam runway. Rafe pulled up to the plane just as the stairs descended.

Car doors opened and closed as everyone piled out of the

SUVs. Elle caught sight of a tall, dark-haired man unfolding himself from the driver's seat of the second SUV. With a full beard and dark eyes, he looked a bit older than the rest of Alpha. His hair was still more pepper than salt, but there was something in the way he carried himself...almost as if he carried the weight of the world on his shoulders.

This man had seen a lot, Elle thought to herself.

He spoke with Vince and Rafe a minute before letting the two men head toward the plane.

"Miss Monroe." He approached, holding out his hand, and introduced himself. "I'm Sean Stone. Sorry we couldn't meet during better circumstances."

Logan sauntered by, a heavy duffel braced on his shoulder. He clapped Sean hard on the back and kept going. "This here's Alpha's head honcho. The Boss Man. The Captain."

"So you're the one who can tell me exactly what's happening?" she asked directly. "Or are you the one who gave the order to keep me in the dark?"

There were a few throat-clearings as people shuffled around.

"I'm sorry for all the hush-hush, but it's what's best for now." Sean's apology didn't really sound like an apology. "Just know that we have your safety in mind. Which means that we need to get you on that plane."

Elle wanted to disagree, but she also knew staying in the open probably wasn't a good idea.

Sean turned to Trey, who stood just behind her shoulder. "You and Elle are taking the plane back to headquarters. Vince and Rafe are going with you. Chase, too, so he can help keep an eye on her head. The rest of us will drive the SUVs back."

"Sounds good," Trey acknowledged. "We'll see you back at headquarters."

They boarded the plane, and Vince raised the stairs before he and Rafe disappeared into the cockpit. A third man she didn't recognize stepped out from a back room—an entire freaking room—on the plane. Sweet heavens. She was starting to think Trey didn't have any ugly friends.

Tall, blond, and broad, he flashed them a smile. "Was starting to think I was going to have this entire bird to myself."

Trey palmed the small of her back and introduced her. "Elle, this is Chase, our medic. He's going to take a look at your head."

"I'm fine." She waved off the concern.

"But he's checking you out anyway."

Trey's tone of voice made his words sound more like a demand than a suggestion. Hands braced on her hips, she turned to look him in the eye. "I'm a trauma nurse. I think I'd be able to tell if I have a concussion—which I don't."

He folded his arms across his chest and didn't even blink. "And as the person who carried your unconscious body out of the hotel, I say you need to get checked."

From somewhere within the plane, a clock ticked. No one had ever infuriated Elle so much—not even her father or James. When she went toe-to-toe against them, she wanted to throttle them. Period. When she butted heads with Trey, she had to stop herself from throwing herself into his arms and shoving her tongue down his throat.

"This plane isn't taking off until it happens, sweetness," Trey warned.

"Fine." Elle clenched her teeth and turned toward a waiting—and uncomfortable-looking—Chase. "You can check my pupil reactions, but I'm telling you that they're fine. I don't even have a headache anymore. I know my name, the date. The only thing I don't know is where I am or where I'm going, and that's because no one will actually tell me."

Elle took a seat on the leather couch and waited. Chase knelt warily, his penlight in hand. "I'm beginning to see why you and the doctor are friends."

Shay.

A swarm of guilt flooded Elle at the thought of her best friend in this madness because of her. God, Elle wouldn't blame Shay for disowning her—or moving and not sending her the new address.

"Were you the friend that Trey said was with her?" Elle asked.

Chase nodded as he studied her pupils. "I was. That woman could curse the paint off walls—especially when she's worried about you."

Elle smiled, wondering if Shay had pulled out the curses she'd learned from her Sicilian grandmother. "The feeling goes both ways. Are you sure she's okay?"

"Oh, she was seriously pissed at first—at not being with you. But she eventually realized that you're where you need to be." Chase skated a look to Trey, who was watching from a distance, and murmured, "And go easy on him, will you? I know he makes not throttling him really damn hard, but he means well... and just wants to make sure you get where you need to be too.

"You're all good," Chase announced a little louder, and stood. "I think I'm going to keep Vince and Rafe company up front—unless you kids need a referee."

"Bite me, Kincaid," Trey offered.

Chase laughed and clapped him on the shoulder. "Careful. I hear you may need a little backup when we get to headquarters. Be nice or I'll take away my support."

Chase disappeared toward the front of the plane, leaving

her and Trey alone. Trey's presence filled the interior of the plane. He tracked her as she finally took the time to study her surroundings, making her feel like a bug under a microscope. She wasn't sure what he was thinking, or if he expected her to say something.

Heck, she didn't know what *to* say that didn't sound awkward or ungrateful. He'd given her the best sex of her life and had also saved her rear end—twice.

"You can relax here on the couches." Trey gestured to a pair of leather sofas. "Or there's a bedroom in the back, if you want to lie down. It's not a long flight, maybe an hour and a half max. Bathroom is halfway down the hall."

Elle took one couch while Trey took the other. Their knees brushed from the close proximity, and she had to fight against doing it again, but on purpose.

"So," she broke the silence, "I'm sure this is probably shocking to hear, but my father has the tendency to rub people the wrong way...rub them to the point of blisters. If I had a security detail every time it happened, I'd never, ever be alone. What makes this time different?"

"You mean other than the fact that these are more than just threats?" Trey lifted a single eyebrow and propped his elbows on his knees. "They've attempted to abduct you twice now, each time a more brazen attempt than the last. Are you seriously about to try and downgrade it?"

Elle's smarted at his words. "Considering I've had a gun drilled into my ribs *twice* in the past twelve hours, no, I'm not downgrading it. But I'm wondering who my father pissed off, and the list is too long to narrow down easily— or at all. You know what? I think I *am* going to go lie down."

She stood, planning on getting as far away from Trey as the private jet allowed, when his hiss of pain stopped her. His arm was outstretched in her direction, but his attention—and hers—was focused on his red-tipped fingers.

"What happened?" Elle crossed the distance to him in a rush. Despite his protest, she turned his arm to search for the source of the blood and found a frayed slash in his dress shirt and a painful-looking scrape on the back of his bicep.

Trey tried pulling his arm from her inspection. "It's just a scratch. I don't even know how it got there. I'll slap a bandage on it and it'll be fine. No worries."

Elle drilled him with her best nurse's glare, the one known to strike fear in even the unruliest of patients. "I've seen ingrown hairs put men bigger than you in the intensive care unit. It doesn't take much for *just* a scratch to get infected. Tell me, Mr. Commando, how will you do your job then? Can you work your gun trigger with your tongue?"

"Don't underestimate the talent of my tongue, Elle."

Like she could. Her face heated with the not-so-hidden innuendo, and when Trey's lips twitched in the formation of a grin, she looked back to her task. She felt marginally better seeing it with her own eyes. The fabric of his dress shirt had protected him from a more serious laceration.

"First aid kit?" she asked.

He nodded toward the small kitchenette. "Under the cabinet in the corner, but this really isn't necessary."

"Yes, it is." She gently pushed him back down onto the couch. "Sit and be quiet."

Elle retrieved the kit and used the time to try and pull herself together before kneeling between his outspread thighs; thighs that strained the fabric of his suit pants; thighs that practically hugged her waist. She fought to get the jitters out of her hands as she worked.

Trey's proximity affected her like no other patient she'd ever had. Three seconds ago, she wanted to wring his neck.

Now she was dangerously close to begging him to take her to that aforementioned bed down the hall and strip her out of this dress.

Work. She needed to focus on work. "Take your shirt off."

"Excuse me?" Their eyes locked. There was that damn smirk again.

"Shirt. Off." Damn, those words were a lot harder to summon than she'd like. "I need to clean the entire thing, and your shirt's going to get in the way. You may be the professional when it comes to guns and grunting and stuff, but this is what *I* do. Shirt. Please."

"Well, since you said 'please.'"

Elle thought she'd sufficiently prepared herself to come face-to-chest with Trey again. She hadn't. He started undoing his dress shirt, and each time another button popped through the hole, Elle's mouth got a little drier. Her gawkfest started at his chest and slid down to where his abs put a generic six-pack to shame. No wonder she'd gone a little out of her mind back in that Thailand bar.

Whoa boy. Her gaze caught the line of tattooed script skating up the right side of his torso, reminding her that only a few short days ago she'd counted—and tasted—every colorful ink work on his gorgeous body.

"What does the tattoo on your side say?" She returned her focus back to his arm.

"Always fight. Always live. Always love."

Well, that wasn't what she expected him to say. "That's kind of poetic. Do you read poetry?"

He watched her clean his scrape and reach for the antibiotic ointment. "Do those songs they make you recite in kindergarten count?"

Danger! Danger! Humor and sexiness definitely didn't help keep her mind from wandering to dangerous places.

She needed metaphorical distance, and quick. "Guess you probably don't get a lot of reading time in with a job like yours. Rescues. Bodyguarding. Although I have to admit, it's pretty smart of you to sleep with your...What did you call me? Asset? It ensures you're close to them at all times, right?"

Mission accomplished.

Trey's smirk melted, doling out a sliver of guilt to go along with her much needed buffer.

She finished cleaning and bandaging his bicep, then stood, with every intention of hiding in that bedroom for the remainder of the flight. Two steps in, his hand captured her wrist.

Elle couldn't look him in the eye. Instead, she studied his fingers, long and wide, with the exact right amount of callus to let a woman know he didn't work in an office. He used his hands and he used them well...both in his job and on her.

And that right there was the problem. He affected her too much not to make her nervous.

Chase's voice announced their impending takeoff, and Elle was forced to sit. She chose the couch opposite Trey and prayed for a quick takeoff. He didn't speak. She didn't even know if he blinked. He stared, silently searching every inch of her face before his focus dropped to her mouth. On reflex, her tongue flicked out to moisten her dry lips.

The second the unbuckle sign lit above them next to the PA system, Elle did so quickly. But Trey was quicker. He was unbuckled, on his feet, and standing in her way before she could make an escape to the back of the plane.

Gently cupping her cheek, he tilted her face—and her eyes—up to his.

"Is that what you seriously think?" His thumb faintly

brushed over her dry bottom lip as he questioned her. "You think I'd sleep with you just to keep you close?"

"Honestly, I don't know what you'd do—because I don't *know* you."

"You know me, sweetness. Biblically."

She slipped from Trey's touch, despite the fact she longed to close the gap even more. It was like her body was magnetized toward his. "I know what you look like naked. I know you're badass with a gun in your hand. And I know you obviously don't like to be argued with. But I don't know *you*, just like I don't know a thing about what the hell's happening in my own life."

"We're going to tell you everything we know. We're just going to—"

"Make sure I'm out of danger first," Elle finished. "That's what your boss said too. But it doesn't mean that I have to like it."

"When the hell would you have liked me to give you an update? While I was preventing you from getting abducted the first time, the second time, or when you were lying unconscious in my arms?"

"How about before you slept with me!" Elle shouted. It wasn't often she raised her voice. Maybe it was that she'd never been quite so fired up. She took a deep breath and summoned her inner calm. "You know what? It's fine. What we had was one night, and one night doesn't deserve life stories and meaningful conversations. So you can keep your secrets and your agendas to yourself."

"Is that really what it was?"

She gave him a confused look. "What do you mean?"

"Is what happened really a one-night thing?" Trey clarified. He took a small step closer.

The question, innocent enough, made her heart jump.

"Considering that it happened the *one* night...in technical terms, that *is* what they consider a one-night stand."

Trey's heated gaze feasted on her face. He took another step. "One-night stands are meant to be fast." Step. "Forgetful." Another step. "You do what you need to do to get that release and then you move the fuck on."

Elle's throat went dry.

Trey stepped so close that their shoes touched, and despite the fact that she knew she should move, she couldn't. Her feet were rooted into place. "You're right on all fronts."

Trey's arms wrapped around her waist, so slowly, so gently, that she could've pulled away at any time. She didn't. She rested her hands on his bare chest and felt the quickening thump of his heart beneath her palms.

"So then tell me why I can't get that night out of my head," Trey added. "Tell me why, for the first time in my life, I couldn't give a fuck about not mixing business and pleasure and want nothing more than to have you right here and now."

"But I still don't know y—"

"Former Major Trey Michael Hanson. Delta. Thirty-four. Taurus. A son. A brother. Never married, although I hope to be, when the right woman comes along. I haven't been all that interested in anyone for a damn long time—and then I saw you sitting on that bar stool and couldn't think of anything else but having you in any way—or amount of time—I could. Still can't. Now, your turn for a bit of honesty." Trey paused. "Why did you take a stranger up on his offer?"

Elle didn't know if she could handle much more of this honesty thing. Her pounding heart threatened to burst through her sternum. "Because you looked like you were the type of person who did what you wanted, whenever you wanted, and didn't apologize for it. Ever. I hoped some of that would rub off on me."

Maybe she shouldn't have been quite so honest. Trey looked at her as if trying to read her mind, and she was thankful that he couldn't. Right then, it was a huge mess of contradictions.

"So then why the fuck are you so ready to bolt?" Trey's question was no more than a whisper. "Is it because of your ex? Did that asshole hurt you that badly that you're unwilling to take a chance?"

Yes, but not in the way he meant. She'd already been hurt by the time she found out that James was a cheating bastard and her father an emotionless one. When she'd formally broken things off, she'd been . . . numb.

"No," Elle answered truthfully. Her stomach clenched, and she wished she could blame it on turbulence. "James didn't hurt me, not even when I caught him half naked and bending his secretary over his desk."

"Then why the push back?"

"Because I don't want to get drawn into a relationship with someone who could."

CHAPTER SEVEN

Elle wished she could rewind time and say something different because, the second the words left her mouth, Trey's eyes lit up with something akin to challenge. That was the only way to describe it.

She needed to retreat before he acted on the look in his eyes, because once he did, she didn't know if she was strong enough to resist. As it was, she was in a constant battle with her body's natural desire to navigate into his personal space.

"I think I'm going to lie down and take that rest after all." Elle made it as far as the end of the hall, her hand braced on the half-open bedroom door, when she felt his presence behind her. "Trey, this isn't a good idea."

His mouth caressed the back of her neck, making her tremble. He gently turned her around and skated a palm up the length of her arm. Over her shoulder and into her hair, his fingers combed out what was left of her updo and then gently fisted near her nape. A chill zipped along the path of his touch.

"I know." Trey skimmed his mouth down her cheek until it hovered over her lips. "And I don't care. Tell me you don't fucking care right now, sweetness."

God help her, but she didn't.

She gave her head the barest of shakes, unable to say the words aloud. But that was all Trey needed. He walked her backward into the bedroom. His boot kicked the door shut, and then his mouth descended on hers in a kiss that made her body release a little sigh.

Elle clutched his forearms and held herself steady as he slowly slid his tongue past her lips and retreated. Over her jaw and to the soft spot beneath her ear, he sucked and nibbled, rolling her lobe between his lips before giving it the barest of tongue flicks.

"What the hell have you done to me?" Trey murmured.

He gently backed her into the wall, using the stability behind her to anchor his body against hers. His arousal nestled into her stomach, but it was when he lifted the hem of her dress and inserted a muscled thigh between her legs that her knees went weak.

"I need to hear you come, Elle." Trey groaned against her ear, the sound an erotic whisper. Flick. Lick. Nibble. Every caress of his mouth drove her nearly out of her mind.

"Yes," she panted, arching into the palm of his hand as he thumbed her cloth-covered nipple. "God, yes."

If this was his idea of keeping a strong line between personal and professional lives, she couldn't imagine what it would be like if that line were erased.

He shifted his knee and urged her hips into a slow rotation that ground her damp panties on top of his thigh. Elle's eyes rolled backward as a hefty dose of heady desire washed over her whole body. She was wet, ready, and so freaking needy.

Trey brought his hand between her legs. Gently dragging a knuckle over the spot where her clit ached for attention, he waited until her hips bucked into the touch before breaching the edge of her panties with that same finger.

"You're about to go off, aren't you, sweetness?" He rubbed against her wet folds, careful to avoid where she wanted him most.

She rolled her hips and he pulled his hand away. Elle let out a frustrated growl and gripped his wrist in an attempt to hold him where she wanted him.

Trey chuckled against her mouth before giving her lower lip a gentle nibble. "Do you want me to make you come, Elle?"

"Yes! Stop teasing me."

"I'll never tease you." His eyes fixed on hers and, finally, one wide finger glided through her wetness and into her more-than-ready body. "At least not more than you can take."

One finger, then two. He thrust slow and steady before brushing his thumb over her clit. Elle grabbed the back of his neck and pulled him in for a kiss that this time made *him* groan. Her tongue tangled with his, and he met her stroke for stroke, both in the kiss and in the unhurried plunge of his hand.

Her muscles tensed and clenched, the low drumming ache building with each thrust and stroke.

"Oh my God," Elle panted between kisses.

"Let go," Trey demanded against her mouth. "Let go so I can feel your body wrap around my fingers."

Elle never knew she could come on command, but she did. Hard. Her entire body went up in a flash of pleasure.

The rush flooded over her, so intense she didn't know how to contain it—she couldn't contain it. Trey silenced her cry with his mouth and kept up the same slow momentum, thrusting and rubbing his hand against her until the very last quiver rolled from her body.

Only Trey's arms kept her from hitting the floor.

It took forever for her to catch her breath and, thankfully, she wasn't alone. Trey panted heavily, his voice husky with lust. "I need you to know that it's bringing me true physical pain to fucking say this, but we better put on the brakes."

Likewise, but he was right. Not only was this not the time or place, but Elle had a nagging suspicion that Trey could easily become an addiction—the more she savored, the more she wanted.

She shouldn't want because she couldn't *have*.

Trey removed his hand from her panties and stepped back, clearing his throat. "I'll leave you to take that nap."

"Okay."

After one more heated look, he left her alone. Her body still hummed from the orgasm that had crashed through her body when she plopped facedown onto the full-sized bed and screamed into the pillow. "I'm in *so* much freaking trouble."

* * *

Trey grimaced, shifting his cock in his pants to a less painful position. A throbbing dick was his penance for not letting Elle go like he should have. When they'd been together the first time, he hadn't known she was his assignment. This time, the blame was on him.

He changed into jeans and a T, and then waited in the rear fuselage until his erection went down to semi before letting himself into the cockpit. Chase, lounging back and appearing to be asleep, had his feet propped up on the only vacant seat and Rafe fiddled on his phone, no doubt talking to Penny. Vince was the one navigating them closer to headquarters.

Trey pushed Chase's legs off the chair.

"What the hell, man?" Chase startled awake, and then seeing Trey's face, sat up a little straighter. "How's the patient?"

"She's going to lie down until we get to headquarters." Trey sat and glanced over toward Rafe. "How's my little sister doing? She come to her senses and decide she can do a hell of a lot better than you?"

Penny wasn't really his sister, but thanks to her father's inability to parent, she and her niece, Rachel, had come into his mother's house at the ages of twelve and nine, and made his own teen years as hellish as any little sisters could. He'd been the big brother to their skinny pains-in-the-asses until a string of fucked-up ideas created a nearly ten-year rift. And now, Penny was engaged to his best friend.

Once upon a time, the idea of Rafe and Penny together bugged the ever-lovin' hell out of him, and on the occasions they sucked face in his vicinity, he still felt the need to bleach his eyeballs. But bleach be damned, he was glad two of the most important people in his life were now the most important in each other's.

He hadn't booked a fucking wedding venue, but he couldn't deny that he wanted to wrap himself around the same body every night too. He wanted someone comfortable enough with him to tell him when he was acting like a jackass. And caveman-like or not, he wanted someone to protect and worship, someone who wouldn't be deterred by the fact that he'd keep her in bed all the damn time.

He wanted it all.

Rafe put his phone away, but his grin remained plastered on his face. "You know Penny. She's trying to save the world, one unfortunate soul at a time. Last week, we visited Rachel at the clinic, and the second Doc Stevens glanced Penny's way, he got the hell out of Dodge. No lie. I've never seen him move so fast *away* from a woman. It had to have been a fucking record."

Trey snorted. "She tried to fix the good doctor?"

Rafe chuckled. "Poor fuck didn't realize what he was doing when he off-handedly mentioned his recent slew of odd-ass dreams. But you bet he won't make that mistake again."

Trey asked the question that was probably on all their minds. "Did she say how Rach was holding up since we've been gone?"

As quick as a snap of the fingers, the mood in the cockpit went from light to dark. There wasn't a day that went by when Trey didn't want to kick himself in the ass for abandoning his family. He might not have hand-delivered Rachel into the arms of drug lord Diego Fuentes, but he sure as fuck hadn't been there when she'd gone missing. He hadn't been there when Penny had traveled to Honduras to get her back either—*herself*.

Fate and a mutual enemy had returned Trey's family to his life, and now that he had them there, he wasn't about to let go. Rachel fought a constant battle against Freedom, the nasty-ass super-drug Fuentes had pumped into her system and even though he couldn't fight it for her, he was sure as hell going to be her back-up.

They all were.

Rafe's jaw flexed with the effort to keep his own emotions under wraps. "It's one step forward and then a few steps back, but she's a tough cookie. Right now, h̶[...]y problem's that she wants to kick Freedom to the curb too fast to let her body adjust."

A menacing growl emanated from Vince. "If those Fuentes bastards weren't dead already, I'd drop a building on them a second time."

"And I'd be the one to push the fucking detonator," Trey agreed.

Chase gave him an encouraging fist-bump. "Amen to that."

"Speaking of bastards"—Rafe diverted the subject and twisted in his seat—"what the fuck's up with your lady's daddy dearest? Christ. I thought I was going to have to pull you off him."

Vince snorted. "And I would've pulled you off Trey. That ass-wipe deserved a good beating more than anyone I know—except for that hemorrhoid he called an assistant. What the fuck was his name?"

"James," Trey growled. "Elle's ex."

Vince's eyes widened. "The hemorrhoid was the bastard she reamed into at the gala? I should've let Charlie pummel his ass like she wanted to do. How the fuck did Elle ever end up with a first-class ass like him?"

Trey shrugged, not knowing himself. The Elle he was getting to know and like didn't take much shit from anyone—him included. He couldn't imagine her linking herself to a fuckwad like James Worth.

Rafe's sudden burst of laughter broke the brewing tension, catching Trey's attention. "I thought our little nurse was going to have to administer CPR to her own father when you basically told him to shut the fuck up about that damn gala business. The man was one vein-bulge away from having a coronary."

And Trey hadn't cared. Still didn't. His father had engrained into him the proper way to treat and talk to a lady, and it pissed him off when he witnessed others doing the exact opposite. That Elle's own father treated her that way made him see all fucking shades of red.

Trey barely kept his voice even. "First thing Stone's going to need to understand is that the Senator's done calling the shots on Elle's protective detail. There's no more working with him and trying to calm the waters."

Three sets of eyes landed on him, and he made sure to meet each and every one. "Don't look at me like I've lost my fucking mind. There was no goddamned reason—at least a good one—for her to be at that fucking event. And because we did what that asshole wanted, she was put at risk. Never again."

The cockpit went quiet for the second time. Vince looked to Chase. Chase looked to Rafe . . . and Rafe cursed.

"You need to tread really fucking carefully, my man," Rafe stated.

"What the hell's that supposed to mean?" Trey demanded.

"It means that it's awfully fucking easy to blur lines, and I think you're halfway to smudging that shit up real good."

"Coming from you, that's awfully fucking priceless. You know that, right?"

Rafe held up his hands in surrender. "I love Penny, and I don't want to imagine what my life would be like without her in it, but I have tunnel vision when it comes down to her safety. I cringe just thinking about the number of times things could've blown up in our fucking faces in Honduras because of it. I was lucky—pure and simple. I just don't want you to put that same kind of risk on your shoulders."

"Elle's safety is paramount, too, but it's not the same."

Rafe's raised brow silently called him on his bullshit answer.

"Seriously. We happened and it's done. Besides, she's already said she's not looking for anything serious, and I'm not in the market for quick fun. Makes the clean break an easy one." He wiped his palms on his jeans as if cleaning his hands.

This time, Chase was the one choking down a snort. "Yeah, brother. We hear you. We also heard the two of you a little bit ago. If that's what you call making a clean break, I'd be curious to hear what a messy one sounded like."

Trey knew that in order to talk himself out of this corner, he'd have to lie through his fucking teeth. He took complete responsibility for his actions. Always. "It was a brief lapse. It won't happen again."

The guys all exchanged a look, but wisely stayed silent. They razzed the hell out of each other at every opportunity, but they knew when to draw the line. All of Alpha was the same. They were a brotherhood with boundaries. Unfortunately for him, they were headed to headquarters where there were two people who didn't give a flying fig about personal no-fly zones.

CHAPTER EIGHT

Elle's thirty-minute power nap lacked both napping and power—unless you counted the powerful vividness with which she replayed the bedroom-wall interlude with Trey. Over and over, and maybe in reverse, too. But when she wasn't reliving every detail of the event itself, her mind drifted to dangerous places—like Trey's uncanny ability to slip beneath her defenses.

She'd gotten lucky with James, barely feeling a twinge when she broke off their engagement. Heck, she'd been relieved. But if she handed her heart to someone and then watched him look at her differently when she shared that the accident that had hijacked her life with surgeries and doctor's appointments had also stolen her ability to have children?

It would shatter her.

It couldn't happen. She couldn't *let* it happen. And that's where her rules came into play.

No expectations. No relationships. No futures. No messy strings.

As long as she focused more on those rules than on Trey's broody gaze, or his talented hands, or wicked mouth, she'd be safe. Unfortunately, an hour later, when she was the middle of a Trey and Chase sandwich in another SUV, it was practically impossible not to dwell on how the Alpha operative could light her body up like a bonfire. So instead, she focused on the passing scenery.

Mountains and more mountains, with the occasional green valley nestled between. The sun faintly started peeking over the long cascade of treetops, giving them a gorgeous blue halo.

"Those are the Blue Ridge Mountains," Chase said, noticing her look of awe. "They're a small segment of the Appalachian Mountains. Gorgeous as hell, but a clusterfuck to drive through in the winter."

"And we're home," Rafe announced from the driver's seat.

Elle glanced out the opposite window and did a double take. As far as headquarters for a clandestine private security firm went, a country bar was the last thing she expected. Somewhere in the depths of the one-story stone building, a single light illuminated panes of stained glass. A string of small banners lined the overhang, advertising burger specials and beer brands that could be found within. And above that, was the sign.

Alpha.

"Is this the bar you told me about when we were at the gala?" She looked to Trey for confirmation and got a small nod.

"It is."

"But I thought we were going to the Alpha headquarters."

"You're there, hon." Chase gave her a grin before slipping out of the car.

Everyone followed, unloading bags from the trunk while she inspected the front of the building.

"I pictured something a little less…domesticated," she admitted.

Rafe hoisted two large duffels in each hand and led the way to the front door. "What did you expect? A castle with a moat and a dungeon?"

"Maybe not the moat. Now, if you told me that there was some kind of underground bunker built into the mountainside, I could believe it."

Rafe chuckled. "Then you'd be pretty damn accurate."

She widened her eyes, bouncing her attention from man to man before settling on Trey. "Seriously? Wait, how were you allowed to build *into* a mountain?"

"Because we own most of it," Trey answered. "At least for miles in all directions. The entire mountainside used to be a training facility for the Army Reserves."

"Then how did you all get it?"

"Rough economic times and government cutbacks had them closing down some of their smaller facilities, this one being one of them."

Elle's eyes widened. "So the bar…"

Trey held the front door open and finished her trailing sentence, "Is what allows us to do our job without raising local alarms. To them, we're just the owners of their favorite watering hole."

Elle stepped through the door. Her first glimpse of the interior reminded her of a perfect blend of neighborhood bar and Irish pub. Worn wooden tables and chairs and a small row of antique pool tables separated the one room into two, with the other side dominated by a plank-board dance floor and modest corner stage.

Elle fell into step beside Trey as Vince led the group toward the back of the building. "So you mean to tell me that a bunch of men like...you all...bought part of a mountain and no one asked any questions? I thought small towns don't usually like being invaded by outsiders."

"Hell no, they don't," Chase agreed. "Only the government knows about purchasing the mountain, and the rest was handled because Trey, Penny, and Rachel practically grew up around the corner."

Elle's eyes snapped to Trey. "You grew up here?"

"I was a military brat so I grew up everywhere. But this is where I spent my teenage years until I joined the Army."

"Years and years of his mama's red-beet eggs and chicken potpie." Chase scrubbed a hand over his face and groaned. "And you haven't lived until you've tasted Mama Hanson's opera fudge. It's fucking transcendent."

Vince growled. "Shut the food talk, Kincaid. You're making me goddamned hungry."

"So exactly how clandestine are you guys?" Elle had to ask. A secret bunker in the mountain. A private plane to get them where they needed to go. This was no fly-by-the-seat-of-their-skivvies operation.

It wasn't until Rafe stepped next to a shelving unit that Elle realized they were all crammed in a storeroom. Being crowded in a five-by-five space with four overgrown men should've made her damn nervous, but she wasn't. Not even when Rafe flicked something behind him on the wall, and the entire shelving unit shifted left, revealing an elevator door.

"We're so clandestine that even our families don't know the particulars about what we do here," Trey admitted.

"So why are you trusting me? Doing what you all do, I'm sure you've made some enemies along the way. Aren't you worried that I'll sell your location to the highest bidder?"

"We've probably made more enemies than we can count," Trey agreed. "But tell me, Elle, *should* we be worried about bringing you here?"

All eyes landed on her, waiting. Trey had kept his voice light, but she knew she needed to give him the right answer.

She cleared her throat and pushed away the sudden rush of anxiety. "Of course not. All of your secrets are safe with me. I'm just…nervous. I've never been inside a secret non-government facility before."

"You've been inside the White House, haven't you? Trey asked with a smirk.

"And yet it's got nothing on a hidden base built inside a mountain."

It was apparently the right thing to say. Rafe leaned his right eye down to a scanner and, after a second and a faint *beep*, the elevator door opened and they stepped inside a steel box.

When the doors closed again, the car moved. Elle jolted, taken by surprise by the sideways movement, and grabbed onto the nearest stable object—Trey's arm.

"Sorry," she murmured, letting go quickly.

"Don't be." He braced his arm behind her back, his wide palm on her hip. Even through clothes, his touch sent a tingle to the pit of her stomach. "It's not a conventional elevator. It's almost like an escalator—goes up and down, but also deeper *into* the mountain. It takes a little getting used to."

Finally, the elevator stopped. A second after the doors opened, a flying wall of red hurtled into Rafe, the momentum knocking the operative back a few steps. He laughed, right up until the redhead locked his lips in a kiss that nearly made Elle blush.

"Jesus Christ," Trey complained and pushed past the kissing couple. "Can't you save that shit for your bedroom? The gas station burritos I had after breakfast are gonna stage a reappearance if you don't knock that off."

"Fuck you, Hanson. It's been nearly two weeks since I've seen my Red, so you're just going to have to deal." Rafe settled the woman's legs around his waist and walked them into a spacious room that looked more like the common area in an expensive frat house than an underground headquarters.

Chase urged Elle into the spacious dwelling. "Don't mind the lovebirds. Once you come to grips with the fact that they're part rabbit, they're easier to handle."

The redhead giggled and untangled herself from around Rafe's body before turning to Elle, hand extended. "God, I'm sorry," she apologized. "So much for first impressions. I'm Penny—the girlfriend. Just so you know that I don't usually go around accosting men in elevators. Well, just Rafe."

"Damn right, just me." Grinning, Rafe playfully swatted Penny on the ass as he passed, "and you're the *fiancée*, Red."

A pretty pink hue rose on her freckled cheeks as she smiled. "Oh, yeah. That's right."

Penny slipped an arm through Elle's and pulled her deeper into the studio-style space, which had a small kitchen tucked into the corner and a couch and plush chairs spread throughout. Everything had clean lines and warm tones, and fit the men who stayed there perfectly.

"So I had a room ready for you just in case you made an appearance here in the Hole," Penny was saying, "and we picked you up a few things...or *I* did. I wouldn't let any of these guys buy me a toothbrush, much less toiletries or, God forbid, clothing. It was a bit of a challenge not knowing how long you're going to be with us, but if you run out of something, or if I forgot something, let me know, and I'll get it for you."

"Penny," Trey warned.

"Oh, stuff it. I'm not trying to get the dirty details." When he cocked up a disbelieving brow, she added with a chuckle, "Okay, maybe I'll try a little bit, but let's not forget that you guys are the muscle in this circus, and I'm the bended ear. It's my job to listen. Now go away."

Trey looked a little insulted, and Elle couldn't help but chuckle. She liked Penny already. Any woman who could hold her own against this group of guys was obviously a special person.

Vince rummaged through cabinets, pulling things off shelves until he found something he liked. "Have you heard from the rest of the horde? How far out are they?"

"About a half hour," Penny answered. "And Stone said that he wants everyone in the situation room before he gets here. Something about a shit-storm and a clusterfuck and a bigwig with an overinflated head. And I'm not sure he was talking about the one on his shoulders."

Rafe ripped the bagel from Vince's hand and took a huge bite. "Babe, you need to stop calling it 'the situation room.'"

"Fine. I'll call it the War Room. Or the Room of Testosterone. Ooh, I like that one better. Anyhow, you all need to shower before you can even think about planting yourselves on any of the furniture." Penny cut a glare to Vince, who looked about five seconds way from doing just that.

The guys, laughing and ragging on each other, headed toward a back hall, looking more like overgrown teenage boys than badass security operatives. Trey lingered, staying toward the rear of the group.

"You going to be okay?" he asked, voice gruff as though he had a problem forming the words.

Penny propped her hands on her slender hips. "What am I? An ogre? She'll be fine. Seriously, Trey. Don't suffocate the girl. Where the hell's she going to go in this mountainous box?"

Trey grumbled under his breath and started trailing behind the others. He spared the girls a quick glance over his shoulder, for which Penny dramatically shooed him away with her hands.

"You two almost act like siblings," Elle chuckled.

"We are," Penny admitted, surprising her. "Not *really*, but in all the ways that count. Anything horrible an older brother could do to a little sister, Trey did to me. And considering that I lived with him and his mom from the time I was twelve, he had both opportunity and ammunition." She looped her arm back through Elle's. "It's a long story that I usually don't tell until after at least three drinks, heavy on the alcohol. How about I give you the not-so-grand tour?"

The not-so-grand tour turned out to be pretty grand. And twisty. And turny. And probably covered more ground than a football stadium.

"This place is an underground maze," Elle said as they turned into another long corridor. "You didn't happen to pick up a GPS in those toiletries and things you mentioned, did you?"

Penny laughed and looked around as if trying to see it for the first time. "It is pretty massive, isn't it? But then I think about the size of the men stalking the halls. It wouldn't be pretty if they had to be practically on top of each other."

"Is it just the six of them?"

Penny pushed through a set of double doors. "Right now, yeah. But we're slowly growing. We're currently vetting a few guys—and that's before Rafe puts them through the gauntlet to see if they're made of the right stuff. Stone's very particular about who he lets climb on board. It's one of the reasons why only a select few people in the government even know about Alpha."

Elle wondered how her father had managed to get his name on that list, but then again, he got his name on a lot of lists—blacklists, hit lists. He was versatile that way.

Eventually, she and Penny reached the sleeping quarters. Doors lined the hall, some closed, some open and revealing surprisingly spacious and well-organized rooms. Elle wondered which one was Trey's.

"Do all of you live here?" Elle forced her imagination away from a Trey-inspired bedroom theme—which included his sheet thread-count and the size of his mattress.

Penny nodded and continued to lead the way down yet another corridor. "For the most part, but we all have regular apartments closer to town, too. It would raise more than a few eyebrows if a dozen people holed themselves up in what appeared to be a small business and never came out. This is rural Pennsylvania...if we started doing things like that, they'd peg us as some kind of weird religious cult and call the feds."

Elle chuckled. "Yeah, I guess you're right. That would look a little odd."

"This is our testosterone-free zone," Penny announced.

They stepped into a mini version of the main room, but this one sported a much gentler style, with coordinated but mismatched furniture and a modest television instead of a gargantuan movie screen.

"If any of the guys come in here, they know to tread carefully." She pointed to three doors on the far wall. "That's my room, when I'm not staying with Rafe—which I do nearly every night unless I'm trying to teach him a lesson. That room in the corner is Charlie's, and the one to the right is yours."

Her own room. Elle peeked in, pleasantly surprised by the size—and the bathroom. Not to mention the mound of clothes sitting on the bed. Penny urged her inside. "Go. I can't imagine walking around in a dress and heels for longer than thirty minutes, and you must've been in that get-up for hours. Shower and change, and I'll be out here when you're done. Or I wouldn't blame you if you wanted to collapse."

Elle wrapped the other woman in a hug before she even realized what she was doing. "Thank you *so* much, Penny. I don't know how I can ever repay you for all of this."

"Please, you don't need to thank me." The redhead returned the hug and waved off the gratitude. "Oh, and there's also a walkie-talkie on the bed—just in case you get lost in the maze and need to send out an SOS."

Elle didn't wait longer than five seconds after Penny closed the door before she was shedding her gown and kicking off the shoes that had definitely given her at least two blisters. She turned the water to scalding hot and stepped under the spray with a sigh. Now, if only the last few hours would go down the drain, she'd be all set.

Elle washed her hair and then her body, and, loving the shampoo Penny had put in the bathroom, washed her hair again. After drying off and dressing in a T and yoga pants, she decided to rejoin Penny in the small testosterone-free common room.

"Well, well, well. Look who decided to grace us with her presence," a familiar English voice sang when she came out from the bedroom. Charlie, wearing a sports bra and shorts, lounged in one of the plush chairs, her feet propped up on the coffee table. "I was about to send a search party to see if you tried escaping through the plumbing. Not that I would've blamed you for making a break for it. I swear to God, one of these days I'm going to snap and go postal on every single thing of male Alpha origin that currently resides in this mountainous bloody crater."

Elle's step faltered as she glanced at a laughing Penny. "Is she okay?" Elle asked the redhead.

"No, I'm not okay!" Charlie's feet thudded to the floor, a look of pure lethal intent glinting from her brown eyes. "When we *finally* get to Alpha after two hours of being trapped in a car, I head to the gym to work out a few of the kinks, and who do you think makes an appearance? *Navy!* But only to point out everything wrong with my sparring stance, and then fly out of the room like someone lit his jock strap on fire."

"By Navy," Penny fake whispered to Elle, "she means Vincent. He and Charlie are *special* friends."

Charlie's brown eyes narrowed on Penny. "You are so bloody lucky that I love you to pieces or I would totally have you in a headlock about now."

Penny blew the other woman an air kiss.

Charlie turned that wicked gleam in Elle's direction. "Speaking of special friends..."

Penny's head snapped back and forth between Elle and Charlie. "What? Wait, who? I have no idea what you're talking about, and you know I don't like being left in the dark. Tell. Spill. Dish."

Charlie's smirk widened, and she even threw in an eyebrow wiggle for good measure. "Not my story to tell."

Penny's gaze twisted to Elle, and Elle reached for the bottle of water in front of her.

"There's not much to tell," Elle lied. *There was so much to tell.* "I'm here because my father must've pissed off someone—again—which is no real big surprise for anyone who knows him. It's happened before and I'm sure it'll happen again. The only difference is that this group doesn't seem to mind getting their hands dirty. So now I'm here, and I'm still waiting for my explanation—or at least an update on where we go from here."

Penny nibbled on her bottom lip, her face scrunched up as if in deep thought. "Somehow I don't think that's what Charlie meant, but let's keep rolling with it for now. The guys haven't given you any kind of inkling as to what to expect in the next few days?"

"Days?" Elle snorted. "Try minutes—or even seconds into the future. All I keep being told is that once I'm *safe*, they'll finally clue me in."

"Maybe that's what they're discussing in the Room of Testosterone."

Charlie's previously teasing smile vanished in an instant. "What do you mean?"

The redhead shifted in her chair, looking a bit uncomfortable. "I mean that they're all having a little powwow in the strategy room. Stone had me tell the guys when they landed. I assumed that you already knew about it, but just couldn't take their presence anymore."

"It must have slipped their minds," Charlie said through gritted teeth, not looking or acting like she believed that for one minute. She erupted out of her seat a second later. "Let's go, ladies. I think it's about time we bring a little estrogen into the Room of Testosterone—and maybe we can get Elle some bloody answers while we're at it."

Elle wasn't sure exactly what the petite blonde had in mind, but if it erased a few—or any—of the looming question marks hovering over her life right now, she was game.

"Let's do this," she agreed, getting to her feet.

CHAPTER NINE

Everyone had lost their damn minds. It was the only rationale for anyone thinking their current topic was a remotely good idea. Trey shook his head in disgust, not bothering to temper down the snort that had all eyes swiveling to him, including his boss's.

"You have a problem, Hanson?" Stone asked from his seat right across from Trey.

Sir Stone and his Knights of the Oblong Table.

When everyone had arrived, they'd gathered in their strategy room as expected, and the seating arrangements went like they always did—first come, first served—with no particular throne for the boss to sit in because he liked to keep things on an even keel.

Stone rested his unyielding gaze on Trey. "Keeping Elle here at the compound makes the only logical sense—especially since we've yet to identify who we're dealing with."

"It's not the keeping her here that I have a problem with—it's the fact that we're going to let someone else deal with the bastard who's threatening her when we should be hunting him down ourselves."

Logan grunted his agreement from his seat two spots down. "A-fucking-men to that."

"I'm telling you, Stone," Trey added. "I *know* him from somewhere—or I feel like I should know him and it's driving me fucking crazy."

"Guys, I get it." Stone sympathized with their frustration, scrubbing his hand over his beard and looking like he was about to start pulling it out, roots and all. "But it's not like we're going to be sitting down with our thumbs up our ass. Charlie's already loaded the main bastard's facial sketch into our databases and shared it with the investigators the Senator hired to look into the threat. If we get a hit, we'll pass it on to Secure Solutions so *they* can use it to track the bastard down, but our focus needs to be on keeping Elle Monroe safe."

Ever since the morning in Thailand, her safety was all Trey thought about. At least, when he wasn't thinking about how she felt against his mouth. Or in his hands.

Trey ignored the sudden hush that swept over the room and leaned back, balancing his chair on its back two legs. He felt the fucking looks—from Rafe, from Vince, from Logan—from all of them, including Stone.

"What am I missing here?" Stone asked, his dark eyebrows lifted up in confusion as his attention bounced from man to man.

Chase chuckled. "I told you we should've had the water tested before we bought this crater—and then I said it again after Ortega came down with jungle love fever."

"Hey, now," Rafe half-heartedly defended himself, and then grinned, no doubt thinking about his lusty little redhead. He shrugged. "That was it…just *hey*, *now*. Because he's right. There's no sense in me denying it."

Vince got up and helped himself to one of the bottled waters in the corner fridge. "Why the fuck do you think I suck down these things? The shit here isn't safe."

Stone growled, "Would someone care to bring me into the joke?"

"There's nothing happening between me and the Senator's daughter that wasn't mutual or short-lived," Trey finally defended himself to his asshole friends. "Maybe instead of worrying about my fucking love life, you all should start worrying about the storm clouds that are going to brew when you tell Elle that she's going to be stuck here for the foreseeable future."

Logan peered over Trey's shoulder. The former sniper, always cool and laid-back, thunked his boots to the floor with a softly muttered expletive. "Too late, man. It's already fucking raining."

Trey turned and immediately swallowed a curse. Charlie and Penny flanked Elle, not a smile or hint of a grin between the three of them as they stepped into the room. It was like watching a pack of velociraptors from that dinosaur movie, the three of them spreading apart and making it near impossible to keep track of them all at the same time.

"Babe," Rafe acknowledged Penny.

He stood to greet his fiancée and was left standing alone when she took his seat instead. Vince stole a glance at his empty spot. He wasn't so diplomatic about giving up his chair. He made a quick grab to mark his territory, getting Charlie's pointy elbow drilled into his midsection for good measure.

"Goddamn it, woman," Vince growled.

Charlie ignored him, lifting her sneakered feet onto the

conference table. "We figured that our invitations to your party got lost in the mail, but now we're here, and the fun can start." She patted the empty chair next to her, urging Elle over—within direct sight-line of Trey's own position. "Come on and have a seat, love. Let's hear what the boys have to say."

Stone looked weary as he leaned his elbows on the table. "We were only going over our options, Charlie."

"You mean the ones that involve me?" Elle chimed in, sitting next to Charlie.

Fuck if she didn't stare down Stone until he shifted in his seat. Sean Stone made uncomfortable by a woman half his size—unreal, although justifiable.

"I think you said back in New York that I'd get answers to my questions once I was safe," Elle reminded him. She looked around the spacious room, blatantly passing over him. "I don't think I'm going to get much safer than here."

"You're not. Nothing and no one is getting to you here," Trey spoke up in hopes of getting her to look his way. It worked, and her blue eyes nearly knocked him off his fucking chair.

Something about the woman turned off every brain cell in his head whose goal wasn't getting her naked and in his hands. That's what had happened in Thailand and on the plane...and they needed to have a conversation about what they were going to do about it.

His underlying hope? Not a damn fucking thing.

But being surrounded by his friends wasn't the prime time to hash things out. He needed to wrestle his dick into behaving and lift his mind out of the fucking gutter. For now.

"Well?" she eventually urged him to continue. "Then start talking. Tell me what's happening."

The woman didn't mess around. Stone gave him the

small nod to go ahead. Yeah, make him be the harbinger of bad fucking news. "The bottom line's that a few days before you were scheduled to be back in the States, someone contacted your father's staff with threats against you, and they're credible—as you figured out by the airport and the gala. They're not fucking around."

"Why?" Elle asked.

"What do you mean, 'Why?'?" Her question surprised him.

"Why are they using me? Why not threaten my father directly?"

"Because it's more efficient for them to threaten the family than the individuals themselves. It's what they call the Paparazzi Effect. Celebrities often don't care about the gossip rags talking shit and photographing them, but when their children get caught up in the storm, it's a different story."

"So they threaten me and get my father to do—or give them—something they want?" Elle snorted on a laugh, but the humor didn't come close to reaching her eyes. "Then they're going to be sorely disappointed when he tells them to take a leap. They'd be better off threatening James if they want my father to do something for them."

Elle's adamant belief in her words made Trey wish he'd punched her father when he'd had the chance. Christ. She was the man's only daughter, his family. Trey didn't even want to think about what she'd had to deal with growing up in the Monroe house for her to be so settled with the fact that her father didn't really give a damn.

Elle cleared her throat, breaking the sudden awkwardness. "So what happens next?"

Stone joined the conversation. "Ideally, the authorities will find the person responsible for the threats, and once he's taken into custody, the payday for our men in black doesn't happen. They go away. You're free and clear."

"And the less-than-ideal scenario?"

"The more roundabout way is focusing on the bastard who keeps popping up like a damn rash," Trey answered. "Once we get him and his friends into custody, we use them to get to whoever hired them."

"But that's if you get him."

"He can't hide forever, Elle," Trey needed to reassure her. "Most mercenaries that pimp themselves out for business like this have some kind of military background, and I can tell you from tangoing with the bastard, he has some kind of training."

"Oh, so I have a *trained* mercenary trying to hunt me down. That makes me feel so much better."

"It also means that's it's just a matter of time before we find out who the hell he is, and once we do we'll—"

"Put the information in the hands of the authorities and the security firm your father hired to let them deal with the takedown," Stone interjected, shooting Trey a stern look before addressing Elle. "Our job is to ensure your safety, and we can't do that until all people involved in the threats are apprehended."

"And what happens if that doesn't happen?" Elle asked, interpreting what Stone was telling her. "I can't be expected to stay here forever. I mean, I know everything about my life is one big blank space right now, but I do still have one."

* * *

After taking a much-needed nap, Elle checked in with Shay on Alpha's secure line and felt marginally better knowing that she hadn't ruined her best friend's life. And Shay, despite the fact that she didn't like being kept in the dark about what was happening, understood the need for it without any elaboration. That's what made her so freaking wonderful. Everything was wonderful—Shay, the compound, her two new best friends...

And the drink in her hand.

Unlike the strong *zap* and forceful tingle that happened whenever she was in the presence of a certain green-eyed operative, the hum currently riding shotgun through her body was like something she'd feel rubbing against a person-sized balloon.

"You're running low, love. Let me take care of that." Charlie took Elle's empty glass from her hands and replaced it with one filled to the top.

"I don't think I should have any more." Despite the words coming out of her mouth, Elle wrapped her fingers around the drink and took a long sip.

"Oh, please. If anyone deserves another bloody round, it's you." Charlie grabbed the blender and filled the two remaining glasses. She kept one for herself and passed the spare to Penny.

Actually, they'd bypassed the cute little daiquiri glasses an hour ago, opting for something that held a larger volume. The swapping of the drink-ware had roughly correlated to the time Elle started experiencing that pleasing little hum.

Elle let out a messy slurp that conjured three sets of giggle fits. "These things should be illegal, they're so freaking delicious. If my head wasn't slightly spinning right now, I wouldn't even realize that they have alcohol in them."

Penny looked to her friend with a spark of pride. "Charlie happens to be a mad genius at disguising the alcohol. He'll deny it to the end of days, but even Trey got knackered after having only two of her drinks. *Two*. The guys didn't let him live it down for months."

"Do you know that I've never been drunk?" Elle divulged. Both women's heads swiveled in her direction, their mouths dropping open in shock. "I know. I'm almost thirty years old and I've never had to hang my head over the toilet and puke up my insides."

"Never?" Penny asked, incredulous.

"Never. Not even on my twenty-first birthday. I spent the night like any other birthday or holiday—wearing formal wear and *dining* with people about thirty years my senior—and older."

"That's..."

"Bloody sad," Charlie finished, still looking horrified.

Elle pointed at them and corrected, "*That* was being a Monroe. My mom tried her best, but when she was diagnosed with cancer, priorities shifted—as they should've. She just didn't have the strength to go toe-to-toe against the great Senator Monroe. What he said was law."

Sympathy misted Penny's eyes. "My mom passed away when I was young, too. Is that why you became a nurse?"

The flood of *what-ifs* that always came when Elle thought about her mother had her taking a cleansing breath. She nodded. "Cancer takes control of every corner of a person's life. The nurses who took care of her toward the end helped give a little bit of that back to her—and I wasn't too young to notice."

"It takes a special person to be able to perform that kind of service." Penny lifted her mug in the air. "To nurses—God's angels here on earth."

Charlie and Elle stared at Penny—and burst into laughter.

"God's angels on earth?" Charlie snorted. "Where the bloody hell did you read that? A greeting card?"

"I may or may not have seen it on a bumper sticker, but that doesn't mean it isn't true," Penny defended herself, and ended up joining in their amusement.

"So it looks like we have a twenty-first birthday to celebrate...about nine years too late." Charlie topped off Elle's drink before she had a chance to decline. "I'm not even going to tell you what I did for mine. I don't want to put you into shock."

"Why? Were there police involved?" Penny teased. Charlie gave the redhead a coy smirk that made Penny choke on her drink. "Are you serious?"

Charlie avoided the question. "So you've never had a proper snog with the Porcelain Princess, and you've never experienced a true birthday celebration—including your twenty-first. Love, you can forget tonight's previous goal of making you crawl to your bed. If I've done my job right, you won't even be able to make it off this bloody couch."

They tapped their mugs together in solidarity and tipped their heads back for another drink.

"Did you see the look on the guys' faces when we showed up at the Room of Testosterone?" Penny giggled. "Oh my God. Especially Trey—it was freaking priceless. I seriously think they didn't know what to do about their turf being invaded—even Stone looked a little out of sorts, and *nothing* rattles him."

"Bloody Caveman Club," Charlie muttered before lasering her gaze Elle's way. "Don't let the overabundance of testosterone distract you while you're here in this hole in the ground. It's bad enough that the redhead over there was a sellout."

"You say that like I'm the only one." Penny gave Charlie a pointed glance.

The female almost-operative pushed a pink-tinged lock of hair from her face and looked deceptively calm. "Maybe we should think about cutting you off, Penn. You're starting to talk nonsense."

"Yeah? Then why is one of my fears stepping into the training room to find you and Vince in a naked sparring match?"

"Navy? Not bloody likely."

Penny's grin widened when she shot a look to Elle. "She'd like to think it wasn't so bloody likely, but I have a sense about these things. Just like I have one about you and Trey."

Charlie flung herself on the couch, forcing Elle to clutch her drink tightly. "Talk about naked sparring matches. Panties are at serious risk of catching fire by being in the same room as you two."

"Now I think *you've* had too much fruity goodness." Elle tried to play off the too-on-target statement.

"You may wish that was the case, but we both know it's not true."

Elle shook her head and ignored the faint spin that followed. "Trey's an intense guy. I'm sure he's like that in every aspect of his life."

"He is." Charlie agreed with a nod. "They all are, and they have that brooding, protective thing down to a bloody art form, but Trey—compared to the others—has always been a bit more low-key. Lately, though, he's rivaling Vince in the doom-and-brood department, and that's saying something."

The pull to spill her guts was strong, and got stronger the more the bottom of her mug came into view. This was what she'd always imagined it would be like to have girlfriends and slumber parties. Sure, she had Shay, but she'd come into her life when they'd both already been bogged down with responsibilities and professional futures.

Instead of puking up her emotions, Elle asked, "Do either of you have any suggestions on how to ignore the draw of the brood? Because I have to be honest, if I keep going in the direction I am now, I'm going to smack into it head-first... possibly naked *and* head-first."

Penny gave her hand a sympathetic pat. "I know from personal experience that the more you try to convince your-self that you're not drawn, or the more you try to keep your distance, the harder and deeper you'll fall. Love is a fickle, fickle little bitch."

Charlie choked on her drink, coughing until her face went crimson. "You said fickle little *bitch*."

"I swear. I can swear. Why does everyone think I'm inca-pable of swearing?"

"Screaming '*Oh, God*' when you and Rafe are shaking the compound walls during a vertical mambo doesn't really count."

Penny tossed a pillow into Charlie's face, initiating an-other string of giggles. It took a few minutes for them to settle down, but then the root of Elle's concern came roaring back.

Trey. Her. And that undeniable draw to have his hands on her at all times.

Penny angled sideways into the plush chair and draped her legs over the arm. "In all honesty, Elle, you really could do a lot worse than Trey. He's one of the good guys. He says what he means and doesn't play into drama. He's loyal. He's steady."

"So he's not an overbearing alpha type?"

"Oh, no. He's *totally* overbearing. Sometimes it's so bad I call him a Helicopter Brother." Penny laughed. "But I'm reserving hope that he'll get that out of his system when he works off all the stored guilt. At least that's what I tell my-self so I don't kill him with my bare hands."

Guilt. She wondered what would make a guy like Trey

feel remorse, but the conversation was already starting to feel a little gossipy. Lord knew she didn't want anyone dissecting her feelings—past or present.

Elle felt the heat of someone's scrutiny and looked up to see both women watching her carefully.

A smile bloomed on Penny's face. "I think what Trey needs is someone determined enough to rip through that guilt and strong enough to throw a kink into his hovering. Once that happens, I think it would be happily ever after with church bells and a gaggle of kids."

Charlie chuckled and nodded her agreement. "Couldn't you imagine? Green-eyed, blonde-haired, with little dimpled, cherub cheeks? People would die from the level of cuteness."

At the mention of children, a sumo wrestler could've sat on Elle's chest and felt light. While Penny and Charlie exchanged laughs, Elle quickly sobered, and she didn't blame her new friends. After all, it was the "normal" progression expected by the majority of the population—James and her father included.

It was almost ten months ago when she'd finally accepted that it wasn't *her* normal progression. But it wasn't until much more recently that she'd stopped blaming herself for it. Sometimes, she wondered if she even had.

A solid lump formed in Elle's throat. She had to swallow a few times for it to go down. Trey's happily ever after shouldn't matter to her—but it did.

"Is that something Trey's looking for?" She barely managed to keep her voice even. "The marriage and kids and dogs barking in the backyard?"

Oblivious to Elle's inner turmoil, Penny played with a lock of her red hair. "I don't think it was even on his radar a year ago, but he bought his house a few months back, and there's really only one reason why a single guy needs *that* many bedrooms. And then there's that whole guilt thing, and his mom's not-so-subtle comments about being the only woman in her kickboxing class without grandkids."

"Who's kicking grandkids?" Vince's question had all three women turning in their seats, but it was Penny's balance shift that sent her to the floor in a chaos of giggles.

"Looks like someone's been hitting the sauce a little hard." Rafe stood next to Trey in the open doorway, smirking at his fiancée.

Penny struggled to her feet and then stumbled toward him, her finger wagging. "Strawberries, not sauce. And fruity margaritas are the beverage of choice when men are being misogynistic douches."

"Harsh words, Miss Kline," Rafe teased. "Harsh words."

"Damn right, they're harsh. And I'm telling you right now, Mr. Ortega, if you ever think for even a hot second about keeping something from me *for my own good*, or make a decision *on my behalf*, you better hide all the pointy objects."

Rafe effortlessly tossed Penny over his shoulder and didn't bother smothering his laughter. "Threats *and* swearing. You're turning into the regular hard-ass, Red. Let's go experience this new side of you together in our room."

Penny's curses could be heard echoing down the hall. Charlie answered Vince's low chuckle with a curse and a slam of her bedroom door, and with no one to amuse him, the tattooed operative said his good-byes and disappeared.

Elle was alone at last . . .

Except she wasn't.

CHAPTER TEN

Elle teetered when she stood. It took a good few seconds of clutching the back of the couch to make sure she wouldn't fall head-over-behind, and then she busied herself taking the empty mugs to the sink.

"Don't let me prevent you from doing what you need to do. I'm sure it takes a lot of hours to hone the fine art of evasion." Elle kept her back turned toward Trey but felt the warmth of his stare on her neck.

That was one of her problems—she *felt* him even when he wasn't touching her…even when he was clear across the room. Hell, he didn't even have to be in the room, because the second an image of him popped into her head, her body started revving its engines.

"Is that what this margarita-fest was all about?" Trey asked. "You being under the impression that I was keeping you in the dark somehow?"

Anger spun Elle around, and suddenly, he was inches away. He hadn't made a noise when he moved, and yet if she took a deep breath, their bodies would touch. His gravity started to draw her even closer until she managed to pull herself together.

Lifting her shoulders back and holding her ground, she stated, "There was no *impression* about it. It's taken well over twenty-four hours to finally be told that I may as well make myself comfortable and forward all my mail."

"When would you have liked me to sit you down and have a heart-to-heart? When you were about to be abducted or when you were unconscious on my lap?"

"How about anytime between sticking your hand down my pants and us walking through the doors of Fort Wilderness? Or better yet, before you even slept with me!"

The muscle in Trey's jaw flexed wildly. "I already told you that I didn't know you were my assignment when we met in Thailand."

"Actually, no, you didn't. What you *did* was ask me if I thought you capable of doing such a thing, which led to me saying that I didn't know you, which led to the whole *'I'm Trey Michael Hanson. Son. Brother. Taurus. Never been married.'* After all, I needed to know your astrological sign before I was told why I was being threatened with guns every time I turned around."

"What exactly are you pissed off about? That you think you've been getting the information dodge, or the fact that we slept together at all?"

"Yes!" Elle tossed up her hands.

"Yes to what?" Trey asked, his tone patient, as if he were dealing with a petulant child.

"Yes to all of it—for keeping the little woman in the dark and making decisions that involve *my* future and then expecting me to go along with it, no questions asked. And yes, for sleeping with me when you've been off buying big houses with empty rooms that need to be filled. All. Of. It."

Freaking margaritas.

Trey shuffled closer, obliterating the nearly nonexistent gap between their bodies. Her ass pushed into the edge of the sink as he slipped his arms past her waist and caged her against the counter. In their close proximity, the mini apartment shrank two sizes.

Trey leaned down, stopping when his mouth was a breath away from hers. "If you want to talk about this, then we're going to talk about it once those damned margaritas are out of your system and not a second before."

"Why? Are you trying to *evade* again?" she pushed.

"Nope. What I'm trying to do is make sure you remember everything I have to say to you because, babe, I have quite a bit. The first topic's going to be that shit about sleeping with you under false pretenses."

"Why? Because you're above using people?"

Trey's eyes flashed, and Elle clamped her mouth shut. She didn't even know where that had come from, but while the margaritas dropped her walls, they amplified her insecurities. She liked to believe that she'd shed them all when she left for Thailand, but it was obvious that they'd come sneaking back—at least when aided by alcohol.

"I'm giving you a pass on that comment but only because these last few days have really sucked ass—that, and I've had the displeasure of meeting your bastard father and ex," Trey said calmly. "I have a feeling they put you through a hell of a lot more than I know about, but one thing I'll tell you right the hell now is that I'm not them. I have never *been* that kind of man, and I'm sure as fuck not going to turn into one anytime in the future."

"No guy's going to come right out and admit to being a manipulating jerk." *God Elle. Shut. The hell. Up.*

"That's it." Trey bent at the waist and pulled her into a fireman's hold.

"What are you doing?" Elle squealed, giving his butt a smack as she dangled from his shoulder. "Put me down. Right now."

"No can do. Actually, I could, but I'm not going to. You're going to sleep this off." Trey stalked from the room and turned down the hall—and kept walking.

"Great. Sounds good. But my room's where we just were." She smacked him again, but he didn't even break his stride. "Take me back!"

"Nope. Because when you finally sleep this off, we're going to have a little talk, and I don't want to have it with Charlie's ear pressed to the door."

There was nothing to do but hold on. Elle gave up trying to squirm away and braced her hands against Trey's lower back. Each up-and-down movement of his steps churned an unpleasant storm in her stomach.

The second her feet hit tiled ground, Elle lost her battle with the nausea. She leapt for the toilet as the margaritas staged a reappearance, and then she prayed for death by toilet water. It felt like a lifetime had passed when the last twist finally ebbed. Her hair, dampened with sweat, stuck to her forehead, and her eyes watered.

"You okay?" Trey asked.

Oh, God. He released her hair—which she hadn't even noticed he'd been holding away from her face—and handed her a damp washcloth.

She closed her eyes and buried herself in the cool cloth. "I think so."

"Good."

Trey lifted her limp body off the floor and deposited her on a bed of clouds. At least it felt like clouds, her suddenly sore muscles nestled by nothing but softness.

Elle buried her face into a downy pillow that still held Trey's spicy scent. "God, you always smell so freaking good."

"Glad you think so."

Elle was too busy trying to get the world to stop spinning to enjoy the humor lacing his words. She groaned and clutched tightly onto the pillow, as if it could anchor her to the ground. "Can you flick the off switch on the carousel?"

"Afraid not, sweetness. Looks like you're stuck going on the ride."

Elle groaned again, barely registering that her shoes were being pulled off. Next came her yoga pants, as steady hands began gliding them down her thighs. She tried to help with her shirt, but got brushed away. It was probably for the best, because she could barely manage flipping onto her stomach when the blanket was tucked around her body.

"Tomorrow." Trey's mouth brushed against her ear in a low murmur.

Tomorrow.

Ell burrowed into the mattress...If anything happened tomorrow she hoped it would be an incurable case of amnesia.

* * *

Someone dared Elle to eat cotton balls. That was the only explanation for why her tongue was a useless mass of grossness in her mouth. She rolled to her side, gasping when the mattress fell out from beneath her body. A sluggish foot-plant to the floor was the only thing that saved her from breaking her nose.

"I'm dying," Elle groaned. With her head playing out a tom-tom drumbeat, she pried her eyes open a millimeter at a time and pushed herself upright on the edge of the bed.

Her vision was slow to focus and, when it did, the memories of the night before started slinking their way back—her diarrhea of the mouth, the embarrassing porcelain prayer. There was a vague recollection of being undressed—which must've happened, since she was now sporting a dark gray T-shirt that hit her about mid-thigh...and smelled of Trey.

Stupid. Stupid. Stupid.

Elle slipped from the bed and said a little prayer of thanks for the bottle of water and aspirin left on the table. Her body ached, muscles stiff, as if she'd lain in the same position for a week. But with no clock in sight, there was no way to tell how long she'd actually been out. It could've been minutes or hours or even days.

She peeked into the hallway, happy when she found it empty, and hustled as fast as she could to her own room. She made a beeline for the bathroom, and what she saw in the mirror made her cringe. Red-rimmed and bloodshot, her eyes were the only thing on her face that wasn't an unseemly shade of pale.

She brushed her teeth—twice—and hopped into a shower hot enough to melt skin off bones. Once she could stand her own smell, she changed clothes and retraced her steps from the day before, when Penny had shown her around the compound.

Ten minutes of walking later, she realized she was lost in the maze of corridors. At ten and a half minutes, she realized she'd left behind the damn walkie-talkie.

As she was about to eenie-meenie a direction, a loud metallic echo rang through the hall. Elle followed the sound to find Charlie standing in an indoor shooting range.

On a table to her left, an eclectic array of handguns was spread out.

The female operative's back faced the open door as she aimed a gun at a target and fired off a quick succession of rounds.

When she was finished, she turned with a grin and pulled off her headphones like she'd known she wasn't alone. "Look at you, all red-eyed and limp-tailed. I thought you'd been exaggerating when you said you've never gotten drunk, but you weren't, were you?"

"There's a boatload of things I've never done."

At Charlie suggestive eyebrow lift, Elle couldn't help but laugh. "Except *that*. I've done *that* before, although I can't really say I find it as invigorating as some people do."

"Then you've been with some lazy sods. I swear, between you and Penny, I feel like such a worldly woman—or maybe a social deviant." Charlie chuckled, shaking her head as she turned toward her weapon table and swapped handguns. "That redhead claims to be all fire and spunk, but when I checked on her an hour ago, I got a pillow thrown at my head. Lightweight."

"And you didn't check on me," Elle teased, leaning against the wall. "I'm heartbroken."

"Oh, I tried checking on you, but then His Royal Moodiness appeared and warned me away. I admit, I caved, but only because I knew you'd come out sooner or later."

Trey had warned her away? Or more importantly, Trey had been in and out of the room checking on her himself? Elle wasn't sure if the thought was comforting or if it made her feel even guiltier for the things she'd said.

"You don't have to worry about running into him for a bit," Charlie said, as if reading her mind. "He's making an appearance topside along with a few of the other guys. We have to keep up the pretense of normal lives. Civilian stuff. I'm sure he'll be back bothering us before you know it. Make good use of the time alone."

"Then don't let me stop you." Elle nodded toward the target. "You looked like you were doing some serious damage."

"I do my share. Do you want to stick around? That is, if your head's not playing the bongo drums?"

"Aspirin and water did my body good."

"Then watch and learn." Charlie passed Elle a spare set of headphones before placing her own over her ears.

Elle definitely watched—and studied the ease with which Charlie held her gun. Each shot blew a larger hole in the paper target's chest and, when there wasn't much left, she aimed for the head.

"And one more for good measure," Charlie called out before releasing another shot.

"I think you finally missed," Elle joked.

Charlie flicked the switch to bring the image closer. "Look again."

Elle looked...and looked. By the time she pulled it from its clip, she couldn't stop laughing. Instead of aiming for the head or chest, Charlie's last round had ripped right through Paper Guy's crotch. "Never mind. Bull's-eye. Tell me again why you're not a full-fledged operative yet?"

Charlie tossed her headphones on the table and motioned for Elle to do the same. "Because I have a vagina. Okay, so maybe not entirely because of the lady bits. It boils down to the fact that I've never been in the military boys club, and the closest I ever came to being on the police force is riding in the back of the car."

"So you have more to prove."

"Exactly. And it didn't help that Stone hired me as the brains behind the brawn. The guys are the epitome of old dogs and new tricks. They're used to me being the one behind the computer and their new toys. But I'm getting there. Slower than I'd like, but Stone's started letting me go on assignments here and there. Actually, Thailand was my first one."

"You were in Thailand?" Elle asked.

"We were down there for about three days before we finally got the file on you." Charlie gave her a steady look before shrugging. "I'm saying that because I think it's something you should know."

Elle bet there was a bit more reasoning behind her mentioning it. "Thank you, Charlie."

"Anytime, love."

"And if it's any consolation, I'd feel safe as a clam with you watching my back."

Charlie smiled, an honest-to-God smile that softened her eyes and made her look years younger. "Thank you, but I think you'd much prefer having your dimpled Adonis watching your back, because while I think you're damn adorable, you and I wouldn't be snogging in the corners of empty rooms."

Charlie's wink stole Elle's denial and brought a blush to her cheeks. "There's no snogging...at least not anymore."

"You're forgetting that I'm with these guys *all* the bloody time. No matter what anyone says, the hero types—especially the misunderstood ones—are bloody catnip to anyone lacking a Y chromosome. No one would blame you for partaking of the snog."

"Does that mean you are, too?" Elle teased, remembering Penny's good-natured jibing from the night before.

Charlie waved off the comment. "Please. These gorillas love taking care of the damsel in distress, and I haven't been a damsel in a long, long time."

Charlie's words echoed painfully in her head. That's what

Elle had been, too. A damsel. Someone who *let* things hap- •
pen to her. But then she decided that if one slick road could
take away a small chunk of her dream, then she was sure as
hell going to control everything else within her ability.

In an odd way, the news that biological children would
be next to impossible for her had given her the fire to take
back her life, and she'd started with ending her engagement
to James and accepting the position in Thailand.

And she was going to keep up the trend.

Elle eyed the row of guns sitting on the table. "Do you
think you could teach me how to shoot one of these things?
At least well enough that I won't shoot myself in the ass?"

Another smile melted onto Charlie's face. "Sure thing. I
was heading over to the gym afterward. You're more than
welcome to come with me."

"Will there be kicking and punching?" she asked eagerly.

"And quite possibly maiming. Neither chocolate nor
shopping therapy has anything on beating the crap out of a
heavy bag. Not only is it cheaper, but you don't feel guilty
afterward."

Guilt-free stress relief sounded wonderful.

CHAPTER ELEVEN

Even on the nights when people blamed the full moon for all the crazy shit they did, Trey enjoyed being topside. He enjoyed having that little slice of normal that didn't involve memorizing strategic points of entry and exit. But tonight had been an exception and he couldn't have been happier to be on his way down into the Hole.

After dealing with a malfunctioning tap machine, fending off a dozen lame pick-up lines, and getting caught in the crossfire of a woman trying to verbally castrate her boyfriend, he was on edge and ready to climb into his fucking bed...next to Elle.

The last time he'd checked on her, she'd been out cold and still wearing his shirt. He'd never thought himself a masochist, but trying to be gallant by making sure she was comfortable for what would no doubt be a rough morning anyway had been the sweetest kind of torture.

That didn't mean he was stupid. He knew his limitations,

and sleeping beside her was way too much temptation, so he'd tried grabbing a few winks of shut-eye in the chair, and instead spent most of the night replaying the conversation leading up to him hauling her over his shoulder.

Losing his temper hadn't been one of his finest moments. She'd had a gallon of margaritas to blame for her loose tongue, but what the fuck did he have? *Nothing*.

"I'm telling you, I was equal parts nervous and turned on...but mostly fucking nervous," Logan was telling Vince when Trey stepped into the common room.

He grabbed a water bottle from the fridge and downed it in one drag before grabbing a second. "What's making you nervous? Finally getting that prostate checked?"

Vince guffawed. "Yeah, you wouldn't be so glib if you saw what your girl's been doing for the last eight hours."

"Six," Logan corrected. "Two hours before that they were taking turns neutering some poor fucking paper target in the target range."

Trey polished off his water and tossed it into the recycling bin. "I don't know what the hell you're talking about, and if you want to actually tell me, then you need to make it quick because I need a shower, food, and sleep—not necessarily in that order."

"It's not something that can be told, man. You have to see it to get the full effect."

"You've got five minutes."

It took them that long to reach the training room, and then Trey's feet stuck to the ground. When he'd seen Elle earlier, she'd been wearing nothing but his shirt and bedsheets. Now, stretchy black yoga pants and a short racer-back tank top revealed a tantalizing amount of golden skin.

Charlie held the heavy bag steady, instructing Elle through a series of kicks and punches. Five minutes ago, he'd been ready to fall facedown on his mattress. Now he couldn't sleep if his life depended on it.

"They've been at this all day." Logan seemed nearly gleeful as he leaned against the doorjamb. "After the shooting range, it was hand-to-hand, and let me tell you, that was fucking life-changing, man. Now it's boxing. I suggested a solid hour on grab-and-escapes, but I had a five-pound weight tossed at my head."

Trey snorted. "Your fault for poking the lion. Charlie's been in rare form lately."

"It wasn't Charlie that hoisted the weight like a fucking shot put."

Trey diverted his attention to Logan. "You're shitting me. *Elle?*"

"Those two hanging out should make us all fucking nervous. That's all I'm going to say."

Logan was right, but Trey still couldn't help being impressed. He turned his sights back on Elle, not caring that he was the butt of a joke, while Vince and Logan turned and left.

Charlie taught Elle with the same high-energy, no-nonsense attitude she approached her day-to-day life with, and Elle listened, using her quick reflexes to duck and weave. On occasion, she'd ask for a repeat, until he would be hard-pressed to identify the difference between student and teacher.

Breathing heavily, Charlie lifted her hands behind the sparring bag. "All right! All right! I'm crying bloody uncle before my hands go completely numb. Don't take this the wrong way, but I thought you lived a life of folding cloth napkins and studying seating charts."

Both women lay sprawled face-up on the mat, yet to notice Trey by the entrance.

Elle let out a breathy laugh. "No offense taken—and that

actually had been my life for a good long while. But then I started placing sworn enemies at the same table solely for entertainment purposes. You could probably imagine the reaction that got out of my father."

Charlie grumbled, "Bloody arse...and so's that ex of yours. I know it's none of my business, but I hope you got a good jab at his juniors for screwing around on you."

"You want the honest truth, Charlie? By that point in time, I didn't even care about the cheating. What bothered me most was that they seriously believed I'd just turn a blind eye and accept it as one of those things."

"They?"

"Yep." Elle nodded. "My father knew, and as a matter of fact, he claimed that my mother had done as much for him when she was alive—ignoring the cheating."

Charlie chanted a long string of curses before getting to her feet and grabbing a nearby towel. "Then I guess that's my answer for why you have the right hook of a terminator. You could've become a medal contender if you hadn't gone into nursing."

Elle laughed. "I probably could've."

Charlie caught sight of him, but turned her attention back to a heavily panting Elle. "I'm going to go for a run before heading to my room. Are you going to be able to find your way back?"

"I'll manage. I don't think I can move just yet, anyway, but thank you, Charlie. For everything."

Charlie waved off the thanks. As she approached Trey, her eyes narrowed. "Don't do anything I may have to punch you for, Hanson. Behave."

"I always behave," Trey retorted.

She threw him a glare before disappearing out of the training room. Trey contemplated leaving, but after hours apart from Elle already, he couldn't stay the fuck away. He casually strode over to where she still lay face-up on the mat, admiring the way her chest lifted and fell with each breath.

"You look a half inch from death." He smirked through the lie because the truth was that even sweaty and tired, she still looked fucking incredible.

Her eyes fluttered open. "I feel it. Were you watching?"

"Maybe."

"For how long?"

"Long enough to know you have a lot of pent-up aggression—and a lot of reason for it." And even though some of the things she'd said in her margarita-induced speech still chafed, he was starting to see that it had less to do with him and more to do with the assholes she'd had in her life.

Elle gave him a little shrug and sat upright. "Shay used to drag me to a self-defense dojo because she said the same thing, but there wasn't exactly one nearby in Thailand."

Trey knew it was a bad idea before he suggested it, but his mouth moved anyway. "I can show you a few floor escapes . . . if you're not too tired."

She looked torn, nibbling her bottom lip. "I'm not tired after sleeping the day away, but are you sure you have time?"

"Always got time for you, sweetness."

He gently pushed her shoulders back down to the mat, lifted her hips, and inserted himself between her bent legs. While his cock twitched out his pleasure at their new closeness, his head told him this was a fucking stupid idea.

He propped his hands on either side of her shoulders and hovered inches over her body.

Stupid. Stupid. Stupid idea.

* * *

Trey's body heat diffused through the small amount of space between them and soaked straight through Elle's skin. Floor escapes required a physical intimacy that she'd forgotten about until the firmness of his growing erection rubbed against her mound.

Elle cleared her throat, suddenly overwhelmed by a flood of nerves. "Maybe we should try this when I'm not so…" *Horny.* "Sweaty."

"Doesn't bother me." His green eyes went darker as his attention dropped to her mouth. "First thing to remember when someone has you pinned to the ground is that you don't necessarily need to be stronger to break away. You just need to know the proper mechanics."

Trey lowered his body until a piece of paper couldn't have been inserted between them.

"When I drop down closer to your chest, lock your arms against my shoulders and then shrimp your way out by planting your right foot and rolling left."

They worked through the beginning moves again and again. When she finally ignored the instinct to pull him closer—the exact opposite of what she was supposed to be doing—the escape became one fluid movement. Soon after, they added the next step, and the next, and then Elle readied herself to put on the final touch.

"Good." Trey nodded once she'd succeeded in pushing free. "Now you kick out to either the groin, midsection, or chin. I'd go for the—"

A vicious cramp attacked Elle's thigh muscle. She gasped, reflexively extending her knee to seek relief when a thud and a string of curses slowly pulled her out of her pain-induced fog.

"Oh my God." She stared in horror as blood seeped through the fingers Trey had cupping his nose. "You're bleeding?"

"That's what usually happens when you get blasted in the nose with a sneaker," he said, his voice muffled. "Goddamn."

She grabbed a nearby towel and wet it with a bottle of water before crawling back and wiping away the bloody carnage. "I am so sorry. I had a massive cramp and it hurt so freaking bad, my muscles kind of did their own thing. Shit. I hope I didn't break your nose."

"Wouldn't be the first time it's been broken." Trey laughed at her sickened expression. He gently removed the towel she held in place, but kept hold of her hand, and sniffed. "Elle, it's fine. See. Still works. Now imagine the damage you could do if you have your mind actually focused on it."

"I still should've been careful."

"Why? Because I'm such a delicate flower?" Trey slid his hands beneath her thighs and dragged her close. "No harm done other than to my pride. We're good. No apologies. But I'm pretty damn thankful we weren't working on crotch shots because then any hopes of future Trey juniors would've disappeared instantly."

Elle's heart stumbled. It had been a casual comment, had rolled off his lips so effortlessly, yet it stole the breath right from her lungs. *Act normal. Act cool. Act like there wasn't an invisible dagger prepped to slide straight into her heart.*

Trey was too perceptive. His eyes narrowed in on her as if trying to figure out what was going through her head. She forced a small smile and let her hands drop to his shoulders.

"No damaging the man-goods. Got it." She nodded in agreement. "We certainly wouldn't want to deprive the world of miniature Treys."

"What was that?" he asked.

"What?"

"You're sitting in my lap, straddling my waist, and yet I felt you pull away just then. I'm asking why."

Why the hell couldn't he be the stereotypical unobservant male?

"Because even if I don't owe you any apologies for kicking you in the nose, I do owe you one for last night." Elle prayed he took the topic change without question. When he stayed silent, she continued. "The things I said were rude and inconsiderate, and I'm really sorry."

"Yeah, well. You had a right to know, and I had more than ample opportunity to tell you. That's all on me, and I'm sorry for that. But one thing I don't appreciate is being compared to some jackass who evidently soured you on men. I don't use women, and I sure as hell don't sleep with them under false pretenses. Any women who I invite into my bed get a full disclosure on what to expect. And they get one whether they want one or not. It's how I'm wired."

"I know. Charlie mentioned that you didn't get your assignment until after you'd already been in Thailand for a few days…but I should've believed you." Elle swallowed the embarrassment that was no doubt making her face fire-engine red.

"Why? You were right on that plane, too. There's more that we don't know about each other than we do. But I'm trying to rectify that, if you'll let me."

Elle searched his eyes for some kind of clue as to why Trey Hanson seemed so…*different* from other guys she'd met. "Even before you knew I was your job, you were insistent on keeping me around. Why?"

Something flickered in Trey's eyes, some emotion she couldn't identify. He palmed her cheek and kept her face directed toward him. "It fucking kills me that you think someone wouldn't want to get to know you unless they were obligated to, sweetness. And I'd love nothing more than to get my hands on the bastard who made you think like that."

Trey took a slow breath, and his thumb brushed over her bottom lip. "I want to get to know you—because who *I* am really fucking likes who *you* are."

"Who I am is not the woman who's going to help you fill all those empty rooms." The words were out of her mouth before she could stop them, and then she waited as each passing second stretched on for what felt like forever.

"That's the second time you've mentioned something about empty rooms; I'm going to take a wild guess and say that Penny or Charlie told you about my house," Trey said carefully.

"If what you want is to find a woman who's going to help you fill that house with a lot of little Treys, then that's what you should do. But I can tell you right now, that woman isn't me. A fling is all I have to give."

When he didn't say a word after the fifth blink of her eyes, Elle shifted in an attempt to stand, but his hands clamped down on her hips and prevented her from moving.

"I'm not going to deny that I'm done with flings," Trey finally stated. "I told you that once before and I meant it. But just because I don't have my minister on speed dial doesn't mean that I'm going to walk away if someone special happens to fall in my lap."

His palms skated from her hips to her thighs, and his body shifted beneath her. She thought he was about to release his hold, but then he pulled her so snugly onto his lap.

Elle tried not to read into it. She tried—and failed. "I should go," she murmured nervously.

"Do you really want to?" He stole a quick glance at her mouth.

"No, which is why I really should."

"You obviously have a hell of a lot more willpower than me."

"It's not so much willpower as knowing what I can get away with." She knew he didn't get it, and that would definitely be one conversation they'd *never* have. Elle's gut told her that delving into any sort of relationship with Trey—with strings or without—would stretch her rules and heart beyond their limits.

"You're not looking for a relationship," Trey repeated her earlier excuse. "So what are you going to do? Live the rest of your days in a nunnery? Somehow I don't see that going all too well."

As if to demonstrate his point, he traced his hand up her spine. A trail of goose bumps immediately burst from her skin. Her body definitely didn't give a damn about keeping an emotional distance. It wanted Trey like nothing else and didn't bother with worrying about the repercussions.

"I didn't say that sex wasn't in my future," she finally admitted. "Just all the expectations that usually go along with it."

"So it's going to be one-night stands for you from now on?" He didn't raise his voice beyond a bare whisper, but the edge in his tone took her by surprise.

"Maybe," she admitted truthfully. "Or I'd take a page from your book and make sure everyone I take to bed knows the rules."

"And what are these rules of yours?" His hand cupped her nape, his large fingers twining into the hair that had fallen from her ponytail. Gently holding her in place, Trey demanded her attention.

"No expectations. No relationships. No futures. No messy strings," she answered softly.

"Sounds clinical, and sex is anything but a medical intervention...at least if you're doing it right."

"Then I'll find someone who only does it wrong." *Boy, was that the wrong thing to say.*

Trey's green eyes darkened like a storm-shrouded jungle. "Like hell you'll find someone else."

His mouth fused to hers, his tongue pushing past her lips and coming into direct contact with hers. Elle groaned as they took turns taking the lead in a kiss that quickly stole every ounce of her breath.

"You're not going to be giving those breathy little moans to anyone but me," Trey murmured. He took his mouth away and peppered kisses and gentle nips down the length of her neck.

"Boundaries," she said breathlessly, hoping to God that she could remind him why this was a bad idea because she sure as hell didn't care right then. "You don't mix business with pleasure, remember?"

"Fuck my boundaries. There's no way in hell I can be near you and not touch you. It hasn't even been twenty-four hours since I had you in the palm of my hand, and I'm so goddamned twitchy I can't even hold a freaking water bottle." He took her mouth in another searing kiss before cupping her cheek and holding her gaze steady with his. "You want sex without strings? Fine. But you get it with me."

Elle forced her shocked mouth closed. Her heart pounded in her ears. She needed to make sure she'd heard him right. "No expectations?"

The muscle in his jaw tightened. When she thought he'd changed his mind, he agreed with a faint nod. "No expectations."

Could she do it? Could she really be with Trey and stay emotionally unattached?

"If things change for either one of us, we split...no hard feelings, no questions." If Trey took her at her word, she could maybe escape the arrangement with her heart battered and bruised instead of shredded to pieces.

"I have one question for you, Elle."

"What's that?"

"Floor, bed, or shower?"

Elle's inner vixen, whom Trey always managed to conjure without trying, lifted her mouth into a coy smile. "Which is closest?"

"Floor, but the gym doesn't have a lock on the door, and if I wasn't about to share you with some nameless asshole, I'm not about to share the sight of you with the assholes I call my friends." Trey brushed his thumb across her aching nipple. "But you happened to mention that you were all sweaty, and we have a perfectly close, and lockable, shower room just on the other side of that door."

Elle slid off his lap and put a little extra sway into her hips as she walked toward the locker room. She stole a glance over her shoulder and caught him staring at her butt.

"You coming or not?" she asked, dropping her voice to a sexy purr.

"You're going to be the one that's coming first."

Trey jumped to his feet. Elle ran, barely into the locker room when his arms swept her off her feet. He kicked the door closed, flicked the lock, and strode to where the mother of all showers took up a corner wall.

Tiled and with more than enough room for two people, multiple shower heads hung in different places, but all pointed in the same direction. Trey turned on the water and tested the temperature before using the band of her yoga pants to pull her flat against his solid body.

"I wasn't expecting to get ravished today, so my clothes aren't exactly designed for easy removal," Elle admitted.

"Don't worry. I haven't had the pleasure of putting my mouth on you for almost two days. I have a lot of incentive and, if all else fails, a pocket-knife to cut my way through." He groaned, his head dropping to her shoulder. "But goddamn it, there is something I don't have."

"What's that?"

"Condoms."

Elle got his meaning and instantly felt a wave of disappointment. "I've never done anything without one."

Trey let out a sigh. "I understand. Completely."

"But…" Biting her lip, she gave him a nervous look. "I know I'm clean. And as far as pregnancies go, I'm basically a sure thing—for it not to happen, I mean."

He raised a brow at her choice of wording, but didn't comment. "What are you saying, sweetness?"

"That I'm okay with going without…if you are."

He waited a beat before replying. "I'm clean and I've never gone without either. I'd never put you at risk. But this can only happen if you're completely on board with it. If you have any reservations at all…"

"There's no reservations here," Elle whispered. She slid her hands beneath his shirt and slowly peeled it up and off his sweat-dampened body.

"None?" Trey asked, doing the same to her exercise tank.

Elle shook her head, getting breathless as he slowly lowered his mouth to her breast. "Not a single one."

At least not about the condom use.

CHAPTER TWELVE

Trey's sexual stamina had no limits, and when it came to him, neither did Elle's. In the week and a half since their locker room interlude, she'd found herself a wanton, carefree woman she didn't recognize—and the feeling was almost as addictive as the man who elicited it.

In the hopes that they'd stick with repetition, she'd started reciting her four rules every morning in the bathroom mirror. Some days she said them twice. And on those days, she made sure Trey got a refresher too.

But she hadn't needed to do that today because it had been almost eight hours since she'd laid eyes on him—or on anyone else, for that matter.

Everyone was topside. Stone and Chase were following a lead regarding the mysterious Alley Man, which took them out of town, and Rafe surprised Penny with a night away from the compound. Everyone else—Trey included—was upstairs putting in their appearances at the bar.

Eight hours of no Trey, no people, and way too much junk food had Elle standing in front of the elevator doors when it hummed to life. This far into solitary, she didn't care if it was a vacuum salesman coming to visit.

The doors opened, revealing a lone Charlie.

"I guess I'm not the one you were hoping to see sneaking out of work early." Charlie chuckled as she stepped into the room. "Your boy's still working hard at not doing much, but it's soon time to shut things down."

"It's almost closing time?" Elle heard the hope in her own voice and cringed. Being stuck in a hole in a mountain was starting to get to her.

"About another hour." Charlie grabbed a baseball hat someone had left on the table and tossed it into her hands. "Put this on, love."

"Why?" she asked while she pulled her ponytail through the back and settled it on her head.

"Because even though I doubt anyone upstairs would know the difference between a senator's daughter and a pole dancer, I don't want to tempt fate. You've been cooped up in the Hole long enough. It's time we got you some fresh air. Well ... *air*. I don't think it could be considered fresh. We get a lot of hunters and there's some bloody nonsense about soap scents scaring the animals away."

"Are you serious?" At Charlie's raised brow, Elle grinned. "Not about the soap. You don't think going upstairs would be a problem?"

Charlie threw her arm over Elle's shoulder and led the way into the elevator. "I wouldn't have suggested it if I thought it would be an issue. The guys have squirreled you away down here out of an abundance of caution, but it's not like Frederick is a beacon for mercenaries searching for blonde nurses. But just so you know, the only one who knows about our side jobs is Shiner. I call him Alpha's Grease Technician, but he calls himself a cook. He kind of came with the place."

Elle nodded. "Got it. Keep my mouth closed."

The elevator came to a stop and, a few seconds later, a beep indicated the coast was clear for them to step into the storage room. The smell of sizzling grease hit Elle's nose before they'd even fully walked into the kitchen.

"You're gonna drop them there patties, kid!" Armed with a shock of white hair and a loud bark, an older man made the kid in question jump inches into the air. "No one's gonna pay for burnt patties! You best work faster and get the shake out of your hands."

Charlie planted a loud kiss on the older man's whiskered face. "Who are you trying to fool, Shiner? These Yanks will eat anything as long as they don't have to run across the field and catch it themselves."

Shiner barely managed to smother a smirk. "Yeah, but the kid don't need to know that."

Charlie chuckled. "Shiner, this is…Laura. Laura, this is the one and only Shiner."

Shiner raised his white, bushy eyebrows, and gave her a flirty wink. "Laura, huh? Yeah, you look like a Laura. I used to know a woman named Laura…and *oh, boy*."

"Of course you did." Charlie gave his weathered cheek an affectionate pat.

A loud plop and softly muttered curse turned everyone's attention toward the greasy mess on the floor—and the kid standing in front of it. Shiner looked up at him with a growl.

Charlie steered Elle toward the swinging doors. "It's best we let them have their moment alone. Shiner's usually a big ol' teddy bear, but he can be a bloody grizzly when he's in a snit, and he's been trying to teach Ryan how to flip a decent burger for close to a month."

Elle stepped into the main bar and did a double take. Unlike the time she'd been in the room before, bodies filled every table and corner. Music blared from the speakers. Pool balls cracked together. People laughed and danced and drank. There didn't seem to be a soul in the place that wasn't having a good time.

"What do you want?" Charlie ducked beneath the bar's counter, where Vince was filling two huge mugs from the tap.

"Just a water."

Charlie nodded and pushed her a bottle before jumping into action alongside Vince. The tatted operative said something in her ear that had Charlie squirting him with the water nozzle in her hand. The spray hit him in the face and dripped down to his shirt. Elle couldn't help but grin at the show the two put on without even realizing it.

On the other side of the bar, Logan stood talking with one group of patrons before laughing and moving on to the next. It was all a little surreal. Logan schmoozing. Vince and Charlie running tabs. No one knew that the people who poured their drinks and replenished the peanut bowls were badass heroes of the selfless kind.

And then there was Trey.

He'd yet to see her, but her attention drifted to him like he had a homing beacon pinned to his clothes. Across the room, he leaned casually against the wall, his arms folded across his chest in a drool-worthy display that emphasized the contrast between his black T and sleeve of tattoos—and the redhead glued to his side Siamese-twin style.

The woman pushed her impressive cleavage against his arm and danced two red tipped fingernails up and down the center of his chest as she whispered something in his ear.

Trey listened intently and then tossed his head back and laughed.

It was a sad testament to her love life that Elle had never cared about anyone enough to invoke jealousy—not even James. But there wasn't a doubt in her mind that it was responsible for her sudden desire to claw out the redhead's eyes—especially when she lifted herself to her toes and planted a solid kiss on Trey's cheek.

Elle had no right to get upset. It was her decree of no expectations that gave him free rein to do as he pleased, and now she had to deal with the consequences. But that didn't mean she had to stand by and watch.

Elle approached two men who looked to be wrapping up a game of pool. "Does someone have dibs on the next game or is the table free?"

From the corner of her eye, Elle caught an encouraging wink from Charlie.

The man in the blue plaid work shirt and worn jeans flashed her a smile and offered her a cue stick. "It's all yours, sweetheart. This one looks like a good fit for your little self. Why don't you try it on for size and go ahead and break apart those balls."

She accepted the cue. "Thank you."

"No, thank *you*." His friend nudged him as she leaned over to take her first shot.

She bit her bottom lip in concentration and let the cue fly. Balls flew apart, at least four dropping into various pockets. Elle barely refrained from jumping up and down. She'd played a time or two before, but it had been a while. She called stripes and systematically started clearing the table.

"*Day-um*, sweetheart," the plaid-wearing stranger drawled. "You sure know how to work that stick, don't you?"

"Jealous?" Elle returned.

His friend chuckled. Elle barely resisted the urge to roll her eyes at the juvenile joke. In her periphery, she caught a glimpse of Trey, no longer looking casual and relaxed. He glared her way—and his little friend didn't look amused.

Elle couldn't help but put a little extra sway in her step as she walked to the other end of the table. One ball left to go and about a million and one ways for the shot to go wrong.

"You sink that ball, hon, and I'll pay for your drinks all damn night." Plaid Man chuckled, obviously not worrying about the thickness of his wallet.

"I'll start with a martini." Elle bent down to the table, examining the lay of the felt between the cue and the eight ball, when she felt a wall of warmth sidle up on her left.

"Keep ogling and I'm going to let Charlie serve your eyeballs in that fucking martini," a familiar voice snarled.

"Hey, Trey," Plaid Man confirmed what Elle had already guessed. "It's been all in good fun, I swear."

"Yeah, well. Get gone before I have fun with your face."

Plaid Man and his friend scampered away without so much as a backward glance.

Whatever. Trey could growl and snap all he wanted, but he wasn't ruining her good time. She threw her concentration back to the table when his spicy masculine smell drifted around her, at the same time as did a set of corded arms.

"Move now or risk getting a cue stick drilled into your gut." She gave herself a mental pat on the pack for sounding so normal.

"I'll take my chances." Trey's low voice, brushing against her ear, sent a warm tingle straight between her legs. "What do you think you're doing?"

"I should think that was pretty obvious."

"You know what I mean, sweetness."

Elle looked across the room to where he'd been chatting

up his little friend and found the redhead sending her a death-glare. Elle gave a little wave and turned toward Trey before she could see the other woman's reaction.

"Charlie said it wouldn't be a problem if I came up, and so I did," Elle explained easily. "Contrary to popular belief and my current circumstances, I do still have *some* control over my life."

Trey's silence hung heavy in the air before he murmured, "Sweetness, you have control over a hell of a lot more than you even know. If you've been up here for a while, why didn't you come over and say hello?"

"I didn't want to bother you when you were...busy."

Well, crap. That sounded catty, even to her own ears.

Trey's lips twitched. "I was playing nice with some of the locals. It's part of the job."

"Your job must have a lot of perks...two of them, to be exact."

Elle bit the inside of her cheek as Trey's smirk split into a shit-eating grin. God help her, she didn't have alcohol to blame this time for her loose lips. But it was too late to back down now, and she wasn't entirely sure if she wanted to, either.

"Careful, sweetheart, or you're going to have me believing that you're jealous."

She snorted and rolled her eyes. "Please. Why would I be jealous?"

"That's the million-dollar question, isn't it? Because you're the one who reminds me of our agreement every chance you get."

"Because it's something that can be forgotten pretty quick if we're not careful." She did her best to hold on to her mad, but it was hard to do with his body still so freaking close. "And I'm not jealous," she lied. "I just don't understand why women feel as though they have to flaunt the lady bits in order to get attention."

"Because those women don't think they have a whole lot else going for them, so they try to amp up the goods themselves. You don't have that problem."

Heat rushed to her cheeks. "Are you saying I don't have the goods to amp up?"

Trey let his hands drift slowly from the table to her waist and anchored her hips to his. "No. I'm saying that you don't need to paint yourself up like a clown and wear a shirt three sizes too small to grab someone's attention. You do that by being yourself."

Words escaped her. That was sweet...much sweeter than her catty self deserved.

"Last call! Start settling up," Charlie shouted. A chorus of complaints echoed through the room. "Hey, Laura! Get your cute little arse over here."

Elle cleared her throat. "Uh...that would be me. I'm Laura."

"Then I guess you better go." Trey took a small step back, but not one large enough that she didn't brush against his body when she slipped away.

Elle's knees wobbled as she returned to the bar and to Charlie's knowing smirk. "You looked like you needed a save."

"From who? Myself or Trey?"

"Both."

CHAPTER THIRTEEN

Elle *thunk*ed her head on the countertop and groaned. "What the hell is the matter with me, Charlie? It's like my brain isn't attached to my mouth, and my hormones themselves have gone ape-shit crazy."

Charlie gave her hand a sympathetic pat. "It's the Alpha Syndrome, love. I told you, these men pack quite the wallop."

When Elle lifted her head and brought it down for a second time, a soft pillow cushioned her *thunk*.

Charlie gestured to the rag under her forehead. "Use that to work your sexual frustrations out on these mug rings. My arms have never been as fit as they've been since this place opened."

Why not? She didn't have anything else to do, and if it took away even the smallest bit of stress, then it was well worth it. Elle started attacking the mug rings down the length of the bar, but instead of clearing her head, the harder she wiped at the stains, the more confused she got.

"Some women prefer to eat their way through a box of chocolates because of man problems, but I'm in the same category as you, hon. Work through it. May as well get something accomplished while you're trying not to wring their necks," a friendly female voice empathized.

Elle glanced up. Somewhere in her early- to mid-sixties and dressed in pressed linen pants and a button-up top, the older woman didn't exactly mesh with the other clientele at Alpha. But she sat on the bar stool as if she'd been coming there for years.

Elle returned her friendly smile. "It's a little pathetic to admit this, but I'm not used to having these kinds of man problems. Probably because I've never met this particular kind of man before."

"And is that a good thing? That he's different?" the older woman asked.

There was something both disarming and welcoming in the way her green eyes glittered in the bar's dim lighting. She studied Elle carefully, almost as if reading beyond the words she said aloud. Something told her that this woman would recognize a lie the moment it left her lips, so Elle didn't bother trying to fabricate one.

"Yes and no," she said honestly. "Yes, because I've been unfortunate enough to have been around some real jerks. No, because I don't know what the hell to do with him. He's flipped me upside down and inside out so many times I don't know which way is up."

"If you ever find out what that something is, you let me know, because his father—God rest his soul—had the same knock-you-for-a-loop effect on me."

It took Trey dropping his arm around the older woman's shoulder for Elle to truly decipher her meaning.

With his eyes lit up with affection, Trey planted a kiss on

the woman's cheek. "Ma. What are you doing out this late at night?"

Oh. My. God. His *mom*.

"Seems to be the only way I get to lay eyes on my one and only son these days." Trey's mom, with the same deep green eyes as her son, flashed Elle a conspiratorial smirk. "But now I can understand why you've been working yourself so ragged lately."

Elle wanted to bury her head in the nearest hole—strike that. A crater would be better. On another planet.

Trey's mom chuckled. Reaching over, she squeezed Elle's hand, obviously reading her embarrassment. "We didn't get to the pleasantries yet, honey. I'm gathering from Charlotte's vibrant bellow that your name's Laura. I'm Sophie Hanson, this one's mother...though his lack of visits suggest I'm nothing but a mere stranger—or a pit stop to occasional bathroom breaks."

"Actually, most people call me Elle." Keeping a low profile or not, there was no way in hell she was going to lie to Trey's mother.

Sophie didn't bat an eye. "Well, it's very nice to meet you, Elle."

"It's been busy, Ma," Trey half-heartedly defended himself. "But I was going to come over soon."

"You mean like tomorrow? At the Sled-tacular?"

Trey stared at his mother for a minute before muttering a soft curse, which earned him a raised brow. "I know I said I'd help out, but things at work are a little crazy."

Sophie leaned casually against the counter and stared at her son—who had to be a foot taller than she was. "What time does Alpha open for business, Trey Michael?"

Elle watched in fascination as Trey stumbled over his words, and a faint rosy color rode high on his cheeks. He stole a quick glance her way before meeting his mother's eyes. *He was blushing!*

"Not until late afternoon but—" Trey tried explaining.

"And how many partners do you have who could easily do whatever tidying up may be required before opening?" Sophie held up her hand to silence him and nodded to where Charlie stood a few feet away, devouring the show like live theater. "Charlotte, sweetheart? How many partners does my son have in this little venture of his…including you, of course?"

"Then that would be six other partners, Soph." Charlie grinned mischievously.

Sophie turned to Trey, still looking the epitome of calm and cool. "That's right, six. So tell me again why I'm going to have to disappoint an entire youth center full of children when I announce that you're not going to be there to watch them race the sleds that *you* helped them build?" Sophie caught Elle off guard when she turned toward her. "How would you like to go the Sled-tacular, Elle?"

"Ma," Trey groaned out a warning. "You can't just go around—"

"As in sledding?" Elle ignored Trey's deep sigh. "In the snow?"

"Well, it's definitely not summertime, so yes." Sophie chuckled. "I happen to run Frederick's youth center, and we're fortunate enough to have a prime spot for sledding right beside our little building—one of the benefits of being on a mountain."

"I've only ever been sledding once—and I don't really remember much of it. I'd love to go."

Sophie clapped her hands excitedly and turned to her son. "Then it's settled. I'll see you two tomorrow at noon. The community center." She slipped off the bar stool and pulled

Trey's head down for a forehead kiss. "And don't forget to wear an extra pair of socks, hon. It's going to be colder than your Aunt Edna's brass bra."

With a little wave, Sophie Hanson disappeared out Alpha's front door.

Trey still looked a little shell-shocked. Charlie chuckled in amusement. And Elle tried wrapping her head around all of it.

"So"—Elle plunked her ass down on the stool Sophie had vacated—"that was your mother."

Trey rolled his neck and chuckled. "All my life."

"I just made an ass of myself…in front of your mother."

Trey lifted an eyebrow. "*You* made an ass out of yourself? And here I thought she made an ass out of *me*."

"It wasn't that bad." Elle tried to be polite.

"Yes it was. It was bloody wonderful," Charlie chimed in gleefully as she hoisted a crate of dirty beer mugs and disappeared through the swinging doors.

Elle laughed. She couldn't help it. "Okay, so maybe it was a tad on the humorous side."

Trey chuckled along with her and scrubbed his face, looking like he'd just finished a marathon. "Christ. I'm thirty-four years old. I've made militia heads and dictators piss their fucking pants, and I come home and my mom's reminding me to double up on my fucking socks."

A sudden wave of sadness hit Elle out of nowhere. She tried to brush it off before he noticed, but of course that didn't happen. He caught her chin before she could turn away. "What's up? Look, if you really don't want to go tomorrow, she'll understand."

"It's not that," she admitted quietly.

"Then what is it?"

She lifted her shoulders in a small shrug. "You're lucky

that you have that—a mom who cares enough to worry that you don't lose any of your little piggies."

"I know I'm lucky. I wouldn't trade her in for anything in the world—even if she does still try to dress me like I'm four."

"Aren't you worried that she probably thinks you and I are an item?"

Points to Trey for not looking completely wigged out. Actually, he didn't look the least bit bothered. "Knowing my mom, that's probably exactly what she thinks. But why would that worry me? And if it doesn't worry me, it shouldn't worry you."

He pulled the damp cloth from her hand and plucked her off her seat. "I think that's the cleanest this counter's ever been. Come here. My show was cut short."

"What show?" She'd barely asked the question when he began racking up the balls on the pool table. "You want to play a game of pool?"

"No, I want to watch you play one, and now that there's no one here to ogle your ass when you bend over, I can actually enjoy the sight of it."

Elle scanned the room. He was right. At some point, *everyone* had vacated the room. The customers were gone, and Vince had disappeared. Charlie, having vanished with the dishes, hadn't returned. They were well and good enough *alone*.

"And what makes you think that I'm going to bend over for you?" Elle weighted her voice in what she hoped sounded like a sexy purr.

Trey stalked toward her. And it was a stalk…purely animalistic in the way his eyes ate her up as he closed the distance between them, only stopping when he looped an arm around her waist and hauled her against his chest. "Aren't you?"

They both already knew she was, but that didn't mean she

needed to give in right away. She slipped from his hold and picked up the cue she'd used earlier. She leaned over the table and enjoyed the sound of Trey's swallowed groan as she made the first shot.

Balls clacked and rolled, two immediately falling into their pockets.

"Excuse me." Elle nodded to where he stood and she needed to be.

He stepped back a half inch, barely giving her enough room to squeeze into the tight space. This time when she bent closer to the table, her rear nestled perfectly against the front of his jeans.

Trey's hands clamped down on her hips, holding her firmly in place as she made her second shot... and missed.

"Game over," Trey growled.

He'd barely turned her around when his mouth claimed hers in a toe-curling kiss. Hands clutching his arms, Elle held on for dear life as he pillaged and plundered. She eagerly accepted his tongue into her mouth and gifted him with hers. The longer the kiss lasted, the more her body melted against his.

Nothing was innocent or easy when it came to Trey. Any gentle caress or lingering look had the potential to go nuclear. Elle couldn't touch him enough. Her hands ran over his chest, fisting the soft cotton as he effortlessly hoisted her onto the edge of the pool table and inserted himself between her jean-clad legs.

"Goddamn." Trey pulled her shirt from her jeans and skated his hands toward her bra-covered breasts. "You have no idea how much I fucking want you right now."

With a strategic hip roll, she brushed her mound across the firmness pushing against his zipper. "I think I may have one," she teased.

"Then what the hell's stopping us?"

"Clothes. A lack of bed. Then there's the fact we're probably on camera right about now."

Trey guided her hips in another swivel that made them both groan. "The clothes we can remedy, beds are overrated, and the guys value their lives too much not to have turned off the camera feed from this sector the second Charlie left the room. I want to be buried balls-deep inside you when you let go," Trey admitted huskily. "Bed or pool table?"

"Didn't you say beds are overrated?" Elle's blood ran hot, every inch of her body feeling as if it could burst into flames.

"Damn straight they fucking are."

They both reached for the button of his jeans at the same time.

CHAPTER FOURTEEN

Trey couldn't keep his eyes off Elle, and it was more than the fact that he was responsible for her safety. She was fucking gorgeous, red-cheeked and laughing harder each time the wooden toboggan pitched her into the snow—which was on nearly every pass down Sandler's Hill, the hilly decline that started at the back of the church parking lot and ended after an exhilarating plummet into the community center's backyard.

"I can't believe how much fun this is." Elle's blue eyes sparkled with something he guessed she didn't experience often—freedom. She grabbed his hand and gave him a little tug. "Come on, you know you want to go up there with me. Please."

He gifted her a faint grin. "I'm content watching you have all the fun right now."

She dusted excess snow off the front of her coat and giggled. "Oh, God, and it *is* fun. Getting away for the day is just what I needed. Don't get me wrong, because I love everyone for what they're doing, but sometimes it feels a little claustrophobic."

A hint of guilt attacked Trey's conscience. As far as she knew, she hadn't gotten away for the day so much as the day—and the team—had followed her there. The fact that no one should be able to track her to Frederick didn't mean he'd leave her safety to chance. That's why Charlie, Vince, and Logan were positioned around the perimeter. Out of sight, but not out of Trey's earshot.

Charlie's disapproving snort chimed from his earbud, and he couldn't tell her to stuff it because, number one: she was right to think him a lying piece of shit; and number two: *because* he was a lying piece of shit, if Trey verbalized his displeasure, he'd end up ratting himself the hell out.

Trey swallowed the guilt and brushed away the clumps of snow that held on to the ends of Elle's hair. "I can't believe how much snow you've eaten this afternoon."

She swatted his chest and created a snow cloud around them. "*I* can't believe you helped them make these sleds."

They waved to a group of youngsters whose parents had already shown for pick-up. Only a handful of children remained, trying desperately to get in a final run.

"They did the hard parts themselves," Trey admitted. "I was more of a supervisor to make sure no one lost any digits."

"Well, then your supervisory skills are superb, because I don't think anyone could buy a better sled in the stores."

"Miss Elle! Mr. Trey! Look!" Three girls who'd been in the youth program since his mother had started it five years before called for their attention. They fell backward into a pile of snow and immediately started flinging their arms and legs in and out. "We're making Elle Angels. Get it?"

Trey chuckled, shaking his head at the kids' antics. "You've been a big hit today, although I can't say that I'm surprised."

She looked pleased, but gave a modest shrug. "Kids are just short adults without all the baggage that comes along with age. It's practically impossible not to get along with them."

Susie Wannamaker, a spritely seven-year-old with a penchant for sparkly things, tackle-hugged Elle's waist. "Miss Elle, my daddy's here to pick me up but he said I could go down the hill one more time. Will you go down with me on my sled?"

Elle clutched her chest with one hand and tugged the little poof on the girl's hat with the other. "You mean ride with a future professional sledder? You don't even have to ask. Let's go."

Trey watched the two climb the hill and was about to tell Charlie to stow her displeasure where the sun didn't fucking shine when Elle's spot was taken over by another frustrating woman in his life. His mother had remained uncharacteristically quiet this morning, and he'd known it was only a matter of time and opportunity until it came to an end.

And it fucking ended.

"Elle's absolutely lovely." Sophie watched as Elle and Susie hoofed it up the incline. "Where did you say the two of you met again?"

"I didn't say." Trey caught the coy smile lifting up his mother's lips. "Ma. Don't."

"Don't what?" she asked way too innocently. "Don't admit that I'm eager to see you settle down with the right woman and give me grandbabies? Do you know that Martha Weatherspoon's daughter just had a fourth girl? *Four*, Trey. And she's five years younger than you."

Trey draped his arm over his mother's shoulder. "My life isn't child friendly right now."

Sophie guffawed. "Please, you're part-owner of your own business so don't give me that nonsense, Trey Michael Hanson. What does Elle think about it? Kids?"

"Don't go there, Ma," Trey warned.

It was a conversation they'd had before. Marriage. Kids. And everything that came with them. But for some reason it felt different this time around, and his hunch was that difference involved a stubborn blonde nurse.

"Elle isn't looking for a forever kind of thing," he reluctantly admitted.

"What?" Sophie's eyes widened. "That doesn't make any sense. I mean, look at her with those kids. It's obvious that they adore her as much as she does them. She's a natural."

"And it's not what she wants. Hell, she doesn't even want a relationship."

"What happened?"

Her question took him off guard. "What do you mean?"

"I thought I saw something in her eyes last night at Alpha, but now I know I did. A woman like her doesn't shy away from a future that's obviously meant for her unless there's a damn good reason."

"Well, it's a reason, but I'm not really sold on how good it is. But she's convinced that it is and there's no changing her mind."

"I'm not saying it would be easy to do it, but *anyone* can be swayed with the right motivation. Have you tried not being so...large?"

Trey looked at his mom and tried to read behind the twinkle in her eyes. "Large? Like you want me to...shrink? What the hell kind of glue are you using in your craft class?"

She smacked his chest and laughed. "Sweetheart, I love

you. You know I absolutely adore you. You are my world...
but you have a habit of being...a little..."

"Spit it out, Ma."

"Controlling." Trey opened his mouth to argue but
stopped when that mom-finger started waving right under
his nose. "Do not deny it, young man. Your father used to
be the same way and I had to re-train him right from the beginning. Hell, he was still working on it up until the day of
his heart attack. It's great that you want to take care of the
people in your life, but sometimes you need to let them take
care of themselves. And most importantly, sometimes they
want to do it themselves."

Trey studied his mom carefully. "You're not talking about
women right now, are you?"

"Actually, I am. I'm talking about myself, and Penny, and
Rachel. Leaving home to start your own life is no reason
to feel guilty...but you need to remind yourself that even
though we missed you, we survived. And some women wear
that kind of survival like a badge of courage..." Her eyes
flickered up the hill toward Elle. "You don't want to do anything to compromise the badge, honey. Make sure it stays on
the jacket. Double-stitched. Maybe super-glued, too."

Sometimes Trey wished he had a translator for his
mother's words of wisdom. "So basically what you're staying is that I shouldn't be a controlling prick and scare Elle
away?"

She gave his cheek a firm pat. "I always knew you had
my smarts—something I would most definitely like to pass
down to a few grandchildren."

Trey couldn't help but laugh, and he'd nearly forgotten
that three of his teammates were silently listening to every
word—until Logan's voice chimed through the mic. "We
have an unknown approaching Elle."

Trey's gaze snapped to the top of the hill and, sure enough, Elle stood, still holding onto Susie's hand, as the tall figure stopped a bare three feet away from them. Trey didn't need to be standing next to her to read the tension in her stance.

"Fucking A," Trey cursed.

Sophie narrowed her eyes, squinting to see in the distance. "Is that one of the fathers? We told the parents to pick the kids up at the youth center."

"Vince, Charlie," Trey barked, "get my mom and whatever kids are still around out of here. Logan—"

"I'm already hustling up the right side, man," Logan panted as he ran.

Trey took off, trusting his teammates to make sure everyone else remained safe. He was halfway up the hill when he heard Elle gently urge Susie onto her sled. The little girl looked confused, but the second her bottom touched the seat, Elle nudged the sled loose with her boot and the seven-year-old shuttled down the hill and toward safety.

Smart fucking thinking, baby.

"We got a sledder coming down," Trey called, letting the others know.

"I'll get her," Charlie stated.

Trey's lungs burned, the cold air freezing his insides as he climbed the embankment. Tunnel vision narrowed his focus on Elle and, the closer he got to the top, the more he knew his gut hadn't steered him wrong. The asshole from the gala had fucking found her, and he had no goddamn clue how that had happened.

About ten feet from the crest of the hill, both Elle and the hired mercenary slithered out of his view. Boots slipping on the fresh snow, he dug his hands into the earth and clawed his way up the last few feet. Logan reached the top at the same time, the two of them approaching the small parking lot from different angles.

"And here I thought nothing could surprise me anymore. You sure do get around, princess," the merc's voice drifted through the lot. Trey ducked and wove, searching for their exact position. "I thought I'd have to pick one or the other, but it looks like I'll be able to get my payday right along with a little retribution."

"I have no idea what you're talking about," Elle's voice followed. "You're the one who tracked me down here."

In hand signals, Trey ordered Logan right as he went left. They closed in on Elle's position from both sides.

"Leave me the hell alone!" Elle shouted a moment before the sound of a scuffle reached Trey's ears.

Trey hustled, skirting around the hood of his SUV and drawing his gun. *One* hair—if the fucking bastard moved one hair out of place, he'd end him. He stepped into the clearing just as Elle executed a flawless uppercut into the bastard's nose.

The merc's weapon dropped while the man himself held his nose, blood gushing from his face as he cursed a blue streak. "You fucking whore! You broke my goddamned nose."

"That's no way to treat a lady, asshole." Logan stepped out from the rear of a pick-up, putting him closer to Elle. He guided her straight into Trey's arms. "Go. I got him. Get her the hell out of here."

Elle shook her head frantically. His little nurse, who evidently packed one hell of a wallop, was starting to lose her shit. "All the kids...we can't leave them out there to get hurt. And your mother! We have to go back down to—"

Trey cupped her cheek. "Everyone is safe, sweetness. I promise. Now we have to get you safe too."

She looked hesitant, but she didn't fight him as he stuffed her into the passenger seat of the SUV and flew around the hood to leave Logan to deal with the asshole. "Vince, how are things looking on your end?"

"Everyone's safe, and it looks like the fuckwad was alone this time," Vince said.

Why the fuck would he make an attempt alone? It didn't make any sense, but then again neither did how he'd managed to find them. "You need to call Stone and Chase and get their fucking asses on this shit real quick, because there's no goddamn way for that bastard to have linked her to Frederick. No fucking way."

"Charlie's already on the horn. Are you taking her back to the compound?"

"Fuck no."

"Good idea," Logan's voice came on the mic, breathless and sounding extremely pissed. "Because a parent showed up at the lot, and our guy used it to his fucking advantage. He's in the wind."

"How many times do we have to fucking lose this guy?" Trey cursed.

Goddamn it. Elle's eyes hadn't left him from the time he gunned the engine and peeled out of the parking lot. She was too smart not to realize that he wasn't talking to himself, but he couldn't worry about the well of hurt shining in her eyes—not right now.

Trey informed his team, "I'm going off the grid, and I'm not getting back on it until I know for goddamned sure that it's safe. I'll get in touch when I can verify that our comm isn't compromised. And Vince, you make damn sure you keep an eye on my mom until we figure this the hell out."

"Got you covered, man. You good on supplies?"

"Always." In fact, he never left home without them. Call

him a paranoid bastard, but this was one time he was fucking glad he always thought to the worst-case scenarios.

* * *

Nature could be found everywhere—in the cracked cement of big-city sidewalks and hiding in the shadows of oversized skyscrapers. And Lord only knew what kind of growth could be found in the subway.

But Elle didn't need to look too hard now. Trees surrounded her, their fresh, pine fragrance permeating the air with their heady scent. And with each step she and Trey took further up the mountain, the smell intensified.

Under normal circumstances and with an above-freezing temperature, the current scenic backdrop would've provided the perfect setting for a romantic picnic, but these weren't normal circumstances.

Each inhale of frigid mountain air brought her lungs closer to turning into two blocks of ice, and in the hour since the sun had sunk behind the treetops, she'd tripped over no less than four overgrown roots and narrowly dodged face-planting into three tall oaks—definitely not a scenario that screamed romance.

"You doing okay back there?" From six feet ahead, Trey glanced over his shoulder, his boots kicking over the large drifts of snow without even breaking his stride. "If we keep up this pace, we'll be at the cabin in less than a half hour. But we can take a break if you need one, or keep going if you're good to go."

"'Go' as in keep walking or 'go' as in *go* numb—because I lost the feeling in my toes about forty-five minutes ago."

After they'd left the community center, Trey had done nothing but drive, getting on and off interstates and weaving through back roads in an attempt to confuse anyone who might be on their tail. It had been hours until they finally pulled into a nondescript garage where he exchanged a wad of cash for a beat-up pickup—a vehicle they'd left in the parking lot of a forest ranger station roughly an hour and a half ago.

It was all a complex, well-thought-out plan—that definitely hadn't been a spur of the moment thing. Once she thawed out a little bit, she'd start thinking about how this exact scenario had evidently been planned—right down to the team being present at the park.

Trey stopped and waited for her to catch up. From less than a foot away, it was easy to register the frown marring his face.

"Why are we stopping?" she asked.

"If you need a break, we'll stop," he offered.

"Nope. Let's keep going. I'm fine."

At his disbelieving snort, she added, "Okay, so I may not be singing-from-the-rolling-hills fine, but I'll survive as long as you promise me that where we're going has a bed and maybe a little bit of food—what kind, I'm not too picky about, although I'd prefer if it wasn't the dried-beef-stew particles I choked down earlier."

"Can't promise there won't be more MREs, but there'll be some canned goods, too."

"Good, so let's go." Just thinking about the Meals, Ready to Eat made Elle cringe. They started walking again, and Trey stayed within an arm's reach. She couldn't help but think it was to keep a closer eye on her. "So, I do have a question for you. I mean, it's not exactly a casual stroll up these mountains. The pessimist in me is wondering what happens if we need to make a quick exit."

Trey stepped over a fallen tree and turned to lift her easily up and over. "If it's a challenge for us to get there, then it's not going to be easy for anyone else, either."

"Well I guess that can be considered a check in the pro column," Elle mumbled.

"You don't need to worry. This place is so far off the radar that unless you've personally been here, you aren't finding it. And in the impossible instance that someone does, it's built like Fort-fucking-Knox." Trey wrapped his hand around her nape and pulled her close enough for her to see small crystals forming on the tips of his lashes. "Still not convinced?"

"Oh, I'm convinced—that I'm in the middle of the Ozarks, where no one but you and I—I mean *you*—know where we are, and we're about to lock ourselves inside an impenetrable box."

Trey smirked. "We're in the Pocono Mountains, not the Ozarks, babe. And there's *always* another way out."

"Too bad that didn't include an easier way in," Elle said drily. "You know those thirty minutes are going to get longer if we continue to stop and start."

"I lied about the thirty minutes."

"You did?"

"Yep. We're here." He spun her around, and Elle's jaw nearly hit the snowy ground.

He hadn't been lying when he called it a cabin, although comparing it to Fort Knox was a stretch—a long one that could probably wind around the state's entire border.

Nestled into the trees, the modest one-level structure was built primarily of stacked aged logs. A massive stone chimney abutted one end, and the rickety front porch looked as if it would give way with the slightest bit of weight. A strong breeze could knock this building down to the foundation—if there even was one.

Elle gave the building a second look. "We have two completely opposite ideas of what Fort Knox looks like, and yours screams nineteenth-century-themed television show more than gold-reserve holding tank."

Elle half expected Trey to laugh and lead her in the direction of the real safe house, but he took her hand and plowed the way to the log home. "It's meant to look like an abandoned hunting cabin; that way if anyone happens to stumble onto it, it doesn't look out the norm."

"I can't believe I left a cement bunker in a mountain for four walls made out of matchsticks," Elle muttered beneath her breath.

Trey abruptly stopped at the base of the stairs and tugged her chin up. "I wouldn't have brought you here if you weren't going to be one-hundred-percent safe. Hell, in a lot of ways, you're safer here than you were back at headquarters."

"I know." At his look of doubt, she added, "I *do* trust you—and everyone else at Alpha. It's just that before I got on the plane back to the States, I told myself that I wasn't going to backslide into letting other people control my future, and here I am, letting some unknown person do just that. It's frustrating. I don't mean to sound unappreciative."

"You're not unappreciative. I can't think of another living person who would've taken all of this shit in such a graceful stride." A strand of hair fell from Elle's knit cap, and Trey tucked it behind her ear. The touch, even muted by thick gloves, tilted her stomach sideways. "And once we're thawed, I'm going to hear more of that backsliding thing."

Not in this lifetime. Not ever. People who had fun and flirty affairs did *not* share secrets, or feelings, or concerns about the future. It was difficult enough to remember that their time together had a shelf life as it was, without confusing the matter with little heart-to-heart talks.

Oblivious to her internal struggle, Trey flipped aside what looked to be a broken wood panel next to the door. Except it wasn't broken, or wooden. A high-tech access pad blinked at them as he typed in a code and pulled off his glove to scan his finger.

He chuckled at her surprise. "I told you. The outside's a façade. Under these wood planks are cement and steel. No one gets in or out without authorization. Now take off your glove and give me your hand."

Getting fingerprinted shouldn't have felt erotic, but Elle's cheeks started warming as she watched Trey gently maneuver each of her fingers onto the pad. When they were done, he feathered a kiss across her wrist and upped the heat to a slow sizzle.

The door gently released with a low buzz and let them in to a small antechamber with another scanner. He entered a different series of numbers and applied his fingers to the pad, and then the second door clicked open.

Elle cocked up a brow. "Paranoid much?"

"What can I say, the entire place is Charlie-ized. That woman's downright scary with a gun, but it's nothing compared to her with a computer." Trey gestured for her to go first. "After you."

Where the Alpha compound was industrial with slight hints of comfort, the inside of the cabin was entirely hunter chic. Aged wood walls and rich dark colors filled every space. Mismatched plush chairs and a worn leather couch made the modest living room nearly as inviting as the impressive stone fireplace against the far back wall. Everything looked used and homey, right up to the scarred end table and white filtered lamps.

"Is there actually electricity all the way out here?" Elle trailed her hand over the fireplace's hand-carved mantel.

Trey dropped his pack on the ground. "Alpha's known for getting the impossible done. That said, most of the generator's juice goes toward sustaining our gadgets, so sometimes the other amenities can leave things a little...chilly. We'll have enough hot water for showers and we'll have the fireplace for most of our heat."

There didn't seem to be much of a need for a tour. The living space melded into the open kitchen, where Trey opened and closed cabinets to verify that it was indeed stocked with a lot of canned goods. On the opposite end of the fireplace, a short hall—little more than a nook—led to two doors.

"There's an actual bathroom in the back"—Trey pointed to the first door—"and the other is the bedroom."

The bedroom.

As in, the only one. Solo. Singular. Not more than one.

For a woman who'd decided to have no-strings sex with her hunky bodyguard, the idea of sharing a room brought more than a small amount of anxiety. Elle couldn't help but look inside, and the sight of the simple iron-framed bed didn't lessen her nervousness one bit.

Trey nestled against her back, his hands on her hips as his mouth caressed her jaw. "It's not much, but it serves its purpose."

Actually, it was beautiful. A bright country quilt covered the full mattress, coordinating with the rich red and cream area rug. And sitting catty-corner to a small wood chest was an antique armoire. The cabin could've been displayed on the cover of *Log Home* magazine.

It was secluded. It was gorgeous. It was intimate. There'd be no hiding in the kitchen with Penny or disappearing into the gym with Charlie. She and Trey would practically be on top of each other for God knew how long.

"If you're not comfortable sharing," Trey broke into her thoughts, "I'll sleep on the couch. I've done it once before. It's actually not too bad. Though I'm not lying—or trying to convince you to lean one way or another—when I say that the extra body heat might make the difference between a bearable chill and frozen toes."

Elle didn't doubt the truth in his statement, but she wasn't so delusional to think that it meant a lot of sleeping, either. Close proximity led to touching. Touching led to kissing— a brush of lips here or a flick of a tongue there—and then before you knew it, you were sexing it up and forgetting all about your rules, a little more with each mind-blowing orgasm.

"We'll see how it goes," Elle stated. Even if keeping some kind of a distance was a pipe dream, she could at least start things off with the right intentions.

CHAPTER FIFTEEN

Falling asleep had been a feat of humility. Left. Right. Back. Stomach. Every attempt to find a comfortable position ended the same way—with Elle's left calf muscle coiled into a knot, the throb so fierce that every attempt to stretch her leg resulted in a chain-reaction of spasms.

She couldn't take it any longer. Elle slung back the covers and prayed the kitchen's nonperishable supplies included hot chocolate or tea. At this point, she'd even consider straight boiling water.

A small wave of warmth greeted her the instant she carefully opened the bedroom door. No longer a full, crackling flame, the dying embers in the fireplace glowed a faint orange.

Elle squinted through the darkness, but from this vantage point, her only clear view was of the back of the couch, which Trey claimed at his bed. She tiptoed around the corner—and bounced off a bare-chested roadblock.

Instincts pulled a shriek from her throat, and thanks to Charlie's lessons, a knee up for a crotch-strike.

Trey quickly deflected the shot and pulled her flush against his body, probably more for his own safety than to prevent her from falling on her ass as she stumbled. "Whoa there, Rocky. Wound tight much?"

"You freaking *scared* me," she scolded him. She smacked his chest and tried to dislodge her heart from her throat. "I didn't know it was you."

"Who did you think it was?" He barked out a laugh.

"I don't know." Thank God for it being the middle of the night. Elle felt her cheeks flush red hot with embarrassment. "It's late, and I'm about one degree from turning into a human popsicle. I'm not exactly functioning on full cylinders, here."

Part of her body wasn't. Everything involved in creating a physical reaction to Trey's bare chest worked absolutely fine. Perfect even. Her flannel sleep shirt—which happened to belong to Trey—did little to protect her nipples from brushing against his rock-hard abs.

She shifted her weight from one foot to the other—and *zing*, the brush of his bare skin zapped another mini flare of heat to her nether regions.

"Why are you not wearing a shirt?" she blabbed.

Trey's lips twitched into a devilish grin. "Why? Am I distracting you?"

"No. Yes. Maybe." Elle gave herself a mental smack across the cheek. "I'm a nurse. I can't help but be concerned that something's going to...fall off."

Well, that comment did nothing to wipe away his smirk. It widened it instead. "Is that you offering to keep me warm?"

Flame-colored cheeks and diarrhea of the mouth, here

comes Elle Monroe. "No, it's a roundabout way of asking why you have a state-of-the-art security system in this place and yet couldn't figure out how to install a thermostat."

For a moment, Trey didn't look like he was going to let the topic-shift fly by without a healthy dose of teasing, but he surprised her by releasing her hips and gesturing toward the couch. "I wasn't kidding when I said most of the generator's power goes to the security system. And to our link to the outside world. We may like that this place is off the grid, but we do need to be able to check in to headquarters."

Which he'd done after they'd arrived.

Elle sat on the floor instead to get closer to the fireplace, and watched him toss a few logs onto the giant hearth.

If shirtless Trey in daylight was a snack, a half-dressed Trey in the warm glow of a fire was a visual feast. He poked a stoker into the ash, the move rippling the muscles of his back and shoulders. The play of dark and lighter shadows mesmerized her, much like everything else about the man. He was strong, capable, loyal to his friends, and from what she'd witnessed during the Sled-tacular, a doting son and a fan of children.

When he'd been Trey-the-Lone-Traveler, he'd been a safe bet for Post-Thailand-Elle to have fun and release a little pent-up tension with. But Commando-Trey combined with a Penchant-for-Getting-Embarrassed-by-His-Mother-Trey and Toboggan-Making-Trey, made Regular Elle really damn nervous.

"Am I too late in stoking the fire?" Humor dripped off Trey's words.

"What?" she asked, startled back to reality.

He grinned. "You went still. I thought you'd turned into that block of ice. This cold front's wicked. I wouldn't be surprised if we had a few more inches of snow on the ground in the morning."

"Snow after living in a sweatbox for months." Elle rubbed her arms until her palms heated. "One extreme to another."

"Your body adjusted to the heat and humidity. It's probably going to take a while for it to remember what it's like in cooler temps."

"I don't know if I'll be here long enough for that to happen."

That seemed to catch Trey's attention. He didn't look at her, his attention still focused on the fireplace, but something in his body language had tensed. "You have someplace to be?"

"Right now? No. But when I can finally get back to my life, I'm hoping to pick up another assignment. It's a sad reality, but there's always someplace in the world that's in need of medical help."

"Thailand was your first post?"

"Yep." Elle propped her chin on her bent knees and wrapped her arms around her legs. "Shay and I didn't plan on staying as long as we did, but everything there was so much worse than any picture could've captured, so we extended our time. Some people lost *everything*—their families, their homes, their total livelihood. And yet they gave more to me than I could ever give them."

Trey finally looked at her over his shoulder and studied her intently. "What did they give you?"

"Perspective." And Elle meant it. "There was no contest as to who'd been through more suffering, and yet they were still trudging along, making the most of a really horrific situation. They made me realize that it was time to stop focusing on the things I didn't have and start being thankful for what I do. Suck up. Buck up. And toughen up."

"You're plenty tough, if you ask me."

Her eye roll–snort combination could've been seen and heard from the Hubble. "Right."

Trey gave her a disbelieving look. "You uprooted your life and moved thousands of miles away to help take care of people who'd fallen on rough times. How the hell is that not the definition of tough? It's brave as fucking hell."

Because I did it to run away from my problems.

The words nearly fell from her lips, but Elle clamped her mouth shut—not because she didn't think he'd listen or care, but a guy like him wouldn't understand skirting past problems by using airline tickets and a few thousand miles of distance. He dealt with them via head-on collisions, as did everyone at Alpha.

"Don't try and turn me into something I'm not," she said wearily.

"I don't need to *turn* you when you're already *it* to begin with."

Trey's intense inspection forced her to look away. Knowing he saw her in that way was nice. It just wasn't the truth. As far back as she could remember, fear of her father's disapproval had fueled every decision of her life—even nearly marrying a man she didn't love.

It was worry of backsliding into that naive, "*Yes, sir*" life that had sent her to Thailand, not the long list of altruistic reasons Trey had just recited. Hell, she'd been back in the States less than a few weeks and was already letting fear influence her decisions again. Instead of a medical clinic in Thailand, her reprieve from reality was Trey's arms.

A live-action landmine would be safer than this conversation.

"You're the brave one." Elle turned back on him. "I'm not exactly a military expert, but even I know that they don't let just anyone into Delta Force. And then when you left the Army, instead of taking a quiet, safe desk job, you joined Alpha. I'm sure you've been to a lot of interesting places. Where was your most memorable?"

"Thailand." Trey stood, not even batting an eye.

He closed the distance between them, his sweatpants riding low enough on his waist to reveal that delicious arch over each hip. Her icicle toes—gone. Ability to talk—vanished. Her panties—dampening. Neither one of them spoke as he sat next to her.

Elle tracked a spark of embers as it cracked and sizzled in the fireplace—anything not to dwell on the burning hole Trey's green eyes were boring through her defenses. She attempted to swallow a lump in her throat the size of a softball.

"Aren't you going to ask me why?" Trey asked.

"Nope," Elle croaked.

"Why?"

Afraid of the answer. Every inch of her was overly aware of every inch of Trey; his slow, even breath; the smell of soap and musk. From the corner of her eye, she scanned the length of his corded arms and the way his long fingers linked casually between his knees.

Hands said a lot about a man. Rough-tipped and callused, Trey's were equally strong and gentle, able to protect her one moment and worship her body the next.

Next to her, he shifted. Their shoulders barely brushed, but it sent a *zap* of heat directly from his body to hers. He looked physically at ease, yet the tension hanging in the air said otherwise.

"Elle." His thumb brushed a strand of hair that had gotten caught in her eyelashes, and then his fingers gently tipped her face his way.

"Don't." Unknowingly holding her breath, her head started going dizzy in a matter of seconds.

"Don't what? Tell you the truth?" His eyes narrowed as he fought to understand the answers to questions even she didn't know.

"Don't say anything you can't take back. Uncomplicated, remember?"

"*Fuck* uncomplicated." His vehemence made her blink before he softened his words and dipped his head to hold her attention. "This whole damn thing's been complicated since that day in the bar, and you know it."

"One-night stands are meant to be *un*complicated."

"What we had—*have*—is not a one-night stand. It's not a two-night stand, or even a three. What we have is different...I don't know how it is, or why. But I suspected it when I first laid eyes on you, and the more time we spend together, the more I know...it just *is*."

She tilted her head away from his touch. "It's because I'm your job."

"No. It's *you*. It's because I've never met anyone like *you* before and I'm pretty sure that I'm not going to again. And it's because I can't get you out of my head, and a huge fucking part of me doesn't want to."

Elle summoned a mental suit of armor and hoped the glare she threw in his direction looked more solid than she felt. "You can't get me out of your head because you've been forced to look at my face every day since I landed in New York. *That's all*. End of mystery. Trust me, I'm nothing special."

"Bull-fucking-shit," Trey growled.

His burst of ferocity stunned Elle still.

He scrubbed a hand over his stubbled jaw and took a breath. This time when he spoke, it was a stern rumble. "Do you know what it does to me when you do that shit?"

"And what shit would that be, exactly?" she asked, hovering between shocked and annoyed.

"When you downplay what you are? You have no fucking clue how much it pisses me off. It makes me want to hold you in front of a mirror until you see what I see—a strong, competent, and caring woman."

She was already shaking her head, but he reached out and captured her gently by her nape, holding her still...and looking at him.

"It makes me want to hold you..." Trey murmured, slowly bringing her closer, "and touch you...and kiss you...until you feel it, too."

Elle let her eyes drift closed, hoping the break in eye contact would dampen the effect of his words, but she had no such luck.

"Look at me." Trey softly coaxed them open again. One second, she worked to fight the pull, and the next, she was on his lap. "The ship *Uncomplicated* has already sailed, sweetheart. It is so damn far out to sea, Poseidon himself can't fucking track it. Get complicated with me, Elle. What do we have to lose?"

Everything.

And God help her, he stared at her like he could read the panic beginning to swell in her chest. And he didn't say a word. The only sound in the room was the faint crackle of the fire and Elle's own heartbeat.

Trey silently eased her off his lap, and after pulling the blanket from the back of the couch, sprawled on the floor in front of the hearth. "Come here."

Elle couldn't bring herself to move—even after he lifted the blanket and tried coaxing her closer with the promise of warmth. "I'm not going to bite, sweetness. At least, not unless you want me to."

Doing the smart thing meant either returning to her room to freeze alone, or finding a separate blanket and cocooning herself in it like a burrito. She did neither. Elle slowly shifted her body beneath Trey's blanket, but before she turned into spooning position, he reached out and tucked her snugly into his arms.

She had no choice but to nestle her cheek against his chest, and when she did, the steady beat of his heart lulled her own into a rhythmic trot. When he was inside her, it was easier to delude herself into believing that the warm tingle she felt at his nearness was physical lust.

But this?

It went way beyond desire. It was more than lust, or even need.

With a feather-soft touch, Trey's hand gently traced a path over her hip. It didn't lift any higher than her panty-line or travel any lower than her upper leg. It was soothing and innocent—and still packed one hell of a punch.

And it was what lovers did—lovers with a lot more on the line than sex of convenience.

CHAPTER SIXTEEN

Trey rolled from the makeshift bed he and Elle had made in front of the fireplace and got to his feet. At some point in the last few hours, the fire had died, and each breath created a white halo around his head—a stark contrast to when he'd fallen asleep with a very warm Elle blanketed over his chest.

Damn. He could still feel the warmth of her body pressed against his, despite the fact that she was MIA. He was about to find his personal furnace when the satellite phone shrieked from the kitchen table.

"Any word on the asshole?" Trey answered in lieu of a normal greeting.

"Good morning to you, too, love." Charlie's voice dripped sarcasm from the other side of the line. "Wake up on the wrong side of the bed this morning? Or did you even make it into one?"

"Charlie," Trey warned.

"Oh, lighten up, Hanson. Stone has me practically chained

to the computer, so I need to get my thrills in where I can. Trust me, thinking about your sex life isn't my first choice of ways to catch a thrill."

"How's my ma?" He peeked into the bedroom, even though his gut told him Elle wasn't there.

"Not as unobservant or as easily distracted as Stone would like. But I guess when you see your only son haul arse up a hill with a gun in his hand, and then he disappears, you tend to have questions."

Trey rubbed his hand over his face. He knew through years of first-hand experience how relentless his mother could be when she was determined. "How bad is it?"

"The guys started drawing straws to see whose turn it is to be on Mama Hanson protection duty. Loser gets the detail—and the foodie equivalent of blue balls, because she goes on a cooking spree and won't let any of them have a bite."

That was bad, because his mom lived for feeding people. The larger the audience, the happier she was. "I'll call her and try to smooth things over, but it's not like I can answer any of her questions. And speaking of answers, do we have any idea how that asshole found Elle at the youth center?"

"Not a one, and he vanished like he's a bloody ghost, which makes me even more convinced he has some kind of military background, but I'm not giving up. I'll track him down."

"I know you will." Trey trudged back through the kitchen and glimpsed out the back window—and froze.

Elle, snow nearly up to her knees thanks to last night's squall, wielded an ax like a sexy Paul Bunyan. Swing. *Thwack*. And back again. The woman swung it like it was her life's mission to bring heat to the northern half of the continent.

"Keep me updated, okay? And tell Stone that I'll try to calm the water with my ma, but not to expect any miracles."

"You're trying to rush me off the phone," Charlie said astutely.

"Damn right I am." Trey chuckled. "Updates," he reminded before signing off.

After watching Elle scare away the wildlife for a full ten minutes, Trey changed and pulled on his boots. He grabbed an extra wool hat that had been stowed away in one of the back closets, and headed outside.

Despite the clear blue skies, it was colder than a witch's tit, his balls shriveling close to his dick in an attempt to keep warm. Elle didn't see him as he approached. She was muttering under her breath, each word adding to the puffy white cloud hovering over her head. And fuck—he'd heard his name…right before she brought the ax down on a big-ass block of wood.

"Didn't know I bedded Lumberjack Elle," Trey said, once the weapon wasn't poised above her head.

She jumped, startled. Her blue eyes shot to him faster than a goddamned bullet. *Fuck-and-him.* That wasn't a look of a woman who'd woken up on the right side of the bed—or floor. Obviously, something had happened between last night and now, and he didn't like the fact that he didn't know what that something was.

"What are you doing out here?" Elle's voice was breathless as he tugged the hat over her already red ears, wondering how long she'd been at this.

"Protecting those pretty little ears from falling off. And I think the more accurate question here is what *you're* doing out here at all, much less alone."

"I've been taking care of myself for a long time, Trey. I

can't exactly be expected to sit back and do nothing now."
Elle tossed the newly chopped log onto an impressive pile.

"Yeah, but jungle living and winter mountain living are
two entirely different beasts. You know that you don't have
to do this, right? We have enough wood to get us through."

"Through what? The day? The week?" She backed him
up with the bump of her ass, and *thwack*. Wood splintered
and flew as she brought the ax down again. "I don't particularly like the idea of freezing to death, plus I was awake and
I needed to do something. In Thailand, I worked at the clinic
until I dropped. At Alpha, Charlie's workout schedule kept
me fairly close to exhaustion at all times. If all I do around
here is sit, I'll go crazy."

Something told him there was a bit more to her madness.
"It's been a while since I've been out here. How about we go
for a hike?" He gestured to the ax she gripped tightly in her
hand. "Or I could rescue you from a few blisters and help
you bring down the entire Pocono Mountain range."

She cocked up a lone blonde eyebrow. "There's only one
ax."

"Then let me have a turn." He extended his hand, and Elle
eyed it like it was a snake prepped to strike. When it became
obvious he was wasting his time, he crossed his arms and
leaned against the back of the cabin. "Fine. I got the message. Continue on, then."

Her pretty blue eyes narrowed on him. "You mean you're
just going to stand there watching?"

He shrugged. "I don't have anything else to do. And the
scenery doesn't get much better than a hot blonde wearing
three layers of flannel."

"Four," she corrected, turning back to her task.

People who couldn't stay quiet for longer than a minute
at a time had always irritated Trey. He liked the quiet, liked

hearing himself think. But mind-reading powers weren't necessary to realize he'd somehow ended up Elle's Shit Creek without so much as a toothpick for a fucking oar.

Trey didn't even last five seconds. "Are you going to continue stewing to yourself or are we eventually going to talk about what I did to piss you off?"

"You didn't do anything," she muttered and added another log to her stack of firewood.

"The glacial dagger you hurled my way when I came outside says otherwise."

If it were Rafe or Vince withholding information, Trey would beat the answers out of him, but he couldn't do that with Elle, for obvious reasons. And even though he wasn't as walled-off to his emotions as Stone, he was far from being an express-your-inner-turmoil kind of guy. So Trey did the only other thing that came to mind... something he would've done if it had been Penny or Rachel giving him the silent treatment.

Trey scooped up a handful of snow, patted it into a perfect palm-sized orb, and then hurled it with dead-on accuracy—smack on Elle's glorious ass.

Mouth agape, she bolted upright and spun in his direction. "Did you throw a snowball at me?"

"Maybe. Maybe not. Are you going to talk to me?"

She scowled at him with all the severity of his second-grade teacher. "I don't talk to overgrown toddlers who don't own up to what they've done."

He hoisted another snowball. It exploded against her puffy jacket in a dramatic powdery spray that left flakes clinging to her lashes. "There. I threw that one. *Now* are you going to talk to me?"

"Guys never want to talk. It's a dominant characteristic of the Y chromosome, or something like that." Her frown deepened. "Why can't you be like every other guy in the world? Why do you have to be so...*you*?"

He would've laughed if he hadn't seen that flicker in her eye. Something in his gut told him there was a hell of a meaning behind her rhetorical question. He molded another projectile and bounced it in his hand. "What can I say except that I'm one of a kind? I defy the laws of genetics, and thanks to my ma, I had a solid upbringing. So, what's it going to be, Elle? Talk...or eat another snowball?"

She pursed her lips. "You can't be serious."

"*Beep*." He buzzed a mock alarm. "Too long. Time's up."

He aimed his next ball at her stomach, immediately followed by a quick one to her thigh.

"Will you stop that?" She held out her hands to deflect the blows.

"Come over here and make me."

"Yeah, that's real mature."

"No, mature would be talking about whatever it is that set you off." He pushed off the side of the cabin. With each step in her direction, she switched more from full-on glare to skittish kitten. "I fell asleep wrapped around a warm woman, and I woke up cold and alone to find that very same woman doing serious damage to a tree stump. What the hell did I miss?"

"Maybe you muttered another woman's name in your sleep."

When he stopped, their bodies were so close he had to angle his attention downward. "Not possible."

She'd trapped her lower lip beneath her teeth and was in the process of nibbling it raw. "Why? Because the great Trey Hanson is infallible?"

"If I were infallible, you never would've disappeared this morning in the first place. But no. I know I didn't mutter another woman's name because the only woman in my life is you. Your turn for honesty. What are you so afraid of that you're out here chopping wood and picking a fight?"

Elle's throat convulsed as she swallowed.

"I don't think it's even this fucked-up threat hanging over your head—or being holed away in this cabin." Trey stroked his gloved finger over her cheek. "You know what I think it is?" He focused on the way her heartbeat thundered at the base of her throat. "I think what has you running, Elle, is *us*."

"There *is* no *us*," she croaked softly.

Trey's internal alarm blared. *That* was the proverbial nail on the fucking head. He could see it in her eyes, and he didn't like the uncertainty one bit—or the fact that her first instinct was to run, even if it was only outside.

And yeah, it was a tad bit hypocritical, considering that he'd once done the same damn thing, except it was from his familial responsibilities. But he'd learned from his mistake and tried making amends for it every damn day. It helped that he had a patient, understanding family—at least, after they'd finished kicking his ass.

He couldn't kick Elle's ass—but he could give it a slight nudge.

"You and I both know that's not entirely true." When she opened her mouth to argue, Trey silenced her with a finger to her lips. "I already told you once that I wouldn't push you into something you don't want, and I aim to keep that promise. But you're not doing either of us any favors by lying to yourself. Denial only increases your chances of missing out on something that could be great."

Elle nibbled her bottom lip again, tempting him to kiss away whatever reservations were currently firing through her pretty little head. "And you're saying that you're that something great?"

"Sweetness, I'm the best."

"You're also too cocky for your own good." Elle stepped back, and Trey took one step forward. Three steps each, and the backs of her knees hit the tree stump and brought her to a stop.

He grinned, knowing he had her trapped. "If I wasn't fucking great, our clothes wouldn't keep coming off."

"Well, you have to realize that I was in Thailand for a really long time. It made for one hell of a dry spell. I could be making up for lost time."

He chuckled at her attempt to brush him off. "Yeah, I don't think so."

"Fine. You're right. It's called *lust*. It's a physical response to the release of endorphins."

"Lust burns out, Elle. Do you honestly feel like we've backpedaled to a slow simmer?"

She was back to biting that plump lower lip and, goddamn, he wanted to take a little nibble, too. But he'd be damned if she was going to distract him into letting her escape again.

"You made it clear that you don't want hearts and flowers and rose-strewn aisles, and I've accepted that," Trey stated. "But while we're in this...*agreement*...you need to be all-in. No half-assed retreats. No hide-and-seek or hot-and-cold. I'm too old for games."

"So you're saying it's an all-or-nothing kind of arrangement? Isn't that kind of odd for something with a shelf life?"

"It's exactly what we decide to make of it, and if you're determined that this thing between us has an expiration date, then yes, I'm saying that while we're in the thick of it, it's all-or-nothing." Trey pulled her to him. Even with mounds of layers between them, the heat they created simply by being in close proximity could've melted the snow around them.

Giving in to his need to feel her skin, he tugged off his gloves and cupped her pink cheeks. Her small hands wrapped around his wrists. She looked a second away from bolting, but she surprised him by grabbing onto the loops of his jeans and pulling him flush against her body.

She whispered, lifting onto her toes. "You're right. This attraction hasn't simmered down at all, has it?"

"Not in the least. And I don't think it's going to happen anytime soon." The back of Elle's hand brushed against the growing bulge in Trey's jeans. "*Definitely* no time soon."

A second after she tugged on his fly, he felt air. His eyes snapped open a split second before his dick took an ice-bath—or more accurately, a direct hit with a fucking snowball. He jerked like a squirrel had chomped on his nuts, but he forced himself still while the snow melted. Tears of laughter streamed down Elle's cheeks.

"This is war, sweetness."

"Oh, come on." She lifted her hands in peace, chuckling nervously. "I was only doing my duty. It's not healthy for a man to run that hot all the time."

"I'd be more than happy to provide you the same kind of service."

She skirted around the stump, stepping backward. "Thanks for the offer, but I don't think that's necessary. I'm pretty cool—chill, even."

"Nope. You're always so damn hot."

Elle squealed as he leapt. She turned to run, but stumbled, hitting the snowy ground. Trey effortlessly flipped her to her back.

Her eyes widened as she tried—and failed—to bat his hands away. "You wouldn't dare!"

"I would. I really, really would." Trey grabbed a handful of snow and smeared it in her face as if it were a cherry pie.

Elle sputtered and laughed, the sound dragging out his own. Fistfuls of snow flew all around them in a winter version of a mud sling-off. Trey couldn't remember ever laughing this hard. Only when they were so frozen they couldn't physically move did they lie there, breathless and panting.

Elle halfheartedly smacked him on the chest and chuckled. "You make it impossible to stay in a foul mood. Do you know that?"

"Good. That's what I was trying for." Trey pulled her into a slow, unhurried kiss. When he finally relinquished her lips, Elle's mouth slid into a mischievous smirk. She rolled, using his chest to push herself to her feet, and with her eyes still on him, walked backward toward the cabin.

"I'm going to take a very hot, very steamy shower in order to stave off frostbite," she announced in a low purr. "But first I'm going to have to peel out of these wet, clingy clothes. Too bad I don't have an extra set of hands to make it a little easier."

Trey didn't wait for an engraved invitation. He caught up to her easily at the mouth of the back door. Piece by piece, they tossed aside damp jackets and soaking-wet shirts. Her bra. His pants. By the time they reached the bedroom, the only thing wrapped around him were Elle's legs.

CHAPTER SEVENTEEN

No backpedaling. No second-guessing every touch. No putting her life into a choke hold. Enjoy now, deal with the fallout later.

That had been the focus during their weeklong seclusion at the cabin, and even though Elle occasionally felt the start of the reversion process, she managed to catch herself before it turned full-scale. Trey's earlier words had shaken her up enough to realize that by strapping her life with regulations, she wasn't so much staying in control as shuffling through the motions.

Now, if only things were moving on trying to locate Alley Man and his merry band of mercenaries—or the people who hired them—they'd be all set. There was a big fat lot of nothing. No facial matches. No leads. Elle heard Trey's frustration when he'd threatened to reach through the video-comm and start busting heads together if some kind of information didn't start trickling in soon.

He probably needed this hike more than she did.

Multiple layers and a puffy jacket made her feel—and look—like a microwaved marshmallow, while Trey had nailed down the sexy mountaineer look with a few days' worth of stubble and a flannel hunter's jacket.

Zipped, buttoned, and covered, they hiked over an area of the mountain that probably hadn't seen visitors, other than the furry kind, in years. Trey effortlessly jumped over a particularly wide joint on the rocky ground and then turned to help her do the same.

"You claim this is a spontaneous trip for some fresh air, but I get the distinct impression that you have a specific destination in mind," Elle teased. She looked up the next hilly incline and blew away the hair that fell into her eyes. "Or you're trying to find someplace cool to get rid of my body."

Trey's chuckle made her look to where he offered her his hand. She took it and let out a soft grunt when he tugged her up the first foot.

"You're right about one of those things," Trey admitted, "but I'm too obsessed with your body to do anything as stupid as get rid of it. You're stuck with me, babe."

It was those kind of words, falling so easily from his mouth, that brought a special warmth to the center of Elle's chest. Once upon a time, they would've sent her running into a blind panic. But now, they made her squeeze onto his hand a little tighter. She just wasn't ready to dwell on exactly why that was, and true to his word, Trey didn't push.

They'd made it to the top of the hill when she felt the weight of his gaze.

"What?" she asked, self-conscious.

He nodded outward, and Elle looked—and gasped.

Spread out in front of them, a snow-dusted clearing stretched from a foot away to the next steep incline—what had to be a fifty-yard distance. But it was the sleek, glass-like surface of the frozen lake that stole her breath. "This is *gorgeous*."

"Welcome to Alpha Lake." Trey urged her closer to the rocky edge. "It's actually called Peterson's Pond, but there hasn't been a Peterson around these woods for probably a hundred years."

He dropped her hand and skated his boots onto the ice. "When was the last time you went ice-skating, Miss Monroe?"

"I was probably eight," she admitted. "And I had actual skates on my feet."

"And you were probably skating around in a well-maintained rink, right?" He crooked his finger and beckoned to her. "How fucking boring. You haven't really skated if you haven't skated on a pond in the dead of winter."

She glanced warily at the ice. "That means I also haven't fallen *through* the ice and died from hypothermia."

"It's perfectly safe. I checked the thickness yesterday and the temps aren't due to rise for at least another two weeks." Even from a distance, Elle could see the determined glint in his green eyes. He wasn't going to give up. "Don't make me come over there and get you."

"Always with the threats," Elle teased. "I'm starting to think you're all talk, Hanson."

Her taunt backfired. When he took his first step back in her direction, she threw up her hands. "Okay! Okay! You're the Big-Bad. I'm coming!"

Elle swallowed her lump of nerves before taking her first tentative step. She pushed down and bounced on the balls on her feet before taking another one.

"It's going to be spring by the time you get out here," Trey joked.

"Hardy-har-har," Elle deadpanned. After a half dozen steps, she felt a little more comfortable.

"Slide on the soles of your boots," Trey advised. "The traction will prevent your feet from flying out from beneath you."

"This isn't too bad." She did as he said, and before long, grabbed hold of his arms. He held her upright, smirking. "Okay, so you were right. This is actually pretty neat. But I'm a little surprised that you guys don't have skates holed up somewhere in the cabin. You seem to have everything else."

Trey snorted. "Do we look like ice-skating kind of guys to you?"

Elle giggled at the mental image of Trey and Vince, dressed in sequined spandex and performing synchronized triple salchows.

Holding on to any part of Trey's body she could, Elle shuffled around him, striking the occasional figure-skating pose that made him shake his head and chuckle. After she'd heard the sound once, she wanted to hear it again. She skidded. She shimmied. Trey took hold of her wrists and spun her in circles.

"I'm going to let go on three," he warned, prepping her for a grand release that would slide her across the slick surface.

"Do it." Cold air whipped past her face as she skidded nearly six feet. "*Woohoo*! Let's do that again."

Elle turned back around and took her first shuffle-step—and froze.

Directly beneath her left heel, a forming fissure began cracking—and expanding—through the ice. "Um...Trey?"

"Don't move, Elle," Trey demanded, a moment before the sound of splintering ice reached her ears. "Whatever you do, don't move even an inch. Do you hear me?"

Fear tossed her heart into her throat, and the soft creak

came again. This time, the hair-like fractures spidering out from her boot lengthened. "I can't hear anything above the pounding of my heart. I need to move."

"*No*. As a matter of fact, stop talking."

This wasn't Chuckling Trey. Or Sexy Trey. The man slowly edging his way toward her was most definitely Commando Trey. His eyes, narrowed in concentration, glanced to her feet and back. He skidded one foot closer, and then another. On the second step, the ice beneath Elle cracked a little wider.

Elle swallowed a screech. "Do you really think it's a good idea to bring your two-hundred-pound body any closer? I'm going to jump back."

"Elle, look at me," Trey demanded calmly. He fixed his eyes on her, steady and sure.

"I'm looking! I'm also looking at this huge-ass crack I'm about to plunge through!"

"You're not going to plunge through, babe. I'm not going to let that happen. Keep your eyes on me and focus on taking slow, deep breaths." When she glanced nervously to her feet, he scolded gently, "Eyes on me, sweetness."

"*Trey*."

"You're doing great." He got closer an inch at a time. At three feet away, he was so close and yet so far away.

Everything that happened next, happened in the time span of a finger-snap. The ice beneath Elle's feet shattered. Her left boot dipped into icy water. Trey shouted, his body a huge blur as he lunged in her direction.

Elle didn't have time to register it all before her body was propelled backward, ass sliding on the ice until she hit the pond's rocky edge with a loud *thwack*. It took a few shaky breaths to restart her heart, and then a couple more to realize she wasn't submerged in freezing water.

Trey. She looked onto the lake and saw nothing except an Alpha-sized hole in the ice and small area of surfacing bubbles.

"No. No, no, no, no." Elle scrambled to her feet, slipping twice. "Trey! *Trey*! I swear to God. if this is your idea of a joke there'll be no place on this mountain you can hide from me."

Running on pure adrenaline, she dropped to her stomach and belly-crawled back to where Trey had plunged through the ice. She saw the outline of his body immediately. His hand reached for the broken ledge and instead, kept bumping into the underside of the ice shelf.

Elle ripped off her mittens with her teeth and immediately plunged her entire arm into the murky depths and latched onto his coat sleeve. She struggled to plant her feet—and pulled. Trey's two hundred pounds of muscle had her straining, but two hundred pounds of muscle and wet clothes had her cursing a blue streak that would shock a sailor.

There was power in the yell. Elle hoped Charlie's words about punches and kicks applied to hauling six feet of Alpha male out of a frozen lake. With each tug, Elle howled. Her arms ached from the exertion, but somewhere after the sixth attempt, Trey finally hit air and gasped.

"L-l-let g-go," he stuttered. "The ice is g-gonna b-break."

"Then I suggest you help me get your ass out of here."

They worked together, but with each passing second, Trey's movements became more sluggish. Elle skidded on the ice as she scrambled to pull him higher. "Trey, damn it! You need to use those freaking muscles of yours! Bring your knee over the edge."

"G-go before you f-fall in, t-too." His teeth chattered.

"Stop talking stupid and lift your damn leg." Elle tightened her grip. An ominous creak beneath her had Elle swearing. "Did you hear that, Trey? If you don't suck it up and help me haul your ass out of this hole, we're both going to be taking a dunk. Is that what you want, huh? Some freaking bodyguard you are."

Trey grunted, and then his knee hooked the rim of the hole.

A-ha! Dare to question the machismo. Works every time.

Elle practically growled as she dragged them backward an inch at a time. Trey's body slowly resurfaced, and she kept pulling—numb hands be damned—until they reached the edge of the pond.

"G-goddamn, it's f-fucking c-cold," Trey complained. His lips had taken on a blue sheen.

"We need to get you out of these wet clothes."

"B-bag. In th-the b-bag."

Elle scrambled to his backpack and back, then immediately started dumping everything. Dry clothes. Water. Power bars. But…*clothes*. This time, there was nothing erotic about undressing him. She tossed the wet things aside and struggled to get him into the dry ones. By the time she wrestled him back into his boots, sweat dotted her brow.

Trey's eyes drifted shut.

"Wake up!" Elle gave his cheek a firm pat. "I swear to God, if you think you're going to freeze to death on me, you best change your plans right now."

His green eyes flickered open, but he looked so damn tired. "Since when d-did you g-get s-so bossy?"

"You haven't begun to see bossy," Elle warned, dragging him to his feet.

Thanks to her hazy memory and Trey's unbalanced coordination, it took double the time to make it back to the cabin. She scanned their way through the front door and dropped him onto the couch.

"Hypothermia. Hypothermia." Elle stopped and took a breath, trying to work through her options. Warming him slowly was the better and safer option. Going fast would only put his vital organs at risk for failure.

She tossed a handful of firewood into the hearth. Then, after finding the matches on the mantel, she lit one and threw the entire booklet in right after. As the flames grew, she heated water and poured it into emptied plastic bottles.

"All right, Popsicle Man. Up you go." Elle hauled a half-sleeping Trey to his feet and stripped him back down to nothing.

"Hmm. I like this idea." He curved his hands over her ass and gave her cheeks a little squeeze. "Are you going to warm me up with your body heat, baby?"

Elle would've laughed if the slurring of his words didn't worry her. "You bet I am, so let's get you on the floor in front of the fireplace."

He didn't even argue. He sprawled out naked on the floor and closed his eyes two seconds later. Elle grabbed every blanket she could find and started stuffing the heated bottles underneath his armpits and between his legs. Finally, she shimmied out of her own clothes and nestled her body against his freezing skin.

For the first time since laying eyes on Trey Hanson, she didn't worry about how to keep him at an arm's distance. Now, she worried she couldn't hold him close enough.

CHAPTER EIGHTEEN

Trey took a deep breath and sighed as a familiar warm, sweet scent invaded both his mind and body. He curled his arms around the source and brought it with him as he stretched onto his back. It was so fucking smooth, and he couldn't stop running his fingers up and down the sleek surface—until that surface moved.

Trey opened his eyes and immediately registered the sleeping Elle in his arms. He didn't want to wake her, but he couldn't help but touch her, running his thumb over her bare arm and nestling her deeper into his hold. Her breathing was deep and even, gently fanning across his chest.

This was how he wanted to wake up every fucking morning. He just didn't want to go to sleep as a block of fucking ice for it to happen.

Elle startled awake, and on their eyes locking, she propped her chin up on her hand. "Are you okay?"

"Never been better." He traced a small circle over the small of her back.

"No heart palpitations? Blurry vision? Muscle weakness?"

"All's perfect." He knew the second she felt his cock brush against her hip. Her eyes widened for a fraction of a second before narrowing into beautiful blue slits.

"You nearly die from hypothermia and *that's* where all your blood goes?"

He grinned. "It goes to all the vital organs, right? I happen to think my dick's pretty damn vital."

"So you're sure you're okay?"

"Perfect."

"Good. Because I'd hate to hurt an injured man." She smacked his chest. "Don't you *ever* do that again."

Trey failed to suppress a chuckle, and she pummeled him with a second half-assed punch. "Jesus. That's some bedside manner. Do you go around physically assaulting all of your patients, Nurse Monroe?"

"Only the ones who scare me half to death. Do you realize how lucky you are?" Elle growled. She tried pushing off his chest, but he palmed her ass and held her in position on top of him.

"I'm thinking pretty damn."

This time when she pushed up, he let her go—but only so far as to straddle his waist. The new position gave his eyes an impressive view of rose-tipped breasts, and his cock enjoyed the sight, too. He'd gone from typical morning wood to Elle-induced granite in less than a second. The only thing keeping him from sinking into the heat of her body was the flames sparking in her eyes.

"Elle."

"Don't." She stood up the second he slackened his grip.

For once, she didn't bother hiding from him as she stalked through the room, collecting halfheartedly tossed clothing. She was muttering something about a sock before he managed to get to his feet. And goddamn. His legs took extra time to lock, but once they did, he was golden.

Trey kept one hand on the back of the couch—just in case. "I want to make sure that I'm not still delirious. You're pissed off at me?"

"Give the man a genius certificate," Elle grumbled. "I *told* you I didn't want to go out on that ice and you goaded me into it. And according to the modus operandi of Elle Monroe, I caved and—"

"And I fell through the ice." He was missing something. "Yeah. I was there, and I now own the fucking T-shirt. What do you mean '*modus operandi*'?"

Elle spun around, eyes blaring blue sapphire daggers his way. "You fell through the ice trying to get me off of it."

Realization started to dawn, and his lips twitched. Her glare from before was nothing compared to the javelin spears drilling into him now. Shirt white-knuckled in her fist, she stalked closer to him in all her naked glory. Easygoing and fun Elle was nothing short of gorgeous. But a pissed Elle was fucking spectacular.

She stormed closer, pushing a finger into the center of his chest. "Do not look at me like this is funny, because it's not."

"That I fell through the ice and could've frozen to death? No. You're right. It's not funny. What's funny is you trying to pretend that you're not pissed because you were worried about me."

"Of course I was worried! I'm a nurse, and there's nothing worse than realizing you could do everything in your power to help someone and it might not be enough."

"Sure, and because you care about me." He trapped her

pointy finger in the palm of his hand. "You care about me more than you ever had any intention to, and that scares the shit out of you."

"You said you wouldn't push." Her tone hovered in between a warning growl and a careful reminder.

"I'm not. I'm pointing out the fact that my little ice routine showed you that your no-strings rule isn't quite stringless." Despite seeing the truth in her eyes, Trey knew her stubbornness wouldn't let her admit the words aloud. And that was fine—for now.

He waited for her next move—which was toward the kitchen. One good thing about this cabin was that there was nowhere for her to fucking hide. He watched her walk away, and then he followed.

He picked her up and deposited her on the counter—bare ass and all.

"What are you doing?" she squealed.

"Having breakfast." Trey stepped between her legs and brushed his nose against the curve of her neck, painfully aware that their still naked bodies touched with every inhaled breath. He trailed his fingers over her goose-bumped torso...across her hip...and down her outer thigh.

He wouldn't downplay or add to her fears by stating that, no strings or not, he wouldn't be making it easy for her to walk away. She'd find that out sooner rather than later and, in the meantime, he'd spend the time figuring out exactly how he felt about her, too.

There was no denying he wanted her body. He'd spent the last few weeks in a perpetual state of Ready-to-Fuck. But she'd never once felt like a job. She felt like a necessity.

"You need to rest." Elle's breathless voice went husky as he hooked her knee around his hip. "And you should eat something. Your body's been through a lot. I know it doesn't feel like it because you've been sleeping, but it has a lot of healing to do. Cold stress can be almost as dangerous as hypothermia."

"We finally agree on something." He nipped her earlobe, teasing them both as he glided his cock through her wet folds, oh so close, but not quite taking that final blissful inch. Then he slid his mouth down her neck. He paused at her breasts, cupping one and holding it steady while he delivered a hard suck to its tip. "I'm famished."

Elle shivered in his arms. Her gaze tracked him as he homed in on the sweet spot between her legs and brushed the tip of his tongue against her clit.

She clamped her hands on his arms and let out a soft, keening moan. "I'm still mad at you."

Trey didn't stop his sensual caress. "No you're not, baby. You're relieved…and I think you need a reminder that I'm alive and well."

Trey couldn't wait to jog her memory, and he started by savoring every inch of her body…and didn't stop until she screamed his name at the top of her lungs.

* * *

Elle slid into one of the two seats in front of the computer just as a beep advertised an incoming video-call. She opened the line and saw Stone and Charlie looking back at her from the screen, the Room of Testosterone in the background.

"Good morning," Elle greeted—and got awkward mumblings in return. "Okay, so maybe not such a great morning. Is everything okay?"

"Where's Trey?" Stone asked, not answering the question.

"Here." Trey sat next to Elle, their chairs so close she

might as well have been sitting on his lap. "What's up? Jesus Christ, Stone. You look like you've just been told you have minutes to live. What the hell's going on?"

"We have some news."

"Obviously, and I'm guessing it's not the good kind." Trey draped his arm over the back of Elle's seat. "No sense in sugarcoating it. Spill."

"Although we don't know who's behind the specific threat to the Senator and Elle, we finally know who's been hired to carry out the intimidation tactics. And you're right. It's not good. It's Black Dunes."

Trey froze. Stone stilled. Both men stared at each other through the video screen.

"How certain are you?" Trey finally asked, his voice gruff.

"One hundred percent," Stone said grimly.

And they were back to staring. Elle's gaze bounced from Trey to Stone's image on the video feed. After an agonizingly long silence, she couldn't take it anymore. "Charlie, can you—"

"Decrypt the man-speak happening right now?" Charlie guessed correctly.

"Please, since these two have evidently lost the ability to string together two words, much less an entire explanation."

"We finally got a hit on your facially scarred friend."

"That's good news, right? That means he's ex-military like everyone thought? He was in your database?"

Charlie shifted, looking uncharacteristically uncomfortable as she side-eyed her boss. "Not...exactly. I may have *borrowed* another program, but it's a good thing I did because your friend, Dean Winters, has been on an international watch list for suspected arms trafficking—which actually makes sense because your dad's most recent fight against assault weapons puts a real kink in his livelihood. And he also happens to be the founder of Black Dunes."

"Which I gather isn't the name of a dirty beach."

Trey removed his arm from her chair and shifted forward, muscles tensed. "They're a mercenary group that's not exactly known for their ethics. Actually, they're the exact fucking opposite of Alpha. They're the ones the *bad* guys hire to get shit done. But what I don't get is why it took so long to link the fucker's name with his face."

Charlie's eyes narrowed in challenge. "Are you questioning my intelligence digging?"

"No, I'm questioning why he looks so damn fucking familiar—and yet doesn't. I've never had a run-in with Black Dunes—or Winters—until a few weeks ago. At least, not that I can remember."

"Charlie's already cross-referenced any mention of Black Dunes to your service record with Delta, and like she said, she's even expanded her search efforts," Stone admitted, before shooting Charlie a stern glare. "None of your missions crossed paths with any ops that Black Dunes has even been rumored to have a hand in, so I have no fucking clue where the two of you would've had a run-in."

"Where was Winters before he founded Black Dunes?" Elle asked.

"Nowhere." Charlie frowned, obviously displeased. "It's like the bloody bastard didn't even exist five years ago. I thought I was a close a few times, but there's always something off about the facial biometrics. If I didn't know any better, I'd say he's Frankenstein's younger brother."

"And there's still no word on who would've hired them?"

"Sorry, love. The authorities are combing through your father's emails and other leads, but so far, they've got nothing."

It wasn't what Elle wanted to hear, but at least they'd learned *some*thing. "So then I guess we still have to sit tight, right?"

"Afraid so," Stone confirmed. "But now that we know who we're dealing with, we can start digging a little more. An outfit like Black Dunes thrives on power trips, and when guys like that start getting cocky, being discreet goes out the fucking window. They'll fuck up and eventually point us in their direction. In the meantime, there are worse places to be holed up than in the mountains."

Two weeks ago, Elle wouldn't have been so sure. Now it wasn't so much the mountain that held the allure of staying, but the man currently massaging the back of her neck. More mountain time meant more alone time. Together. She'd take every day like it was an extra gift because she knew it would eventually come to an end.

"We'll keep you updated if anything new trickles in," Stone offered before standing and glancing at Charlie. "And I'd like to see you in my office in five, Sparks. We need to have a little chat about discreetness."

Charlie waved him off and waited until he was gone before asking, "Did you get those emails I sent?"

Elle opened her mouth to reply when she realized the question was directed to Trey.

"I did," he answered. "And I told you that I already got it covered."

"Are you sure? Because I could—"

"Got. It. Covered."

She tossed up her hands. "Fine. But you better make it memorable, or Penny and I will make sure that a never-ending rain of hell falls onto your head."

"I'll wear a fucking poncho. And Charlie? Don't let Stone give you the speech about proper channels. Do whatever the hell it is you need to do to find out where this Winters bastard comes from, and if Stone gives you a problem, just say '*Colombia*.'"

"Why the bloody hell would I say 'Colombia'?"

"Do it, and he'll get off your back. And keep me updated." Trey clicked off the video link and leaned back in his chair.

"What happened in Colombia?" Elle asked, curious.

Trey's mouth slid into a grin. "I promised Stone I'd keep the actual story to myself. But if mentioning it gives Charlie a little reprieve, then I'm happy bring it up."

"I don't like the idea of her doing *whatever the hell she needs to do*," she said honestly. "If this group really is as ruthless as you all believe, then maybe you should all sit back and let the authorities handle it."

Trey guided her onto his lap. He let his hands coast up her thighs and over her hips. "Babe, this *is* us sitting back. Once Charlie and the guys find the bastard, Stone will make sure the authorities get the info—but it wouldn't surprise me in the least if he requested being in on the take-down."

"I don't want anyone getting hurt because of me." The thought of it made Elle's stomach churn.

"Are you kidding? We wouldn't know what to do with ourselves if we didn't have a bad-ass to pummel into the ground. When things are quiet around headquarters, things get ugly. Really, *really* fucking ugly." Trey guided her mouth down to his for a slow, lingering kiss. "But what isn't ugly is a day away. Go pack an overnight bag."

"We're going somewhere?"

"You'll see when we get there." He eased her off his lap and gave her ass a playful smack. "Now go. And in an effort to make it speedy, you can forgo pajamas because you won't be needing them."

She glared at him suspiciously.

Trey wrapped his hand into her hair and pulled her in for a quick kiss. "If you don't start moving, you're not going to be bringing *any* clothes."

"Just please tell me that we don't have to walk a million miles back down the mountain," she begged hopefully.

"Nope. We're taking the much shorter second route. You'll be staring your surprise in the face before you even know it."

CHAPTER NINETEEN

After a twenty-minute hike down the backside of the mountain to where Alpha kept a back-up vehicle, and another thirty-minute drive, Trey was almost 80 percent sure he'd done the right thing. The other 20 percent had him sweating bullets because he was in uncharted territory.

He could end up looking like either an idiot or a thoughtful romantic—and he wasn't comfortable with either title.

Trey stole a glance to the passenger-side seat. Elle, in an oversized coat and his military knit cap, looked like a kid about to get a sneak peek at Santa's village. Ever since he'd told her about the basics of his plan, she hadn't stopped grinning. And he loved the fact that he'd been the one to do it.

"You know I was kidding about Jonesville being a booming metropolis, right?" Trey warned with a smirk. "The only streetlight is on the way leading out of town and I'm pretty sure they still use some kind of bartering system for gas and goods."

"I'm sure it's charming. I don't even care if the public restroom's an outhouse. We're off the mountain—at least for a little bit—and I get to walk around people without having to worry if they're going to abduct me."

"Didn't realize being stuck with me in the cabin has been that trying for you," he teased.

Elle reached over and gave his hand a gentle squeeze. When she moved to pull her arm back into her lap, he interlaced their fingers and held her hand captive against his thigh. Trey waited five seconds for her to pull away, and when that didn't happen, he waited another ten.

Finally, he released the breath he didn't know he'd been fucking holding. A few weeks ago, if he'd had the audacity to hold her hand, she probably would've run away faster than she had down that Thai alley—*after* she'd kneed him in the groin.

He hoped she finally realized that not all men were wired like her father and her ex. Strike that—he hoped she realized that *he* wasn't fucking wired that way. That's what tonight was about, with the added incentive of making her smile.

He hoped.

Birthdays had been something his mother had always turned into a big deal when he was growing up, but he couldn't exactly hire a balloon artist or take Elle to the circus and call it mission accomplished.

Trey cleared his throat, wincing at how dry it was. "I figured we'd make a few stops before we go exploring the town. Maybe get you some underwear to replace the ones I ripped off you this morning. But I doubt Burl's Grocery and Tackle's going to have pretty, lacy ones."

She shot him a look that made him sorry he had to pay

attention to navigating the mountain roads. "I wouldn't need replacements if someone would stop ripping them off me. Seriously. I'm down to two pair."

"Stop wearing them around the cabin and I wouldn't have to rip them off."

Elle's eyes twinkled when she laughed. "So you're saying it's my fault that you can't wait the two seconds it takes to take them off?"

"No, I'm saying that it's your fault for putting them on in the first place. And if you want to get technical, you're the reason for my impatience, too. Stop being so damn hot that I can't wait to get inside you, and I'll start showing a little more restraint."

Elle's unladylike snort make him grin. He'd lied. When it came to getting inside her, restraint didn't come easy. Or at all. And it probably wouldn't, even if he meditated on a daily basis like Vince. It was all a moot point because when it came to Elle, he didn't want to hold back, and he sure as hell didn't want to watch her walk the fuck away.

Nothing had cemented his moratorium of quick flings more than Elle. He promised her he wouldn't push, but that didn't mean he wasn't going to do everything in his power to show her that he was nothing like the assholes she'd had in her life.

He turned the final corner leading off the mountain and there was Jonesville, a string of brick and stone buildings and cobblestone sidewalks. Elle sat up straighter, her face nearly pressed against the window.

"It's gorgeous." She looked in awe as they drove down Main Street. "Oh my God. It looks like something out of a movie."

"*Deliverance?*" he joked.

"No!" She laughed, squeezing his hand. "This is the kind

of place where people can leave their doors unlocked, and everyone has known everyone else since the beginning of time. If you tell me that there's an antique store nearby I'll burn my remaining two pairs of panties and vow to never replace them."

He cocked up a brow and smirked. "All I need to do is unearth an antique store?"

"That's all you need to do."

"Well then, sweetness, break out the lighter fluid and slip off your undies." With a chuckle, he directed the truck into the nearest empty parking spot.

The second Elle spotted Charming Treasures, her seat belt was unbuckled and she was jumping out of the truck. If they kept up on this path, he wouldn't have to worry about Charlie's threat to rain down hail and brimstone on his head. He'd have Operation Birthday in the bag.

* * *

Elle stepped through the whimsical red door of the country antique store and was instantly transported to heaven. From tables to knickknacks and clothing, displays tastefully accented every nook and cranny of the spacious room.

She didn't even know where to start. Her silent eeny, meeny, miny, moe put her at the table of old clocks. Toward the back of the store, she brushed her palm over the oak tables and a rocking chair that had obviously received a lot of both love and use. But it wasn't long before she found herself standing in front of the elegant jewelry case.

Elle could appreciate a well-endowed ring or a pair of dangly earrings, but her tastes usually ran more toward the simple; a dainty bracelet on special occasions or a pair of studs that could be worn both while cleaning house and going out for a night on the town. With her line of work, she tended not to wear anything at all, but she'd always sworn that if given the ring of her dreams by the man of her heart, she'd never take it off.

She scanned the rows of bracelets and charms before stopping on one that also halted her breathing.

Nestled between a gold heart locket and silver watch, a dainty princess-cut emerald ring blinked up at her. Micro-sized diamond baguettes flanked the small stone, making the deep green even richer in color. Now *that* was a ring she'd never take off—not to shower or cook, or do the most disgusting job thinkable for a nurse. Okay, well maybe she'd put it in a safe spot for the latter, but the second she cleaned up, it would be right back on her finger.

Trey's warmth covered her back.

"Find something you like?" His hands settled at her waist as he peeked over her shoulder.

Comparing the man's eyes to jewelry wasn't exactly conducive to maintaining boundaries, but that's exactly what the ring reminded her of—his eyes, when he went all broody and lusty.

She smiled and tried to sound normal. "What didn't I find? If I had the wallet for it, I'd buy the entire store."

"Hello there! I thought I heard the bell chime. Welcome to Charming Treasures." Wearing a flowery skirt and a beaming smile, an older woman approached. "Welcome to Jonesville."

"Don't get many visitors, do you?" Trey said teasingly.

"Not as many as we'd like, but the town council's trying to change that. Are you passing through or staying with us for a while?"

"We're spending the night at Starry Night," Trey surprised Elle by sharing.

"That's my sister Judith's bed and breakfast! Oh, you're going to love it there." The woman patted Elle's hand. "It's absolutely gorgeous, the perfect spot for a newly engaged couple. I'm Sally, by the way. Lord Almighty, you'd think I've never met new people before."

Elle was slow to register her words. "What? Oh, no, I—"

"Which one are you looking at?" Sally asked, already pulling out the felt-covered tray. "Oh, I bet I know which one it is." With nimble fingers, Sally plucked the emerald ring from the holder and held it in the palm of her hand. "You have impeccable taste, sweetheart. They surely don't make rings like this anymore."

"It really is stunning, but—" Elle could barely take her eyes off of it, even when Sally attempted to put it into her hands. "Oh. No. No, no, no. Really, I couldn't. I was just admiring it."

"Admire up close and personal. It really could use a good home." Sally slid Trey a coy smirk that made Elle's cheeks grow warm. "I have a confession. I saw you looking around, and the way your eyes lit up when you saw this ring—it was like a gravitational force pulled you right to it. It's elegant. Simple. Beautiful."

Unnamed emotions clogged Elle's throat. She gently laid the ring on the counter and stepped away, both from the ring and from Trey. There was no doubt that the ring was beautiful. And perfect. And exactly what she would pick for herself, if ever given the choice.

Sally's looked crestfallen. "Are you sure you don't want to try it on? Sometimes you just need that little extra spark on contact to know that something was always meant to belong to you."

Elle didn't mean to look toward Trey. Her head swiveled sideways and her eyes collided with his. His unreadable expression ratcheted up her nerves even more.

She knew firsthand about sparks and a sense of belonging. She felt both every time he touched her or glanced her way—even now, when it was impossible to guess what was running through his head.

Sweat peppered Elle's forehead, and she suddenly found it difficult to breathe. In the background, she vaguely registered concerned voices, but it wasn't until Trey's arms wrapped around her waist that the room started spinning.

"Thank you, Sally," Trey's voice sounded faraway. "But I think she's going to have to think about the ring."

"Of course. Of course."

Elle didn't start breathing until the shock of cool air hit her face. Her feet moved to the truck on autopilot and got as far as the passenger-side door, when she needed to lean on it for support.

"You okay?" Trey studied her, his face a mask of concern.

"Yep." *No.* Not in the least.

"You sure? You look a little flushed."

"Curse of the Irish. There's no escaping the lobster look, whether it's in the blistering heat or freezing cold."

He didn't believe her, and if he had, she'd seriously start questioning his gut instincts out on the field. But despite not being fooled, he didn't drill her about it and instead suggested they check out the rest of the town.

He'd been right about the town's size. They'd walked a few blocks and had already gone half the length of Main Street when they stepped into a winter festival that boasted of a hundred-year anniversary. Vendor booths lined both sides of the street, some with homemade crafts and others with delicious-smelling treats. Parents laughed and mingled, while kids sped around like miniature bullet trains. In the town's center square, a quaint gazebo was laced with green ivy, despite it being the middle of winter.

Trey flashed her an evil smirk, nodding to the far left where they'd set up an outdoor rink—the man-made, well-maintained kind. "Up for a quick skate around the loop?"

Her lethal glare had him barking out a laugh. "I can't express to you how much I do *not* want to go ice-skating. Been there. Done that. Had the near heart-failure to prove it—and so did you."

Freezing temperatures did nothing to bring down the hot flash that whipped through her. Grabbing the edges of her scarf, Trey hauled her mouth to his. His mouth brushed against hers once, then twice. The kiss started slowly but quickly gained momentum. When his tongue brushed against hers, Elle latched onto his arms—both to hold him close and to keep herself upright. They stood there kissing until a duo of whistles cut through the brisk air.

Trey slowly pulled his mouth away and stroked her swollen bottom lip. "A kiss for the birthday girl." He smirked at her widened eyes. "You didn't think I knew?"

"I guess I shouldn't be surprised that you figured it out. I mean, you probably have a file on my entire life. My apologies if I bored you to tears."

"You couldn't bore me even if you tried, sweetness"

Realization made Elle hug him a little closer. She wrapped her arms around his waist and propped her chin on his chest. "This is what Charlie was talking about, wasn't it? What you had covered?"

"Damn woman kept wanting to horn in on my plans."

"So this was all you?"

Trey almost looked a little nervous. "It was—unless you

don't like it, because then I'll blame Charlie or one of the guys. I still owe Logan a little payback."

Elle chuckled. "I love it, Trey. Thank you. For everything... and especially for today. Birthdays have always been just another day for me," she admitted with a bit of embarrassment.

"Birthdays are supposed to be special." He tucked their interlocked hands against his chest and brushed his mouth over her wrist. "But yours even more so."

"Why especially mine?"

"Because if you hadn't been born, the world would've missed out on an amazing, caring soul. Lord knew I would have."

Cold air gave Elle an excuse for her reddened cheeks and watering eyes. Not trusting that her voice wouldn't crack, she swallowed and worked through the emotions rushing over her. Just when she thought she had a handle on him, he surprised her again—in a good way.

"I don't know what to do when you say things like that," she said honestly.

Words meant to wound? She had her retorts down pat. To control? Yep, she had those covered too. To manipulate? Absolutely. Try to coerce her into doing something she didn't want to do, and you'd wish you'd left it—and her—alone.

But this?

Trey was a man who lived life to the max, didn't shy away from a challenge or danger, and yet his words were the sweetest she'd ever heard—she couldn't imagine him saying anything that could potentially wound another person.

Trey tilted her chin up and brushed his lips against hers. "I'm going to make it my job to say things like that often enough that you get used to hearing them—and expect them."

"That could take a long time." Possibly a lifetime.

"I'm up for the challenge—however long it takes."

That little glimmer of hope that she'd get more time with Trey brought her to her toes. His hand cupped her cheek, holding her close as she initiated the kiss this time. There was no tongue, no devouring, but it affected her more than anything that had come before it. When it ended, her feet barely touched back on the ground.

"What was that for?" He caressed her bottom lip with his gloved hand.

"For absolutely no reason at all." Elle smiled, at perfect ease when they continued to walk through the festival, arms looped around each other's waists.

CHAPTER TWENTY

Breathe in through the nose and out through the mouth. Elle couldn't remember the last time she'd had to focus so hard on not throwing up, but that's exactly what she was doing and had been doing ever since Trey had mentioned dinner.

He hadn't mentioned it in a way that said *"Let's grab some takeout,"* or *"Let's look for a barbecue place that has bibs as part of the place setting."* Instead, the heated look in his eyes hinted at dinner meaning more than the eating of actual food. It was the *more* that was making her feel like a fifteen-year-old prepping for her first date.

Palms sweaty and heart beating frantically, she felt waves of nausea come and go, adding to the ridiculousness. Honestly. She'd had sex with the man after knowing him for mere hours and then repeated the action any time and place that wouldn't get them arrested and tossed in a jail cell.

He'd seen her dry and naked, wet and naked. He'd even

had the unfortunate displeasure of meeting her father and going toe-to-toe with her ex. But it was while wearing a modest above-the-knee dress and heels bought at Charming Treasures and about to go to dinner that she felt the most uncomfortable.

A soft knock pulled Elle's attention from the mirror.

"Dear," the voice of Judith, the bed and breakfast owner, came through the door, "your handsome man's going to wear a hole in my hardwood floors and plunk himself in my basement if you don't come on out soon. Does the dress not fit? I could call my sister to see if she has anything else in the back of the store."

Elle and Trey had checked in to the Starry Night Bed and Breakfast two hours ago, and Judith—much like her antique-loving sister—had been nothing but eager to help. When Trey had first announced his plan to take her to dinner, Judith had witnessed the pure panic on her face and immediately gotten on the phone to call in reinforcements—which led to the gorgeous silk dress she now wore.

"I'm just about ready." Elle opened the door to Judith's gasp. "What do you think?"

"Oh my. I think you look absolutely breathtaking! The moment I saw that color, I knew it would be a perfect match for your eyes. Go ahead and give me a spin."

With warmth spreading to her cheeks, Elle did as the woman asked. She loved the dress too, yet another incredible find in Sally's boutique. The sky-blue wrap slid over her curves as if it had been specially designed for her body alone.

"I don't know how to thank you," Elle repeated the same sentiments she had earlier. "Both you and Sally have been so ridiculously nice."

"Oh, there's nothing ridiculous about it, honey." Judith waved away the sentiment. "It's just the way we were raised.

I should be thanking you and your handsome man for giving an old woman something to do with her time this weekend. But I was serious about my floors. Stan's been doing his best to provide a distraction, but it doesn't seem to be working too well."

As Judith navigated Elle toward the stairs, Elle quickly realized that wearing heels wasn't a skill you could avoid for six months of the year and then quickly resume—at least not without a real risk to loss of life. She clutched onto the banister and took one step at a time. When she was two steps from the main floor, Trey stalked into view, and she nearly forgot how to bend her knee.

Whether dressed in tactical garb or dress pants, the man looked sinful. And delicious. And lethal—though the danger was only toward her sensibilities. His broad shoulders stretched his soft gray dress shirt, and the sleeves, partially rolled, exposed powerfully corded arms. Six feet separated them but he might as well been brushing up against her.

He ran his gaze down the length of her body and back. She'd be uncomfortable if any other man looked at her with such appreciation, but not Trey. "Wow. You look gorgeous."

"Thank you. So do you." Elle's smile trembled. *Yeah… fifteen-year-old on her first date.*

His smirk made her cheeks flush. "I meant that you look beautiful. I mean, pretty. *Nice*. You look *nice*. I'll stop talking now."

Judith stepped around Elle as Stan, Judith's husband, walked out from the kitchen. "Look at these two young lovebirds, Stan. Aren't they just the sweetest thing?"

"Tooth-achingly sweet." Stan said, chomping on something that sounded suspiciously like a potato chip, and judging by Judith's scowl, not something her husband should be eating.

Judith turned back to them with a grin. "Well, you two have a darling time. I've never been to the dining room up at Swallow Falls, but I hear it's intensely romantic. And just so you know, Stan and I will be out late—possibly all night. We're going to a friend's house, and whenever we start talking, the wine starts pouring, and then before we realize it, the sun's poking up over the mountain. The two of you will be okay on your own tonight, right?"

"I think we'll manage." Trey still hadn't taken his eyes off Elle. Her cheeks *had* to be crimson by now.

Elle hated to cover the gorgeous silk dress, but practicality and freezing cold temperatures had her accepting the coat Trey held out for her.

"So what's Swallow Falls?" she asked, trying to ignore the fact that Judith basically told them that they were in the clear to come back from dinner and do the horizontal mambo.

"It's a ski resort about fifteen miles away. They have a restaurant there that's supposed to be the best within the tri-state area, and the chef comes from some fancy place in Paris. Don't ask me to pronounce his name. French wasn't one of the languages I took in high school."

"You made reservations?"

Trey raised an eyebrow at the surprise in her voice and tugged on his own coat. "I do know how to work a phone. Have for a while now. I'm good with my hands...I can press the buttons and everything."

"I know you're good with your hands. I've seen them in action." *Kill her. Kill her now.* "I'm shutting up. For the entire night, because I obviously can't be expected *not* to embarrass myself."

Trey looped an arm around her and tugged her to the front of his body. "I like when you start talking all discombobulated-like. It's fucking adorable."

Elle didn't feel adorable. She felt out-of-sorts, only marginally relaxing as Trey navigated the truck through the dark mountain roads. Each time she did, though, he'd glance her way, and then it was back to square one.

Swallow Falls was nestled a little higher in the Pocono Mountains, the main house a sprawling, two-story gray stone structure complete with white twinkling lights and more romantic ambiance than in a romance novel. A grand front porch was wedged between the front of the building and the long circular drive, where Trey stopped the truck in front of a gangly teenage valet.

Trey opened her door and extended a hand to help her step down from the truck. And then he kept his fingers wrapped around hers as they stepped into the resort's lobby. Rich earth tones complemented the stone and wood accents. A massive fireplace filled the room with the scent of pine and nature. It was country elegance from the baseboards to the open, vaulted ceilings.

Trey led the way to the dining room, where a young male twenty-something greeted them with a flashy smile and led them toward a secluded section of the room.

"Your server will be with you in a moment. Is there anything I can get you in the meantime? Would you like to see the wine list?" the young man asked.

"Yeah, sure. That would be great," Trey said, nodding.

The young man walked away, and in Elle's quest to relieve her Saharan dry mouth, she knocked her arm into her water goblet. She swallowed a curse and righted it quickly. With all her father's political parties and society dinners, you'd think she'd feel a bit more reserved, but nope.

Grabbing her attention, Trey captured her fingers from across the table. "Why are you so nervous?"

"I'm not nervous," she lied through her teeth. At the disbelieving arch of his eyebrow, she amended her words. "So maybe I'm a little nervous, but if you ask me why, I honestly wouldn't be able to give you an answer."

"I know what you mean."

She gave an unladylike snort. "*Uh-huh.* I don't think anything can get you ruffled. You always look the epitome of calm, cool, and collected."

"Then you're not looking hard enough."

"I don't know. I'm looking pretty hard." And the more she looked, the more she liked. The man was two hundred pounds of walking complexities. Whenever she thought she had him figured out and had a grip on how insanely drawn she felt toward him, he did something like this and stole that control from her grasp.

He kept her guessing, kept her on her toes.

"Good evening," a low, sultry voice broke through the moment. A tall, lithe blonde stood next to their table, her thousand-watt smile focused on Trey. The woman was gorgeous and knew it. Her white shirt strained at the buttons from her ample breasts, and her black linen pants looked as if they'd been spray-painted onto her body. "My name's Emmaline and it'll be my pleasure to serve you tonight in any way I can."

Elle barely withheld an eye-roll at the woman's blatant vocalization of interest. She all but ripped her shirt apart and laid supine on top of Trey's place setting.

Trey's knowing smirk—or his attention—hadn't left Elle. "I'm glad to hear that, Emmaline, because tonight's a special night—the birthday of one of the most incredible women I know."

As the waitress's smile dimmed, Elle's grew.

"Well...that's wonderful," Emmaline's tone oozed manufactured politeness. "I'll be sure to let the chef know that you're celebrating. He may want us to serve you from his personal menu, if that's okay?"

Trey looked to Elle for the answer, and she nodded. She'd have to chew her food carefully, judging by the look on the waitress's face. The blonde put a little extra shimmy in her step as she walked away.

"I suppose that's status quo for you when you go out, isn't it?" When Trey acted as if he didn't know what she meant, she added, "Women asking you to make *them* your appetizer instead of the breadsticks. And don't pretend like you don't know the effect you have on women, because I'll be forced to hurt you."

Trey chuckled. "No pretending. But do you want a bit of truth?"

Did she? She wasn't sure. "Go ahead. Enlighten me."

"A long line of half-naked women could be standing in the room, and all of my focus would still be on you and only you."

Elle's heart stuttered a little bit, making her chest tremble. "That's a really, really good bit of truth."

"You look like you don't believe me."

"Actually, I do," Elle said honestly. If anyone else had said it, probably not. If it had come out of James's mouth, *definitely* not. But if she'd learned anything about Trey in their time together, it was that he said what he meant. She was still getting used to that.

When the appetizer came, Trey stared at the plate in front of them and even looked a little pale. "What the holy fuck is that?"

Elle nearly choked on her laugh. "Escargots. In what looks to be some kind of garlic-and- herb sauce."

Trey's throat bobbed as he continued to stare at the shelled delicacy. "Those are snails."

"Yes. Yes, they are. I take it you've never had escargot?" Neither had she and, honestly, she wasn't all too keen on giving it a whirl.

"I've eaten grubs. Scorpions. Snakes. But it was when I was in the middle of fucking nowhere and my choices were to either eat them or die from starvation. They sure as hell didn't come on fine china. This is the kind of stuff that's on the chef's personal menu?"

Elle chuckled. "You did say he was a French chef. I can't wait to see what he has prepared for the entrée."

If possible, Trey's complexion went from pale to ashen, but he picked up a snail shell and inspected it like it was going to bite off his tongue.

"You know, I saw a dive bar on the way here that boasted about having the best fried chicken strips this side of the mountain," Elle interrupted before he put his fork in his mouth.

Trey stopped. "But I wanted…it's your birthday. I wanted to make it a memorable night for you."

Elle's chest ached with the sweetness of his words. She reached over the table and took the fork from his hand. "It already is. And it'll be for *good* reason if I don't have to force myself to swallow snails."

Trey dropped his fork to the plate and signaled Emmaline for the check. "Thank fucking God."

CHAPTER TWENTY-ONE

Trey felt instantly more at home in Dixie, the dive bar within the town of Jonesville, than he had in the escargot-serving restaurant at the ski resort. A collection of stuffed wildlife adorned the walls as well as a decorative chronological history of hunting paraphernalia. Every inch of the place played up the livelihood of the people who lived in the area.

And there was no one set of people. Men ranged from mountain men who looked like they hadn't seen the sharp edge of a razor in close to twenty years to couples who looked to be like him and Elle—out for a night at the only place in town open past ten o'clock.

When they walked through the front door, Elle didn't take a single hesitant step, gripping his hand and leading the way to a beat-up table in the back of the room. The bar's locals only looked half-interested in their presence—until Elle innocently shimmied out of her coat, unaware of the heads turning in their direction. Goddamn, he didn't want any trouble tonight.

He exchanged nods with the nearest table of male admirers, making his warning clear—*eyes back on their fucking beers*. They got the message a second before a waitress sidled up to their table.

"What can I get ya's?" The young woman—who looked barely out of her teens—snapped her gum and gave Elle's dress a cursory glance. "And I'm going to warn ya's right now. We don't have any fancy wines or those pigs in blankets. We have watered-down beer because Tom forgot to pay up to the supplier and grease with a side of chicken fingers."

"Good," Elle gave the woman a friendly smile. "Because that's exactly what I'm looking for."

"Same here," Trey nodded.

The waitress snapped her gum again and rolled her eyes before taking their order back to the bar.

Trey turned back to Elle and shook his head at the smile on her face. "So this is your idea of a birthday dinner, huh?"

"Well, it sure isn't escargot," she teased. She reached across the table to squeeze his hand and, instead of letting her go, he wrapped his fingers through hers and held on tight. "But I think it's really sweet that you tried."

"Yeah, well. Who would've thought that the daughter of . . . you"—he caught himself before mentioning her father's name—"would prefer chicken fingers to buttery snails?"

Her smile wilted slightly. "Is that how you see me? As escargot?"

"No. I see you as a strong, beautiful woman who's not afraid to mosey into a dive bar as if she's done it a million times before. Come to think of it, that dive in Thailand was a lot like this one."

She shrugged. "There weren't a whole lot of options

there. Besides, I'm not a fan of all the stigma that usually comes along with buttered snails."

The waitress plopped down their beers and their chicken strips before disappearing toward the other side of the room. Despite this being a far cry from Swallow Falls, they'd already talked more than they had from over the top of a bright linen tablecloth.

"At the gala, you looked as if you belonged." Trey chose his words carefully. "But anyone who looked a little harder could see that you didn't."

Elle's eyes flashed up to meet his. "And you looked harder?"

He nodded.

"And what, exactly, did you see?"

"Honestly? I saw a woman who mentally tallied the costs of all the gowns and decorations and the platters of food around her and thought of all the good that same amount of money could do for a community in need."

"Well, it's frivolous," Elle said, looking slightly embarrassed as she chomped on a fry. "One of those gowns alone could buy a month's worth of medicine for a clinic like the one in Thailand. And don't get me started on some of those *charities* run by the social elite. If the people who needed the help got a fraction of the money that was spent to hold those fund-raisers, there'd be no more famine in the world."

"And that pisses you off."

"Of course it pisses me off." She looked disgusted. "People who are in a position to do good should use that power *for* the good—and not their own."

"Is that what your father did?" Trey had to ask. The sudden swarm of hurt darkening her eyes made him do it. He brushed his thumb over her wrist. "Did he use his influence for his own personal gain?"

"He doesn't live to serve the people. In his eyes, the people live to serve *him*. And if someone's brazen enough to interfere with his agenda, he'll be right there with a good ultimatum. That's why people don't dare go against my father."

"You did."

Elle laughed, but the humor didn't reach her eyes. "No."

"So you're telling me that your father planned for you to become a nurse with an NGO?"

"No, I'm saying that until I took the position at Caring Hands, I let him bully me into compliance like he did everyone else." At the sight of his confusion, she gently pulled away. "What if I told you that I used to be a Step-ford Daughter?"

His eyebrows lifted. "I don't see you as the type of woman to just fall into line."

"Then you're eyesight's all wonky. At sixteen, I rocked at throwing parties like the gala. If my father demanded that I wear dark blue, I wore it from head to toe. If my father demanded that I date a certain up-and-coming politi-cal prospect, I waited for the doorbell to ring and accepted the flowers with a smile. I made a long tradition out of suc-cumbing to every single one of my father's demands."

"But what about nursing school and your job at the NGO? Your father seems the type to think that profes-sion's…"

"Below him?" Elle nodded. "He does. It was one of the first times I put up a stink and, truthfully, I think it shocked him a little. But then he did as is his norm and demanded I be at his side during his reelection. I nearly flunked out of nursing school because I was trying to be in two places at one time—which I'm sure was his intent. But I graduated and became licensed…and then along came James."

Trey's irritation grew at the mention of the ex, and he stabbed his soggy fries a little too forcefully into his vat of ketchup. "And let me guess...he was one of those up-and-comers your father threw at you."

Elle made a *ding-ding* noise and tapped her nose. "Nail on the head. I deluded myself into believing that I actually cared about James because thinking there were actual feelings was easier than admitting that the entire relationship was orchestrated by my father. And then—" Elle paused, a sudden wave of...something...washing over her face. "I was in the accident, and it wasn't exactly a fender-bender. Then one day after a doctor's appointment, I stopped off at James's office to find him with his secretary—which, as she shared with me all too gleefully, wasn't the first time they'd been together."

Trey gripped his beer mug so hard he thought the damn thing would crack. He'd known about the cheating. She'd glossed over it a few times in passing, and then of course there was the altercation at the gala itself. But hearing the story from her own lips made him vow that if he ever saw that bastard again, he'd rip off his head and stuff it up his ass. "I should've broken his neck when I had the chance."

"It would've been a waste of time."

"Not so sure about that," Trey murmured before taking a sip of his beer.

"I am. Because when I saw him that afternoon with his pants around his ankles, do you know what I felt?" Elle almost looked embarrassed as she fingered the condensation on her mug. "Nothing. What hurt worse was when he told me that it was just one of those things I was going to have to learn to deal with—*and he really expected that I would.* My father did too."

"And that's when you ended the engagement?"

"Right then and there—and again, their complete and to-tal shock only solidified my resolve to start thinking and living for myself and no one else. Shay had already gone on a few assignments with Caring Hands, so she put me into contact with them, and a few weeks later I was on a plane bound for Thailand."

Small pieces of the Elle Monroe puzzle finally started making sense—except one. "So if James didn't hurt you, then why all your rules banning any relationships?"

It took a while for Elle to look him in the eye, and when she did, he saw the slight tremor as she captured her bottom lip between her teeth. "I don't want to be put in the position to be tempted to let someone hijack my life again. It took a pathetic thirty years to break out of it the first time."

It sounded feasible, and Elle looked sincere, but Trey suspected there was a bit more to her Elle Goes to Thailand escapade. He wanted to know it all, but he wasn't about to demand she tell him and give her a reason to pull way.

Elle flashed him a nervous smile. "This conversation is a little much for a first date, don't you think?"

He recognized her need to divert. "Is that what this is? A date? Seems like we've put the cart a little ways before the horse, haven't we? We haven't even had our first dance."

"Then let's remedy that." Elle stood and extended her hand right when a fast-paced country song came out of the speakers. "Come on, cowboy."

Shit. He had to learn to think before he spoke.

She dragged him to the edge of the dance floor, where he came to an abrupt stop.

"What's the matter?" She looked at him curiously while he studied the complicated boot stomp being performed by the handful of couples—all in synch.

"How about we wait for a slow number, because I sure as hell know my limits, and it's way before...that."

"I'll teach you." She tugged gently and flashed him pleading smile. "Nobody expects perfection. It's all about moving to the music."

"Any moving to this music that I do is going to look like I'm having a fucking seizure."

Trey could've pulled away if he really wanted to, but the smile on her face had him reluctantly shuffling his feet onto the dance floor, where she spent the entire song trying to teach him a handful of moves. When the song ended, he sent up a silent prayer, only for it to be answered with another fast song.

Trey followed the direction of Elle's laugh and caught sight of an older woman in front of the jukebox with a mischievous smirk plastered on her face. "Go on, honey. Give it another whirl."

After a few stumbles that had both him and Elle laughing, Trey managed to keep his embarrassment down to a minimum. Still, when a slow number came on, he pulled her into his arms with a low chuckle. "Thank fucking God. That was damned painful."

Humor glittered from Elle's blue eyes. Her fingers absently kneaded the back of his neck, while her other hand rested palm-down on his chest. "If I didn't know any better, I'd say you were a little relieved that song ended. What's the matter? You weren't feeling the Boot-Stompin' Shuffle?"

"Not one fucking bit. This is more my speed." He inserted his knee between her legs and brought her as close as their two bodies would permit.

"I like this speed too." Elle rested her cheek against his chest and smiled. If it were possible, she seemed to melt into him a little bit more, and Trey didn't mind it one damn bit.

* * *

Elle lost count of how many line dances Trey endured all in the name of her fun. And as much as she loved watching him glide his large body so fluidly into spins and slides, she loved the slow songs even more.

The mix of clean soap and male musk invading her nose was all Trey—earthy, comfortable, and really damn sexy. That scent and brushing against his body with each beat of the music escalated Elle's desire from a pleasantly warm contentment to a desperate need to get him alone and naked.

Neither one of them had said much since the last song started crooning softly about love and need and desire. Trey guided his hand up her back and into her hair, leaving a trail of goose bumps in its wake.

"Elle." His voice rumbled against her cheek. "I don't want to rush through your birthday or anything but do you want to—"

"Yes." She didn't even let him finish his thought. Clutching his hand, she towed him to the table to grab their coats, and then they exited Dixie's to the chorus of catcalls and whistles.

"Woman possessed" wasn't an apt enough description for the feelings coursing through her body. She needed Trey, and she needed him now. The second they reached the truck, she gently pushed him against the passenger door.

His eyes widened in surprise. "In a hurry, are we? And here I didn't want to have to end the night early."

"We're not ending the night early," Elle said right before she attacked.

Trey caught her, his palms sliding over her ass while she playfully took his bottom lip between her teeth in a gentle nibble. She couldn't stop touching him—beneath his jacket and over his chest. She undulated her hips in an attempt to get closer.

Trey fisted her hair and flipped their positions so it was *him* pushing *her* against the truck.

"Goddamn it," Trey growled. He nipped his way down her neck, each gentle bite making Elle's breath hitch. "I wish we were closer to our fucking room."

"We have a perfectly good truck right behind us."

"I'm not taking you in the cab of a fucking pickup—at least not on your birthday."

Elle's mouth opened to make a retort about it being his birthday gift to her when she registered the scuffle of stones. Trey must've heard it too because he spun around as two men stepped out from behind one of the parked cars.

Wearing dark plaid hunters' jackets and unkempt beards, both men looked as if they hadn't seen the sharper side of a razor in a few months.

"Get in the truck, Elle." Trey handed her the keys and took a small step forward, giving her room to open the passenger-side door.

"Aw, don't get in the truck, hon," the man on the left slurred. "If it's your birthday, it only seems right that me and my buddy here get a chance to give you a present." He shot a malicious grin to his friend. "Don'cha think, Bruce? Maybe a sweet little birthday kiss."

"That sounds good to me, Les," Bruce agreed. Then in a move meant to shock, he grabbed his crotch and lifted his eyebrows in a lewd expression. "And boy do I have a present for you to kiss, princess."

Trey turned enough to hold the passenger-side door open for Elle. "Inside. Now."

"Didn't we say not to get in the fucking car?" Les howled.

Before the hand even clamped down on Elle's wrist, it

was gone. Trey had Bruce's arm twisted behind his back at an odd angle, and his face practically eating the truck's paint job. Elle saw a flash of movement behind him a split second before a dull *thump* made Trey curse.

He teetered sideways, his grip on the first man loosening. Les stood tall and proud, gripping a bat in his hands like he'd hit a home run.

"Back the hell off now, and I may let you actually walk away," Trey warned. Blood trickled from the gash on the side of his head where a small knot was already forming.

The baseball protégé snorted. "Like fucking hell, dick. Not until we get a little taste of that sweet piece of ass."

Trey blocked the bat mid-swing, and delivered an uppercut that sent both Les and the bat flying against the parked car. It wasn't much of a fight. Before long, Trey had Bruce back to eating the truck's hood.

"I told you to back off," Trey pointed out with a low rumble. "Your ears broken or what?"

Bruce struggled in vain to break free. Les was back on his feet, his trusty bat in hand—and focused on Trey.

"Oh, hell no." She slithered out from the truck, her foot bumping into a discarded beer bottle. She picked it up and armed herself. "Hey, Les."

The second Les turned, she swung. The bottle smacked into his head, shattering on impact and making him stumble—*stumble*, but not go down. Red-faced and furious, he charged. Thinking back to Charlie's instructions, she aimed her strappy shoe toward his kneecap and kicked. It didn't pack as much punch as if she'd been wearing sneakers, but it did the job, making the thug drop to his knees.

People started trickling out of the bar, a few even clapping and offering congratulations for a job well done. Not surprisingly, Bruce and Les didn't have much in the way of friends. Dixie's bartender, a man equal in size to Trey, grabbed Bruce by the scruff of his neck and took over for Trey.

"You okay?" Trey looked her over as he stalked over to her.

"I'm fine." At his raised brow, she added. "Charlie's a good teacher."

He studied her again as if trying to make sure she wasn't lying. By the time he was somewhat appeased, red and blue lights had pulled into the parking lot and two brown-uniformed officers climbed out from the police cruiser.

Penny and Charlie would be proud—a birthday outing that ended with a police presence.

CHAPTER TWENTY-TWO

After giving a statement to the town's lone sheriff, it had taken Trey a few rounds of counting to ten and the entire five-minute ride to the B&B to pull his shit together. When they stepped into its foyer, he was still working on it, which meant he needed to haul out the big guns.

"Come here." Trey pulled Elle into his arms and nestled his nose into the curve of her neck. Having her this close was better than any fucking countdown to sanity.

Her fingers gently ran over his arms. "Trey, I—"

"Just give me another minute."

Elle probably thought he'd lost his fucking mind. Part of him thought so too.

"Are you really okay?" His voice sounded gruff even to his own ears. "Keep in mind that if you lie to me and I find out, I'm going to be hella fucking pissed, sweetness."

"I'm fine." Her answer was muffled against his chest.

He eased her far enough away to make sure. No blood.

No bruises. Relief washed over him a split second before fear made him go stupid. "What the hell were you thinking, going after that guy with a fucking beer bottle?"

Elle's blue eyes narrowed on him. "Excuse me?"

Yeah, he probably could've phrased it a bit differently, but his mind was still reeling from the sight of her being confronted by that brawling redneck.

"What I was thinking," she returned, her voice level, "was that you'd been struck in the head by a baseball bat once already and were, amazingly enough, still standing. I didn't want to test that hard head of yours with a second blow. But if you keep glaring at me, I'll rethink my actions the next time someone comes at you with sporting equipment."

Elle trailed her fingers across his brow, and then both her eyes and her tone softened. "You're the one who got hurt. You're bleeding. And you really should've let them look you over at the emergency room. You already have a goose egg."

"Not going to any emergency room."

"Trey, you—"

"No," he said firmly. "There's no reason to go to the hospital."

Elle snorted. "You could have a concussion—or worse."

He shook his head. "Like you said, I have a hard head."

She looked at him like she wanted to test that theory out herself. Instead, she took his hand and led him up the steps and into their room. Gone was the hot and sultry Elle of earlier. Nurse Elle pushed him onto the closed toilet before rifling through the vanity cabinets and finding a first-aid kit.

She pulled out disinfectant and bandages and spread them out on the counter. "Maybe I should talk with Stone about putting a medical staff on your payroll, because you guys seem to need some kind of care on a routine basis."

Their positions put his head even with her breasts. He

palmed her hips and savored her closeness. "The guys can find their own private-duty nurse. You're all mine."

"You need stitches, Trey. Nurses don't do stitches, and I failed every unit in my high-school home economics class—*especially* sewing."

"So slap a Band-Aid on it. It'll still heal."

"It'll scar."

He shrugged. "I hear some imperfections are like catnip to some women. What about you, babe? You like a man who looks a little rough around the edges?"

Elle muttered something unflattering about him under her breath while she disinfected the cut and applied a couple of butterfly bandages. Her softly grumbled profanities made him grin, and then he gave in to the need to touch her a little bit more.

He didn't know which was softer, the dress or her skin. He took it upon himself to test both, running his fingers up the backs of her legs.

"Doing *that* isn't going to put you in my good graces, Hanson." She repacked the first-aid kit with a little more force than necessary and stuffed it back into the cabinet. "You should be going to the hospital."

"And I said that I don't need one. Come here." He coaxed her closer, attempting to slip a knee between her soft thighs.

Her hands dropped to his shoulders and locked. "I'm not straddling you while you sit on a toilet...probably concussed."

"Fine. Hold on." Palming her ass, he stood. She squealed, her legs having nowhere to go except around his waist as he walked the two of them to the bed.

"Put me down," Elle ordered him. "Trey! Damn it, you're going to hurt yourself!"

"It'll take more than a baseball bat to take me out…
especially when you're wearing that sexy-as-hell dress and
those fuck-me heels." There wasn't a damn thing that could
convince him to keep his distance from the woman currently
squirming in his hands.

The night had been about more than her birthday celebration. Hell, it had even gone beyond proving that what they
had didn't deserve a fucking shelf life. It was about confirmation.

He wanted what Rafe had—a no-questions-asked, no-
holding-back, hearts-all-in relationship that fucked people
up in the head. And he wanted that with Elle.

He was falling goddamned hard, if he hadn't already sunk
the entire way. "You're not going anywhere," he murmured,
more to himself than to Elle.

He lay her by the edge of the bed, kissing his way to
her mouth while his hands skimmed up her silken legs. Her
heels dug into ass, driving him crazy.

"Trey." Elle, already breathless and aroused, danced her
fingers up the buttons of his shirt and released them one by
one. "At least let me take off these shoes before someone
loses an eye."

"The shoes stay. Everything else can go…eventually."
*Meaning after he'd tormented them both to the brink of san-
ity.* As badly as he wanted her, he didn't want this over
anytime soon.

He gently plucked open the neatly tied bow on her hip
and slowly revealed the lace undergarments beneath—strike
that—the *single* lace garment, because she was sans one pair
of panties.

Trey groaned, his eyes feasting on her flesh. "Goddamn,
Elle. This is like opening a present on Christmas morning.
You've been without panties all goddamned night?"

Her lips melted into a coy smile as she rotated her hips. "I gave you my word, didn't I? You conjured up an antique store and I hocus-pocused my underwear."

Trey unraveled her dress the rest of the way and nearly came on the spot at the way her sheer black bra hugged her breasts. The demi-cups presented him with her already firmed, half-exposed nipples. And with no panties covering her mound, there was nothing to hide the fact she was already wet and ready.

"You're so fucking gorgeous, baby." He trailed his knuckles up her torso while his lips skimmed over the fabric of her bra.

She dug her fingers into his hair, holding him close as he nibbled and licked her budding left nipple before leaving it and offering the same attention to its twin. Her soft sighs spurred him on and had him locking gazes with her over the curve of her breast.

He couldn't keep his hands or his mouth off her, especially when she looked at him with a mixture of raw hunger and need.

"My turn." Her voice dripped with pure sex as she sat up, running her fingers over the bulge in his pants.

When she reached his fly, his hand closed over hers. "It's probably safer if I stay clothed for now, sweetness."

"I don't want safe right now, Trey. I want naked skin. Yours. Mine." She gently pushed his hand aside and resumed her efforts on his zipper. Once his pants dropped to the ground, she had him in her hand. "I want *this*. Inside me."

Trey loved Elle's assertive side, loved that she felt comfortable unleashing it with him. He tossed his shirt aside just as her tongue flicked out, catching the drop of moisture beading on his cock. That wasn't the inside he'd been thinking of, but it worked for now.

He gently lifted her hair away from her face and watched her take him into her mouth. Pure fucking heaven—that's what her mouth was. Her blue eyes peered up at him, closing as she curled her wicked tongue around his tip and sank back down. Every swipe snapped another thread of his control, until she emitted a greedy little hum—and then all his damn threads disintegrated.

With a low groan, he cupped her cheek and eased himself away.

Unspoken questions and doubt glittered up at him from her blue eyes. "Did you not like it?"

Trey let out a painful chuckle. Wrapping a hand behind her nape, he nudged her gazed upward. "Baby, it's not possible for me to love it any more. If we were a few hours in the future and on our third or fourth round, there'd be no way I'd be stopping you, but I want the taste of you on my lips when you come for the first time tonight, and then I want you wrapped around my cock on the second."

Goddamn, he'd never in a million years get tired of that lusty look in her eyes. She shivered in his arms, her hands gliding up his chest. "I guess that means we both better get naked then, huh?"

Trey half-chuckled, half-groaned as he kissed her down to the mattress, skimming his fingers along her skin. "I want you to stay…perfectly…still." Not only because it was fucking hot, but because if her hands or mouth came anywhere near him again, he'd lose his shit and forget everything he'd said about savoring.

Her nipples, stiffened from arousal, peeked over the rim of the lace bra, directing him exactly where he wanted to go. He curled his tongue around one reddened bud, giving it a slow suck while he gently rolled the other between his fingers. Elle's breathing hitched, her back arching her breasts into his hold. With a simple twist of her fingers, she gifted him an unobstructed view.

"God, I love front clasps." Trey worshiped her nipple with no barriers, and nearly beat his chest at her throaty little moan.

That sound drove him fucking insane. It fueled him to sample every inch of her body—her collarbone, the gentle swoop of her neck. Where his mouth wasn't tasting, his hands touched. No matter how long they stayed at this, he knew that he'd never quite get his fill.

"You with me?" Trey skimmed his mouth down her torso. He kissed her stomach, slid his mouth to the gentle dip above each hip.

"More than." Elle's mouth curved into a sultry grin. He hovered over her mound, coaxing her legs wide enough to permit his shoulders, and then slid his hands beneath her backside.

Keeping her focus on him, he dipped down for his first taste of heaven. Slow. Savor. Touch. He took his time, enjoying the taste of her against his tongue. One of Elle's hands threaded through his hair.

"Don't stop," she demanded breathlessly, gripping the bedsheet in her free hand. "Please, Trey. Don't stop."

"There's nothing on this earth that would tear me away from you, sweetness."

And he meant it—more than he'd ever meant anything in his damn life.

* * *

Being with Trey was sexual overload waiting to happen. Her body ached to be touched more, yet also craved to be the one doing the touching. When she'd had her mouth on him, her head had gone fuzzy with the knowledge that she'd made him tremble, that she'd pushed him close to his breaking point. Now she was the one close to the edge.

Trey coasted his mouth over her body.

"Please." She coaxed him closer.

"No begging, baby. I'm going to give you everything you want, and then I'm going to give you everything you deserve. Both in and out of this bed."

Oh sweet heavens. She couldn't even wrap her mind around his words, too filled with blinding need. Trey brought her legs over his shoulders, the change in position exposing her like she'd never been before.

It wasn't only her sexual reservations that melted away. It was the ones about everything else: her relationships, her father, her future. In Trey's arms, the risk of heartbreak didn't seem like so much of a risk.

"Eyes on me," he gently ordered.

Elle obeyed instantly. That intimacy was her undoing. Her pleasure erupted against his tongue as she came. Trey stayed with her, rubbing and humming, bringing the peak of her orgasm even higher.

He skated his mouth back to her lips.

"No more waiting." She cupped his backside and, with a firm squeeze, urged him between her thighs, where he teased them both by rubbing the tip of his erection against her clit—and then slid home.

Trey pulled back and thrust again, slow and deep. "You feel so un-fucking-believable. Touch yourself for me, Elle. Help me make you come."

Sensing her hesitation, he gently coaxed her hand into position above her clit and then they played together, alternating between soft strokes and firm brushes. "Oh, God."

Trey pulled out to his rim and slammed back...hard and deep. Again and again.

The clash of their bodies echoed through the room. Skin on skin. Moan after moan. Trey kept up the unrelenting pace until the heaviness of impending release coiled between her legs.

"Please tell me you're there," Trey panted.

"Almost."

"Not fucking good enough. I want you to come with me." With a low growl, he entwined their fingers and slid them through her dampness to the exact spot where his cock slid mercilessly into her body. "Eyes on me, baby. I want to see all of you when you let go."

That was what she wanted and feared at the same time. Looking into his eyes was more intimacy than she thought she'd ever have with anyone. It pushed her past her comfort zone, straight into an emotional minefield. And he'd been doing that since their very first encounter.

Trey's thumb brushed over her pulsing clit, his thrusts getting wilder. She lifted her hips and met each one. It wasn't long before her muscles coiled through her body in preparation for a grand release.

Trey must have felt it too. He let out a low growl, steeling her lips for a searing kiss. And that was it. The fuse lit, fireworks scorching their way through every inch of her body as she flew apart in the most pleasurable way, and took Trey right along with her.

CHAPTER TWENTY-THREE

Twenty-four hours of new experiences had turned Elle's thirtieth birthday into the best by far—even including the time spent outside Dixie, giving statements to the local police. And yeah, there'd been times of discomfort, too, when Trey pushed her way too close—or over—her comfort zone.

But it hadn't been as scary as she'd thought, and it had a lot to do with the man she was with. The more time they spent together, the more she found herself wanting to give in—to being with him—to *trust* him.

That realization made her a quieter than normal on the drive back to the cabin. She'd caught Trey looking at her a few times, but he'd just give her a grin and let her continue tracing the long lines of muscle cording his arm.

But the comfortable silence ended when they stepped into the cabin and the satellite phone rang. Trey dropped their bags and answered on speakerphone. "What's up?"

"Boot up for a video call and then open the email attachment that was sent a few minutes ago." Stone, sounding grimmer than usual, didn't waste any time in pleasantries.

"Doing it now." Trey hung up and loaded the video feed from headquarters onto the laptop. From the Room of Testosterone, Stone and Charlie's faces filled up the laptop screen.

Charlie's smile looked a little...forced. "How was the birthday? Caveman didn't screw it up, did he?"

"It was great," Elle said truthfully. "I couldn't have asked for a better one."

Trey pulled Elle onto his lap and shifted her sideways so they could both be part of the video call.

"So what gives, Stone?" Trey asked what they'd both been thinking. "Did you find out where this Dean Winters is holing up?"

"Did you pull up that email I told you about?" Stone asked, his face blank.

"Doing it now." Trey clicked a few buttons.

"Play it."

Trey brought up the link that had been copied from a D.C. area news source and shrank it so that they could still see Stone and Charlie on the other half of their screen. A podium was positioned in front a dark blue background, and news reporters hovered around. A press conference.

Elle had seen hundreds of them before, but this one gave her a bad feeling...especially when her father walked onto the platform. Trey tensed beneath her and linked his fingers through hers as they waited.

"Good morning," her father's voice echoed from the microphone as he looked into the nearest camera. "I'd like to thank you all for taking the time to come here this morning. I know as well as anyone that weekends are meant to be spent with family."

Elle snorted humorlessly. "Right. He wouldn't know family time if it bit him in the ass."

"Anyone who has followed my career through the years knows that the only thing that rivals my passion for getting assault weapons out of the hands of our enemies," Senator Monroe added, "is my family—my daughter. And now someone is using my love for her as a bargaining chip for their own nefarious plans."

Cameras flashed and reporters called out questions, to which Elle's father simply raised his hand and called for quiet.

"My daughter's life has now been put in danger on three separate occasions, the last happening two weeks ago, while under the nose of her private security detail— and in the presence of children. This audacious and disgusting behavior is the exact reason why these people must be dealt with, and as New York's senator and the country's champion, I will bring these law-breakers to justice and show them that we will not be scared into compliance."

Samuel Monroe stared stonily into the camera in front of him. "Stand in the way of my agenda, and I will bring an end to your tyranny. Threaten our families, and I will bring an end to *you*. Thank you."

Elle's father ignored the slew of questions being hurled in his direction and turned from the podium. He took a few steps and stumbled. Then in a frenzy, people poured onto the stage, and a handful of men whisked him away.

"What the hell happened?" Trey asked.

"We're told he's doing okay," Charlie said the moment Trey hit pause. "They're keeping him in a D.C. hospital for tests and observations, but they expect a heart attack."

"My father's healthy as a horse. There's no way." Elle hated to think it, but she didn't believe that speech or anything around it held even a speck of honesty. And then there was the other little thing…the thing that formed a small sliver of ice in her chest and sent it through her veins. "And what did he mean by three separate occasions? With the last around children? There was the airport and the gala—no kids."

"And then the sled-tacular," Trey pointed out. "The activities were basically over, but Susie was with you on the hill when Winters made an approach."

Elle nodded at Trey. "Right, but who told my father about that?" She focused on Stone and Charlie, and their less-than-amused faces. "That's why you wanted us to watch the briefing, isn't it? No one told my father that Winters made a third appearance at all, much less at an event where kids were present. The only way he could've known that is if…"

Elle felt like throwing up. She got off Trey's lap and forced herself to concentrate on keeping down her breakfast.

Trey didn't bother to temper his anger as he glared into the video-comm. "Are you fucking telling me that her father's been behind this the entire fucking time?"

Stone ignored Trey's string of curses and gently addressed Elle. "Do you think your father would—"

"Hire a mercenary group to abduct me and a separate security group to protect me?" This was low, even for her father, but she couldn't deny the truth. She stopped pacing and met Stone's stare through the screen. "If he thought it would increase his chance of being reelected, he would've auctioned off his mother to the highest bidder."

"What would he have gained?" Charlie asked. "I mean, would he seriously put your life on the line like that?"

"People have been known to stage all sorts of things in the name of publicity," Elle pointed out. "And you said yourself once that Black Dunes will do anything for a paycheck. They had three chances to kill me if that was their plan, yet they tried to take me instead."

Trey didn't look any less livid. "So he knew about the third attempt because—"

"Because he heard about it from the source," Elle finished. "I'd like nothing more than to say that I'm not related to someone who would do something like this, but I can't. Because he would."

Everyone started talking at once. It took a minute for Elle to realize that Logan and a few other Alpha team members had popped up behind Stone and Charlie and started adding their thoughts to the melee. It got so loud, Elle couldn't hear herself think.

Sticking her fingers in her mouth, she whistled. The shrill sound cut through the cabin and evidently through the video link, too. Everyone stopped.

"Bloody hell, that was impressive," Charlie murmured from the feed.

"Do I have everyone's attention now?" Elle asked. But she didn't wait for an answer as she planted herself back in her seat and made sure all eyes were on her—including Trey's. "I want to go see my father."

Everyone started talking again, and their responses ran the gamut from calling her crazy to it being a genius idea. Trey leaned over the back of her chair, shaking his head. "Are you insane? You can't go waltzing into his fucking hospital room."

"Why the hell not?" she questioned. "We've already established that this entire fiasco was orchestrated by my father, and if I'm not in any real danger, I don't see the big deal."

"Because it's just a hunch, not a concrete fact. We could

take you out there and, if we're wrong, practically hand-deliver you to the men who want to hurt you."

"Which part of that statement do you want me to rip apart first? My father would absolutely manipulate my life to get something he wants—*fact*, not a hunch. He knew something he shouldn't have—*fact*, not a hunch. Do you want me to keep going?"

"If she wants to face her father, I say we bloody well let her do it," Charlie spoke up. "It's not like we're just going to toss her out in the wild and let her drive herself. Neither Black Dunes nor her father is aware that we know about their link, so we give them both what they expect and fly her in under the radar."

"It's an unnecessary risk," Trey growled.

"Spoken like a man who's had all the bloody family support he could tolerate growing up," Charlie snapped a little harshly, even for the feisty Brit. "Not everyone is as lucky as you, Hanson. As long as we play it like it's business as normal, she'll be in no real danger. We take her in, let her confront the asshole, and then it's done."

"Then I can get back to my life." When Trey looked like he was about to protest, she added, "I'm not letting people rule my life anymore. Not my father. Not James. And not you. I'm sorry, Trey, but I'm doing this—whether you like it or not."

Judging by his scowl, it was a hard *not*. But it was decided. The team would show up at the cabin in the morning and they'd make plans to sneak her into D.C. Part of Elle felt relieved, while the other half hovered on the border of panic.

Getting her life back was what she'd wanted. She just wasn't sure what—or who—she'd be able to have in it.

* * *

Trey flung open the bedroom door and was immediately accosted by the smell of coffee and sizzling bacon—and the sight of his teammates lounging in various spots throughout the cabin. He glanced at his watch and grimaced—barely seven in the damn morning and they'd already been invaded.

"Jesus. When the fuck did you all get up?" Trey bypassed Logan, who was sprawled on the bottom half of the couch, his booted feet propped up on the coffee table.

"Early," Logan mumbled from beneath his beat-up cowboy hat. It was angled over his face instead of on his head. "And keep in mind that I'm used to getting up before the ass-crack of dawn, so if *I* think it's early, it was a fucking inhumane kind of early."

Stone, who sat at the kitchen table nursing a mug of coffee, acknowledged Trey with a faint head tilt. "He's been bitching since we left. I think he's concerned the lack of beauty sleep is going to mess with his pretty little face."

Logan grumbled incoherently, making everyone chuckle. But Charlie, sitting next to Stone, flashed Trey a mischievous smirk and openly gawked at his naked torso. "Being squirreled away in a mountain retreat is no reason to let yourself go, Hanson. You couldn't find the time to do at least a few sit-ups?"

"This body doesn't need push-ups, baby." He flexed his pecs, making her snort. "So what the hell are you all doing here so early?" He made his way to the coffee machine, which happened to be on the counter right next to where Elle stood in front of the stove. "When you answer, keep in mind that I haven't had any caffeine."

Elle struggled not to look his way, and he couldn't say he blamed her. Part of his hope for waking up early had been for them to clear the air from the way they'd left things. He didn't like her thinking he was out to control her like the other jackasses that had been in her life, but she also needed to accept that he wasn't going to sit idly by and watch her put herself at risk, either. But now that everyone was here, any hope of a private conversation went out the fucking window.

He dropped a hand on her waist and stepped close, reaching around her for an empty mug. He grinned when a corresponding shiver trembled through her body.

"Maybe we've missed your sparkling personality," Rafe answered with a mouthful of food. The cabin door buzzed open and Vince stepped into the cabin. "Vince may be a shining jewel, but he's got nothing on you."

"Fuck you, Ortega," Vince jested without even missing a beat. "And I mean that in the most sparkling, shining fucking way possible."

Trey almost missed his friends' back-and-forth banter. He took a seat and sipped his coffee, realizing fully well that he hadn't gotten a real answer. But he didn't really need one. It was easier to bully him into agreement in person than long distance.

As soon as Trey had the thought, he cursed. Elle had been right yesterday. How they approached the situation should be her decision, and it wasn't her problem if he found it a bitter pill to swallow. That issue was all his—at least according to his mother. And Penny. And Rachel. Fuck. Every woman in his life.

"What do you have planned?" Trey forced the question out.

"You know I don't like leaving anything to chance," Stone said. "So just in case we were all hallucinating the Senator's little speech, I want a fall-back in place to get Elle out of the hospital."

"I don't think we were hallucinating anything." Elle sat

on Trey's left, nursing her own mug of coffee. "I'm going to tell my father that his little game is over. Either he calls it off, or I go to the press and tell them about his acting debut. Well, it's not a debut, really, since he's been acting the part of doting father for years...but you know what I mean."

Stone nodded toward Charlie. "Lay it on us, Sparks."

Charlie already had her laptop running. Vince stalked over, poised to shift the screen more in his direction, when she shot him a volatile glare. "What the bloody hell do you think you're doing?"

"I can't see the screen," Vince said simply.

"Then move your massive body to the other side of the table. If you even think about touching my baby again, I'll change your name from Navy to Stumpy. Got it?"

Vince threw up his hands in mock surrender and received more than a little mocking from the guys when he moved two chairs down.

"As I was about to say," Charlie resumed, bringing up the hospital schematics, "Black Dunes and Dean Winters are still running on the assumption that we're in the dark about their little game. That means that we treat the op like an actual op and we go in low-key and heavy on the detail."

"So what's the back-up plan to get me out of the hospital—you know, if it's needed?" asked Elle.

Charlie grinned. "You're looking at her, love. I'll already be inside your father's room with one of the guys, when you arrive with your very own testosterone-afflicted entourage. If we're wrong about him and he isn't the checkbook behind Black Dunes, we make a switch and *I* come out as you. If Dunes is watching, our hope's that they'll make a play for Fake Elle but really get—"

"An English pixie with a bad attitude," Vince muttered under his breath. Everyone chuckled except for Charlie, who shot him a look that could freeze lava. He shrugged unapologetically. "What? Are you going to stand there and say that you don't have an attitude, *crumpet*?"

Rafe hid a laugh behind a cough. "Hope you can still sleep with one eye open, man."

Trey sensed more than heard Elle's concern. He reached out automatically, rescuing her bottom lip from between her teeth. "What's wrong, sweetness?"

"If Charlie and I have to make a switch, then that means she's going to be the one in danger." She looked to the female operative. "Are you sure you want to do this? I mean, if everything's going to be well controlled, then I can—"

Charlie spoke up. "Are you kidding me? It's about time I'm allowed into the thick of the action…even if it is as bait."

"And it's only going to happen if we're wrong about your father," Stone added, trying to put Elle at ease. "Which, I'm sorry to say, I don't think we are."

Trey didn't think so either. But both avenues put Elle at risk of getting hurt—just in different ways.

CHAPTER TWENTY-FOUR

The team separated into two SUVs. Much like the time they'd slipped Elle from her father's gala, and just as she had back then, Elle had felt Trey's eyes on her no less than two dozen times since they'd left the cabin.

Trey hadn't kept it a secret that he didn't agree with going to D.C. He wouldn't be Trey if he had. But then he'd let it go and jumped on board with planning anyway. Hell would've experienced its first blizzard if James—or her father—had ever done something like that for her. It was all about what *they* wanted... what would put *their* mind at ease.

Stone drove into the parking garage beneath Memorial Hospital and brought the SUV to a stop next to the service entrance. "Everyone remember what they need to do?"

Four nods, including Elle's, answered.

"Then let's get to it. Watch your asses."

With Rafe and Charlie already stationed inside her father's room, and Chase and Stone sticking close to the

SUVs, Elle had three escorts into the lower bowels of the hospital. They bypassed the boiler room and the kitchen. When they hit the cafeteria, Logan broke away with a faint nod and proceeded to the security office, where he would meet up with the hospital's head of security and monitor the building's surveillance cameras.

At every corner's turn, Elle half-expected the boogeyman to jump out, red eyes fixed and dilated, and drool dripping from his mouth. Except she wasn't six years old and she was wide awake—and she had a bad-ass Alpha operative at each shoulder.

With Vince and Trey next to her, people barely spared her more than a quick glance as they walked the corridors. And she couldn't blame them because, even wearing plain clothes, the guys weren't the type to be missed easily.

"You doing okay?" Trey finally asked when they reached a back stairwell and started hoofing it up the three flights.

"No signs of our friends, so I guess I'm good."

"I wasn't talking about Black Dunes."

She knew he wasn't, and despite this being her idea, she still hadn't figured out what she was going to actually say to her father. She knew what she wanted to—that she was done being his pawn, done with the drama.

Done with *him*.

"I just want all of this to be done and over, already," Elle finally admitted. "He's had a firm grip on my life for thirty years. I'm ready to chisel it the hell off."

With one more flight to go, Rafe's voice requested their arrival time via their ear mics. "ETA?"

"We'll be there in five," Vince murmured. "Coming out of the east end stairwell now. Any visuals?"

"Not of our targets, but it's about to get a whole lot more interesting. The Senator's got... visitors."

Vince looked less than thrilled. "Is it anything we need to worry about?"

"Only if Trey's safety is off," Rafe joked dryly.

Elle tried not thinking about Rafe's ominous words, and she succeeded until they reached the double doors of the intensive care unit. Suddenly, her feet became weighted to the ground.

Trey's hand brushed against her lower back. "You're almost there, sweetness. You go in, do your thing, and then we come out. Easy as fucking pie."

"Maybe I should go the rest of the way alone," she suggested nervously. "It's not like they're going let a herd of armed, gorilla-sized men into the unit at the same time and Rafe and Charlie are already in there."

"It's been worked out with the hospital staff and security. We're good." Trey gently rubbed her back.

Of course it had been. Elle had officially run out of excuses.

True to Trey's word, the secretary barely batted her heavily mascaraed eyes when they stepped up to the window. The double doors *whooshed* open, immediately hitting them with an intense medicinal smell. Present throughout the hospital, it was stronger in the unit than anywhere else: a mixture of disinfectant, medicine, and things most people probably preferred not thinking about.

Shay, a worried expression on her face, blasted her way past Vince and Trey and pulled Elle into a fierce hug. "You really did show up!"

"What are you doing here?" Elle hugged her best friend even tighter. "Let me rephrase that...you shouldn't be here. You should be back home in New York."

"*Psht.* Like I'd let thugs with guns keep me from my best friend. I've stayed away long enough." Shay held her an arm's length away and gave her a critical look-over. "You look okay. Are you okay? Your new friends told me that you were, but you know I don't believe things until I see them for myself."

"I'm ready for all of this to be done and over." Elle realized she hadn't really answered the question, but Shay, surprisingly, didn't call her on it or on the tears starting to well in her eyes.

"Do you really think he fabricated the entire thing?" Shay asked in a low murmur. "I mean, that's kind of low, even for your father."

"That's what I'm here to find out."

"Before you go over there, I need you to know that I'm so sorry," Shay said. "*So*, so sorry. I tried everything I could to get him thrown out of here, but your father started putting on one hell of a dramatic performance. The man missed his calling with the theater. Seriously."

At first, Elle didn't know what her friend was talking about—and then Shay shifted left, giving her an unobstructed view of her father's hospital room door. Or more accurately, the group of men standing in front of it. Mixed in with the black suits and ridiculously mirrored sunglasses of her father's security detail was James.

Elle groaned. She did *not* have the fortitude or the patience to deal with him right now.

Shay was apologizing again. "I tried getting him to leave, but those men in black put a big gaping hole in the term 'assholes.'" The brunette finally registered Trey, who'd stayed a few feet away, giving them some semblance of privacy. "Jesus. I forgot how huge that man was."

She gave Elle a playful smack on the arm.

"Ow!" Elle laughed. "What was that for?"

"For lying out of your ass. There's no way in hell a

man like that doesn't know what he's doing in bed. I mean, Christ...*look* at him."

Elle prayed for the floor to open up and swallow her. While she loved Shay like a sister, the woman did not possess an inside voice. But Elle didn't have to worry about Trey eavesdropping because he wasn't even looking their way.

He was too focused on drilling his glare through James's chest.

"This is going to be good." Shay practically rubbed her hands together. "Broadway can't supply this kind of entertainment."

Elle set her sights on her father's door and hoped that by the time she got there, James would disappear. But she had no such luck. He stepped directly into her path. "I think we need to have a talk, Elle."

Trey was there instantly, his sudden appearance causing a chain reaction of halfway drawn guns. "And I think you need to back off. Touch her and you'll have to jack off with a stump."

James flashed his too-white-to-be-real smile; the one meant to disarm people, but which never failed to rub Elle the wrong way. He was primped and immaculately dressed, looking the part of a politician with his five-hundred-dollar haircut and high-end suit. And he looked too damn jovial for a man visiting his supposedly sick father-figure.

James returned Trey's glare with a condescending smirk. "There's no need for barbarics. I only want a little alone time with Elle."

Trey stepped closer. "You can *want* until you're blue in the face, bud, but you're not getting even a second of Elle's time—alone or otherwise. It's in your best physical interest for you to step aside now, or I'm going to show you how *barbaric* I can fucking be."

Trey's hand rested on his hip, where his gun was hidden from view. Despite the fact that Elle had fantasized about shooting her ex in the ass once or twice, there was no doubt in her mind that Trey wouldn't have a single qualm about doing it in reality.

"Now's not the time, James," she butted in before things got too ugly. "In case you haven't realized, there's a lot going on right now."

"That's what makes it the perfect time," James retorted. "With this threat hanging over our heads, we may not have a second chance."

Trey pushed himself within an inch of James's face. "Care to explain to me what the fuck you mean by that?"

Elle shot Vince a pleading look. "Aren't you going to do something about this?"

"Looks to me like Hanson's got it covered." Vince stood still as a redwood.

Men and their freaking testosterone.

"Yep," Shay murmured off to the side. "I definitely like this one. You got my complete approval, Elle. He's a keeper. A-plus material."

Elle braced a hand on Trey's arm. "The only thing James meant by that statement is that he's self-centered and self-serving. It wasn't some kind of threat."

"Could've fooled me," Trey grumbled.

"Looks like a lot of things could fool you," James snapped haughtily, not caring that he stood in front of two large, armed men. "For the love of God, Elle. You couldn't find someone a little less…brutish…to replace me with? Maybe someone with an IQ at least slightly above that of a fifth-grader?"

Hearing his snide remarks attacking Trey, Elle's anger flared. It was her turn to step closer, wedging herself in between the two men. "Keep spewing and you're going to see brutish when I stuff a roll of gauze in your mouth and duct tape it shut."

"Still the lady, I see." James snorted. "Although I suppose I shouldn't be surprised, considering you've been left unchecked and free to go gallivanting anywhere you please. Now that I think about it, I suppose it was smart of you...aiming low, opting for someone who isn't expecting much more than a quick lay and a slap on the ass. No sense in raising anyone's hopes only to rip them away, right?"

Murderous rage glinted in Shay's eyes. She lurched forward. "You little piece of sh—"

"Ah-ah-ah." Vince caught the brunette around the waist only a few inches short of contact. "Let this play out."

"I didn't get it wrong, did I?" James shifted his attention from Trey to Elle. A gradual realization settled his mouth into a wry, knowing grin. "You wouldn't purposefully lead someone to believe something that isn't true, would you? I mean, could you imagine the fallout down the road? Crushed dreams. Chaos and disappointment." He winced. "It wouldn't be pretty."

Elle felt the color leach from her face. Not like this...not from James's mouth. "Don't. Please."

"Elle's the last person on earth who would lead someone to believe something that isn't true—unlike your boss," Trey growled.

"Yeah? Does that mean she's told you that all she's good for these days is to wet your stick? If you have any plans to bring little brutes into the world, it's best to go somewhere else. That's what I had to do."

Elle didn't even see Trey swing. One moment James stood in front her; in the next, his body crashed against the wall.

"You son-of-a-bitch! You broke my damn nose!" Blood seeped through James's fingers as he cupped his nose.

"I'll break every bone in your fucking body if you so much as use Elle's name in a sentence again, asshole," Trey said, his voice deceptively low and mellow.

"Are you threatening me?" James challenged.

"No, I'm promising you. Touch her. Look at her. Even think about her, and I will break off your dick and stuff it down your throat."

Vince must've believed him because the former SEAL finally stepped close, although Elle wasn't sure if it was to stop Trey from fulfilling his promise or to help make it happen.

Her father's door opened, and Charlie stood there, taking in the scene. She looked from Trey to James to the baffled security guards who appeared not to know what the hell to do. Finally, she took Elle's arm and gestured for her to come inside the room. "With me."

"But—" Elle started to refuse.

"Let the boys work out their issues. Navy will make sure your lover boy doesn't go to jail."

Elle didn't want to move. Trey didn't look the least bit calmer.

"Trey." His name fell from her lips in a faint whisper, but he heard.

The stern look he gave her was a knife through the chest. Pain swelled with every breath she took. He didn't say anything. He didn't blink.

"Go deal with your father," he finally said, voice gruff. "Then you can move on with your life."

Charlie gently tugged Elle into her father's hospital room, leaving her heart out there in the corridor, shattering.

* * *

Trey wasn't proud he'd decked Elle's prick of an ex. He was disappointed—disappointed Vince had stopped him before he could send the bastard *through* the wall instead of into it. At some point in the chaos, Rafe had slipped out from the hospital room and now stood at his right flank.

"Don't even think about it, man," Rafe's voice warned. "I know what you want to do, but it'll only create a whole new shit-storm of problems."

"Would you be singing that tune if it had been Penny?" Trey muttered under his breath.

"Fuck no, but you're too pretty to go to jail. I at least have that rugged thing going on."

Trey snorted. Leave it to Rafe to pull him—slightly, and definitely temporarily—out of his dark mood.

"Let's go, man. Your lady's about to put on quite the show." Rafe smacked him on the back before gesturing to Vince. "You got it out here?"

"Got it covered."

They stepped into the Senator's room, and got their first glimpse at the supposedly ailing man. Dressed in silk pajamas and without so much as an IV attached to the arm, Senator Monroe lay in bed and glared at his daughter.

"You look awfully fucking spry for a man who just had a major heart attack," Trey said, pointing out the obvious.

"That's because he didn't have a heart attack," Elle confirmed without looking his way. Judging by the scowl she was throwing at her father, Trey's pissed-off little pixie was back with a fucking vengeance. "Isn't that right, Dad?"

"No, I did not," the Senator snapped. "But you weren't aware of that until a minute ago, and I have to admit, I'm not impressed with your response time. For God's sake, I was rushed to the hospital almost thirty-six hours ago, and it's taken you until now to come see me."

"There's so much wrong with what you said that I don't even know where to begin." Elle shook her head in obvious disbelief. "But let's start with what you were doing when you were rushed to the hospital."

"What about it?" Monroe's impatience irked Trey to high hell.

"You knew about the airport," Elle continued, "because you'd been given an update. You knew about the gala, because you'd been there. How did you know about the third time? About the *dangerous occasion* where there'd been children present?"

Muffled conversations could be heard from the corridor outside the room as the hospital shift continued to move on around them.

"I'd been given an update," Monroe finally stated. "I am paying these men to keep you safe."

"But you weren't. No one from *this* side of the threat told you…which means you got the information from somewhere else, and I highly doubt it was from one of the elementary school kids."

"You're blowing this out of proportion, Elle," Monroe sputtered, clearly getting flustered.

From the other side of the room, Charlie cursed. "'*Out of proportion*'? You hired bloody mercenaries!"

"To make it *appear* as if she were danger," the Senator finally admitted. "Nothing was ever going to happen."

"Tell that to someone who didn't have to check her for a concussion," Trey muttered harshly.

"My father doesn't care about that," Elle reminded the room. "He doesn't care how any of his decisions or actions affect someone's life unless that someone is him."

Her fisted hands dropped to her side, and damn it if her chin didn't fucking quiver. Trey almost intervened. He wanted to take her out of this room and not look back. But he also knew that this was something she needed to do—alone.

"You not only messed with my life," Elle pointed out to her father, "but you messed with the lives of everyone here. For weeks, they put themselves at risk to keep me safe, and you didn't give one single damn."

"Don't make them out to be martyrs. It's their job, one I *paid* them to. It's not like they're doing this out of the goodness of their hearts."

"Actually," Charlie interjected, looking almost gleeful, "we ripped up the bloody check weeks ago because knowing where the money came from gave us indigestion. And we don't charge family—which is exactly what she is to us. They have our protection, whether they want it or not."

Tears welled in Elle's eyes, but she wouldn't let them fall—not in front of her father. Trey couldn't keep his distance anymore. He skimmed his hand down her back and over her hip. "I couldn't have said it better myself, Charlie."

"I know." Charlie smirked.

Elle continued to stare at her father, her voice barely audible when she spoke. "Family's supposed to be a blessing, and you treat it as a tool to work your will. And it's always been like that…even when Mom was alive."

Senator Monroe shrugged, not looking the least bit fazed. "When you have life goals, you make certain to use the things around you to your advantage. If you don't have any, you create them. That's something you never seemed to grasp, Elle. You give up. You let opportunities pass you by, to do what? Hop from one underdeveloped nation to another with the likes of people like *him*?" The Senator glared

Trey's way and shook his head in disgust. "You could've had a proper, well-respected life with a powerful man."

"Who I didn't love, and who showed me in every way possible that the feeling was mutual," Elle added.

"Love is entirely overrated. Common goals are what matters, and what you're willing to do to achieve them. And let's face it, dear, you can't really afford to be too damn particular—not someone in your predicament."

"All right, that's enough." Trey tossed his satellite phone onto the Senator's lap a little harder than was necessary. "Call off Black Dunes."

"You do not order me around, boy," Monroe howled.

"Oh, I *do* order you around...*sir*. You're going to call off your dogs, show us the confirmation, and then this is going to be the very last time you hurt your daughter. If it's not, the next time an ambulance rushes you away, it's going to be for real."

"I could have you arrested for threatening me like that. I'm a United States Senator!"

"No, you're a United States Asshole...now make the damn call."

CHAPTER TWENTY-FIVE

It was over. Finally. After weeks of lying low, Elle could finally move on to the next phase of her life—*do* what she wanted, *go* where she wanted. Before leaving the hospital, Shay had pulled her aside and told her about another assignment from Caring Hands, this one in South America, helping earthquake victims. The spot on the team was hers—if she wanted it.

Too bad she had no idea what she wanted anymore.

As much ridiculousness as James and her father had spewed, they'd had a point. Not all men were interested in damaged goods. Even the good guys like Trey could claim indifference and mean it in the beginning. But then time would pass, and things and circumstances would change—including the hopes for the future.

It was late—or early morning, technically—and they'd all just stepped into the bar level of Alpha. Elle wasn't stupid. She knew she couldn't avoid Trey forever, but before they had their long overdue talk, she needed to figure out what she was going to do...how she felt...what she *wanted*.

"You look like a girl who needs to shoot things." Charlie's voice shimmied its way into Elle's thoughts.

"Yeah, I think I do," Elle answered.

"Then let's go." The blonde operative led the way toward the elevator that took them to the Hole's bottom level.

The second they entered the shooting range, Charlie hopped over the counter and stalked toward the other side of the range. She dragged a box over from the corner and started setting up a long line of canned goods.

"Are those—"

"Vegetables that have no bloody business being in a can," Charlie answered. She came back and started pulling weapons out from the locked cabinet against the wall. "Paper targets are only so therapeutic. Sometimes you need to see stuff actually fly."

It would've been funny if it wasn't also true.

They fell into a rhythm; aiming, shooting, and in Elle's case, narrowly missing. Neither of them had attempted to open a line of communication beyond a change in grip or line of sight. Elle lost track of time.

With a semi-automatic clutched in her hand, she fired off another shot and missed the row of tin cans by a good three feet. Again. "At least I got closer that time."

"Yeah, those green beans can start quaking in their tin," Charlie deadpanned. At Elle's glare, the other woman simply shrugged. "Don't blame me for your sudden inability to hit a bloody semi. If you want to keep up your skills and even learn new things, you need to practice. When was the last time you picked up a gun?"

When she didn't answer, Charlie nodded. "Yeah, I thought so."

Elle narrowed her eyes and gave the trigger another squeeze. This time, one of the tin cans moved…not the one she'd been aiming for, but still. "I did it!"

"Yeah, you nudged the big bad legumes." Charlie lifted her Glock and fired. The can exploded, spraying beans and vegetable juice everywhere.

"You're such a freaking show-off."

Charlie returned her smirk with one of her own. "Practice for a few more days, and you may eventually nudge one off the perch."

Despite the fact that she'd yet to knock down any targets, this was the best form of stress relief a girl could participate in—besides sex, Elle thought, grinning. "Your level of encouragement astounds me. I think you missed your calling as an elementary school teacher."

"Kids barely out of training pants?" Charlie shivered as if the idea was more frightening than a crazed clown on a murder spree. "No, thank you. Send them to me when they hit puberty. Actually, strike that—too many bloody hormones."

"College-aged?" Elle teased.

Charlie unclipped the magazine from her gun. "Too head-in-the-sky, we-can-make-the-world-a-better-place. All that hopeful perkiness makes me queasy."

"Twenties?"

"Maybe. Sure. Twenties—mid. Or late. But scratch the males off the list. Actually, on second thought, only send the women once they hit thirty."

"I'm thirty." Elle couldn't help but chuckle.

"See. That's why we get along so famously. So how's target therapy going?"

"Working wonders," she said, telling the truth.

"Good. Then I'm going to put this here." Charlie took the gun from her hands and, after removing the clip, set it on the countertop. "And I'm going to ask you when you're going to pull your head out of your tiny—though cute—little arse."

"Excuse me?" The abruptness of the topic-change nearly gave Elle whiplash.

"Your ears work fine, love. You're in love with Trey."

Elle opened her mouth to protest—and couldn't. She hadn't wanted it to happen. She'd tried nearly everything in her power to make sure it didn't. But he'd made it impossible.

She loved him—was *in* love. So hard. So deep. He'd shown her countless times that letting someone into your heart didn't make you vulnerable. It made you stronger.

It hadn't been his physical presence at her side that had pushed her to confront her father once and for all. It had been his *support*—his *belief* that she'd see her own strength and handle not only her father and James, but the entire messed-up situation.

What woman wouldn't fall in love with a man like Trey?

"Was that meant to be a question? Because it wasn't one." Elle hesitantly locked eyes with Charlie.

"You want something in question form? Fine. If you're in love with the man, then why are we waiting for someone from a rental company to drop off a car so you can drive the hell away?"

Elle had asked herself the same question for the last few hours, and the answer was always the same. *Because she loved Trey enough to do the right thing for them both—even if it meant saying good-bye.*

Someone clearing their throat turned both Elle and Charlie's attention to the door.

"Sorry to interrupt, darlins," Logan apologized, looking uncharacteristically uncomfortable, "but your rental's here, Elle."

A rush of emotions made Elle's eyes swell with sudden moisture. "I guess that means I should go get my things."

Elle took her time grabbing the bag that held her meager belongings and then headed topside with Logan and Charlie. Everyone was already there, sitting in various locations around the bar.

"I can't believe you're going." Penny rushed over and pulled her into a hug. "You better make sure you keep in touch, okay? No disappearing to far-off countries without a little heads-up. Do you have any idea what you're going to do now?"

"I'm going back to New York, to Shay's, and then I think we're taking the assignment in Chile."

"You be careful," Penny warned.

And then the train of good-byes came, one after another. Logan's fierce hug didn't surprise her, but getting a quick but affectionate pat from Vince had shocked her so still that everyone else laughed.

Stone approached last, his arms wrapping her in a firm hug. "You better take care, okay?"

"Thank you, Stone." Elle dropped a kiss on the Alpha boss's cheek.

"There's nothing to thank me for, hon." He gave her shoulder a faint squeeze. "You're Alpha family now. You better not be a stranger."

The sentiment warmed her insides. Eventually she'd run out of good-byes—except for one. At that point everyone had left, giving her and Trey the entire room to themselves.

Nails would've been easier to swallow than the lump in her throat. Her mouth opened to say *something*. Anything. But nothing came out.

Trey gently tucked a flyaway strand of hair behind her ear. At the soft touch, her eyes closed. God, she loved it when he did that—simple caresses that made her feel treasured and protected...and like a complete and total fraud.

"So this is it?" he asked, his voice low and gravelly. "You're going to leave without us having a chance to talk about what happened at the hospital?"

Their time together had showed her that unrestricted freedom really was possible with the right person, but it also reminded her that the situation itself needed to be right—and hers was far from ideal.

"I don't know if I'm ready for this conversation," she admitted, hesitantly meeting his gaze.

"Are you ever going to be?" It wasn't asked in an accusatory tone. It was a simple, honest question.

"No. I guess not. But talking about it isn't going to change anything."

"Maybe not the circumstances, no. But it could change how we react to it."

Elle needed some kind of distance to think. Even though it physically pained her to move from his warmth, she stepped away and braced her lower back against the bar top.

Trey stayed in the same spot. Waiting. Watching. Looking like he would close the distance between them any second. And despite the thunderous pounding in her chest, she wanted him to cross it, wrap his arms around her, and make the ache go away.

But this conversation wasn't about what she wanted or wished for. It was about accepting her future and not forcing it on another person...on Trey.

"I can't give you a family." Elle ignored the flare of pain in her chest and kept going. "I can't give *anyone* a family. James and my father may be the severest form of asshole, but they weren't lying about that."

Trey didn't say a word. He stood there in silence, his hands hanging at his sides.

"That accident I told you about caused a lot of internal bleeding. They had to remove one of my ovaries entirely, and the one they left behind was so severely damaged that 'miracle' was the term the doctor used to describe my chances of ever getting pregnant."

"And that was your reasoning behind the no-strings sex?" Trey's voice sounded like he'd swallowed a jar of nails. "You think I'd somehow have a problem with your medical condition?"

She offered him a wan smile. "My reasons for no strings were exactly what I told you before. I didn't want to run the chance of giving someone control over my life—again. This...this is something different—completely separate. It's not just about me...it's about *you and me*."

And that was the truth. She'd accepted her medical condition ten months ago and made peace with her new lease on life before leaving for Thailand. But once she'd met him, she allowed herself to start dreaming about those unattainable dreams again.

He didn't look like he believed her.

"I can't fill all those empty rooms in your new house, Trey." Tears dropped onto Elle's cheeks. "I was heartbroken when the doctor told me my chances of ever carrying a baby were slim to none, but I dealt with it. I accepted it. But I also learned pretty quickly that not everyone could."

"You mean your ex," Trey said through clenched teeth. At her faint nod, he added, "You're seriously going to stand there and compare me to that rat fucking bastard? Haven't I proven a dozen times over that I'm nothing like him?"

"I know you're nothing like him," Elle cried.

"Then why are you standing there still trying to push me

away?" He stepped closer and hovered over her. His eyes locked on her with an intensity that made it difficult for her to breathe. "I would *never* hurt you, sweetness. Not in a million fucking years. I want *you*; not an ideal, not someone else's version of the perfect future. Just you."

Elle couldn't stop the tears now. As fast as she swatted them away, more came. "You say that now—and I know you mean it. I do. But that could change, Trey. People change as time goes by. James might not have hurt me by treating me the way he did—but you? I don't know if I could look into your eyes years down the road and handle seeing disappointment—or worse, resentment."

Elle held his hot, furious, and surprisingly level gaze.

"So that's it?" he demanded. "You're going to let some half-assed fear dictate your life? That sounds an awful lot like giving up—or hiding out. The Elle I've had in my bed since Thailand isn't the hiding-out type."

"Maybe she was an apparition."

Trey shook his head. "No. Because I see her staring back at me. Right now. You're just too afraid to let her back out, and all that's doing is hurting you...*us*. And you're doing it *now*, not years from now in some twisted version of the future that you're picturing in your head."

"And what do you expect me to do about it?" Elle raised her voice in challenge. "Cross my fingers and hope for the best?"

"When you care for someone, that's exactly what you do. But I could stand here and say all the right things and it's not going to make a damn bit of difference, is it? Nothing's going to change unless you're not only willing to listen, but to take a chance." Trey stepped back, and with an angry flourish, gestured to the door. "So don't let me keep you. Go do what you need to do. Go to Chile or Thailand. Hell, go to

Tim-buk-fucking-tu. But we both know that if you choose to go instead of staying here—with *me*—that you're not so much living your life as you are running from it."

He was right. Despite her best efforts to do what she wanted, she was still letting fear hold her happiness hostage. Elle headed toward the exit and stopped just inside the door.

"Thank you, Trey," she said, keeping her back to him, unable to look him in the eye. "For everything. It really does mean a lot to me."

Tears poured down her cheeks with each step she took toward the rental sedan. By the time she slid into the driver's seat, she could barely see basic shapes, much less fine details.

If running meant avoiding heartbreak—both his and hers—she didn't understand why it felt like her heart had already been ground into a fine powder.

CHAPTER TWENTY-SIX

Trey watched Elle get into the car. He watched the tears stream down her face too fast for her to wipe them away, and then he watched her pull out of the lot—and out of his life. In his arms one second, gone the next. And not only had he let it happen, he'd practically opened the door and spread out the red fucking carpet.

After everything they'd been through and everything he'd shown her, hearing the lack of trust and hope in her voice had felt like a wild animal ripping its way through his chest cavity. It still gnawed at him, the hole growing bigger each second. If he didn't do something to stanch it soon, he'd fucking bleed out right there in the middle of the bar.

Trey grabbed a bottle of Jack from behind the counter and hurled it against the wall. Alcohol and shattered glass flew in every direction.

"What the fuck, man?" Vince appeared in the doorway, his SEAL-trained eyes soaking up the mess.

"I'll clean it later," Trey growled.

"Not what I was fucking talking about." Vince leaned an elbow against the counter. "I meant why the fuck did you tell her to go?"

"Why would I want her to stay? So I can hear her compare me to that shitty ex of hers again and basically predict that I'm going to break her heart?"

"I heard no such thing," Vince said, calmly.

"Then you weren't fucking listening."

"Were you?" Vince's eyebrows lifted in challenge. "Because what *I* heard was a woman afraid that she wouldn't be able to give the man she loves everything she thinks he deserves."

"Did you have your ear pushed to the damn door?" Trey propped his hands on the bar top and forced himself to take a slow breath.

"I didn't have to, with the way the two of you were shouting at each other toward the end. Look, man. Yeah, you were a raging idiot—and I mean a fucking massive one. And Elle's way of thinking is a little messed in the head, too, but think about where she came from. Her dad's the fucking Picasso of Pricks and that ex is a fucking Rembrandt or some shit. Can't blame a girl for being skittish. But I *can* blame you for walking the fuck away."

"I'm not discussing relationships with someone whose longest and most serious one was with the five men in his SEAL team."

Vince grabbed two pool cues and tossed one toward Trey's head. "You rack. I break."

Trey caught the stick. "You want to play pool? Now? You fucking suck."

"For every ball I sink, you have to answer a question—truthfully and aloud—with no fucking bullshit. Now stop the goddamned whining and start racking."

It took thirty seconds and four sunk balls for Trey to realize he'd been set up. He glared at his friend. "You've been fucking playing us this entire time."

Vince's lips twitched. "I like to keep everyone on their toes. I believe I earned myself four questions."

"You're serious."

"Damn straight I'm fucking serious." Vince propped his hands on the table. "Why the hell are you standing here with me when you should be chasing Elle down and telling her that you're in love with her?"

"I already did. It didn't matter. She was too focused on what-ifs that wouldn't even happen."

"Did you really?" Vince waited, giving his question time to soak in. "At what point did you tell her that you're in love with her?"

"I told her that I cared about her, that I wanted *her*."

"Caring, wanting, and loving are three completely different things, my friend."

Vince was too goddamned observant. Trey, suddenly feeling like he hadn't slept in a week, dragged his hand over his face. "Goddamn. You had four fucking questions and you start off with the hardest one?"

Vince didn't look the least bit apologetic. "No point in wasting precious time when we both know the real deal. I'm also going to assume you know you were a moron. That way, we can skip straight to finding out how you're going to fix the hole you dug for yourself."

"Fuck. You're right."

Vince looked at him like he was stupid. And Trey was. He wasn't *at risk* for falling in love with Elle. He wasn't *in the process*, or ready to stumble. He'd already fallen, smacked his head on a boulder, and was drowning in a rushing river, his head barely above water.

He was *in* love with her...

Fucking-A. He *was* a moron.

He needed to fix it. He needed to fix *them*. He needed to prove to her that he'd do anything to make sure she knew how much she was and would be loved every second of the day, present and future. Children or not. He needed to make sure she knew that the only thing that was a non-negotiable need in his life, was her.

He'd fallen for her at the first bat of her blue eyes, all the way back in that Thai bar, but he'd fallen again and again every hour since. There wasn't a minute she didn't amaze him, even more so knowing what she'd had to deal with through the years. She didn't quit. She acted. She moved. And that had been the real source of his anger earlier...that after all the struggle she'd gone through to live her own life, she was running away now.

If she wasn't going to fight for them or for herself, then *he* would.

"I'm in love with her." Trey said the words aloud, then turned toward Vince. "I love her...and I need to do something about it."

"Well fucking *duh*, man. The question is, what the hell are you going to do?"

Trey dropped his cue stick and headed toward the door. "If you want to come with me, you better get your ass moving."

Vince dropped his cue on the table and followed. "You mind telling me where we're going?"

"I left something in Jonesville."

* * *

Elle couldn't see the road. Tears had turned her vision blurry, and she'd swerved onto the dirt shoulder more than once since leaving Alpha. She needed to either stop and pull herself together, or resign to the fact she was eventually going to wrap herself around a tree.

She wiped her wet eyes and, after catching a brief glimpse of a parking lot and a building on her right, pulled off the road—on purpose this time. The second she shifted into park, she let the tears fall, unchecked. Her nose stuffed up, becoming a hot, slimy mess, and each breath felt like it would be her last.

She wasn't sure what dying felt like, but it had to be pretty close to this.

"Elle, honey? Open the door, sweetheart. It's Sophie." A soft knock rattled the driver's side window. "Elle?" Trey's mom knocked again, a little more insistent. "Elle. Please open up."

Elle blew her nose and dried her cheeks on her coat sleeve. When she finally opened the door, the sympathy shining in Sophie's eyes told her that she hadn't done a very good job erasing the carnage of her sob fest.

The older woman gently pulled her from the car and into a hug. "Oh, my sweet little thing. What's wrong? What happened?"

"I-I'm leaving," Elle managed to hiccup. "I'm going... home."

"And where's home, hon?"

It was a simple question, and it had a simple answer.

She didn't know.

Home wasn't Shay's apartment. It wasn't her father's place. It wasn't in some far-off country where she didn't know another living soul.

As if sensing her turmoil, Sophie guided her to a bench.

For the first time since parking, Elle realized she'd somehow ended up at the children's community center. But with the children in school, the building and playground were eerily empty.

"Where do you want to be, Elle?" Sophie asked quietly, offering Elle the use of her scarf to clean up the mess on her face. "Don't think about anything else and just tell me...where is it that you want to go right now?"

To Alpha. Back to Trey.

Every mile-marker away from him had settled more weight on the center of her chest until each breath felt like it would be the last.

"I don't want to go anywhere," Elle admitted. She sniffed and wiped her dripping nose. "I want to stay here so bad, Sophie."

"So stay."

Elle bit her lip to stave off a fresh wave of sobs. "It's not that simple."

"Are you talking about the men after you? Are you afraid that my son can't protect you?" At Elle's dropped mouth, Sophie chuckled. "Oh, please. My son likes to pretend that I'm oblivious, but I'm not. I know that boy and his friends aren't exactly owners of a bar—at least, that's not all they are."

Elle shook her head. "It's not that. Trey's the most capable man I know."

"Then what is it?"

"I love him...more than I ever thought I'd be able to love another person."

A smile bloomed on Sophie's face, and the older woman brushed a stray tear off Elle's chin. "Then why the waterworks? Loving someone is a special, magical thing, honey."

"But I messed it all up. I *keep* messing up. Every time I

tell myself that I'm going to live my life the way that I want, something stops me."

"And what's that?"

"Fear that I'm not going to be enough. Fear that he'll change his mind down the line and look at me differently… that he'll resent me for the things I can't give him."

"Can you give him your love?" Sophie asked blatantly.

"That's the only thing I *can* give him."

"Then that's all you need, sweetheart." The older woman wiped away another stray tear. "Love is stronger than steel, or any doubt that could ever come along the way. If you're lucky enough to have it, and share it, it can blast through any obstacle."

"You talk about it like it's a weapon." Elle smiled wanly.

"It is."

"No, a weapon's a gun. A lot like the one I have in my hands right here," announced a very low, very menacing voice.

Elle and Sophie looked up, taken surprise by the man standing three feet away. At first, Elle's heart kicked into high gear, and then she recognized the face.

"You're a little late, Mr. Winters," she told her father's henchman. "My father called off your arrangement. I'm sure you can contact him for whatever it is that he owes you, but your services are no longer required."

"I'm not here about that lame-ass assignment." Winters grinned wickedly, making the puckered scar stand out even more than it already did. "I haven't cared about your father for a while now."

"Then why are you here?"

"For her." He pointed his gun at Sophie before slowly sliding it back and forth between the two women. "But now I'm not so sure. Choices. Choices. To take the mother, or the woman he loves. It really is a hard decision. Tell me, Ms. Hanson, on a scale of one to ten, how much of a mama's boy do you rate your son?"

He. *Trey*. For some reason, this guy was talking about Trey.

"Elle, honey, you need to get inside." Sophie stood, squarely putting herself between Elle and Winters.

That was evidently all the answer Winters needed. "Come with me, Miss Monroe, and your sweetheart's mama here won't get hurt."

"Don't you move a step, Elle," Sophie warned sternly.

When Winters stepped forward, Sophie snapped her outstretched palm against his gun arm. His aim momentarily widened.

"Elle, inside," Sophie barked.

Elle wasn't going anywhere. She'd stepped closer to help Sophie, when Winters brought the butt of his gun down on the older woman's head. Elle jumped to catch her as she fell, but skidded to a stop when Winters aimed the gun at Sophie's head.

"Stop!" Elle cried out. "Don't hurt her!"

"Give me one reason why I shouldn't." Winters dug the barrel of the gun into Sophie's temple.

"I'll go with you," Elle said frantically, praying he'd spare Trey's mom. "I'll go wherever it is you want me to go, as long as you don't hurt her."

Please don't hurt her. Knowing how Trey felt about his family, losing Sophie would be something from which he wouldn't return. And Elle wouldn't let that happen.

Winters seemed to contemplate her offer for a minute before giving a slow nod. "We're going to go to the other side of the road, and you're going to get into the trunk of the car. And then you're going to do exactly as I say or I'm going to come back here and finish what I started. You get me?"

"Okay." Elle stepped closer, purposefully transferring Winters' aim from Sophie to her.

He clamped his fingers around her arm and yanked her harshly toward the back parking lot. Unlike the time in the airport, there was no playing or pretending.

Elle's life was definitely at risk.

CHAPTER TWENTY-SEVEN

Trey whistled his way back to the truck, not giving one iota of a fuck that Vince was having a good chuckle at his expense. They'd gotten to Jonesville in record time, and Trey was prepping to sweet talk Charlie into hacking into the rental company's GPS to find out Elle's location.

Stone's ringtone shrieked from his pocket almost the second they hopped back into the truck. "What's up, boss man?"

"Where are you?" Stone asked. No 'Hello, honey, how's your day?' from the former SEAL.

"Vince and I made a quick run into Jonesville. We'll be back in about an hour and a half. Why?"

"Get here sooner."

Trey flipped the ignition and put the phone on speaker so Vince could hear. "Do you want to tell me why you want me to break speed records?"

"Charlie found out why your gut was talking to you about Winters. Does the name Lance Cummings ring a bell?"

Trey's blood ran cold as he flashed back to ten years ago. Stationed in a Middle Eastern desert, his Delta team had been assigned the task of bringing down a group of drug-runners who'd been linked to supplying the insurgents in the area. None of them thought their leads would bring them right to one of their very own—an Army officer—Major Lance Cummings.

The arrogant bastard thought the entire world owed him a fuck-ton of favors—and money—and decided to use U.S. guns to start up his own collection agency.

"He got blown to high holy hell right along with his stolen grenade launchers," Trey pointed out. "And I should know, because I was there to see the fireworks."

"I don't know what to tell you, Hanson, but it's him. And Charlie's finding a scary amount of info on how he was able to reinvent himself, starting with some Middle Eastern plastic surgeon practically jigsawing him back together."

It shouldn't be possible, but there was no ignoring Trey's gut. It was why there'd been *something* familiar about the man ever since their first face-off at the airport. "You're telling me that someone gave him a new face and—"

"And bone structure." Charlie came on the line. "Whoever nursed Cummings back to health literally changed his facial markers. It's why I came out empty-handed in all of my searches. Dean Winters wasn't *in* the Army. He literally didn't exist until years later, and there was absolutely no link between him and Cummings—until I followed a hunch."

"Meaning you hacked another server?" Vince guessed.

"It may have been more than one, and not exactly anyone the United States is on friendly terms with, but not a single damn one of you better be complaining about it because it led us in the right direction—*finally*."

Stone added, "I'm going to take a wild guess and say there wasn't any love lost between you and Cummings?"

"Fuck no," Trey stated emphatically, although he knew Stone would've already read the reports he'd written for his commanding officers. "When we realized we couldn't completely confiscate the weapons, my team and I were the ones who set them to explode. Cummings ran back into the building to try and save his payload."

"What are the chances that he recognized you from that first meeting at JFK?" Stone asked.

Fuck.

"The Sled-tacular," Trey said immediately. "He may not know I'm Alpha, but that's how he got to Elle at the Sled-tacular. He wasn't there looking for her. He was looking for *me*. She just happened to be a lucky bonus."

Trey peeled out of the parking spot and slammed the truck into drive. "Someone needs to get to Elle and my mom."

"Chase and Logan are already on the way over to the youth center."

"And Elle?"

Stone waited a beat too long.

"Where the fuck is she, Stone?" Trey shouted into the phone.

"Charlie's trying to ping her cell now. Get here as fast as you can without getting your asses thrown in jail."

Trey pushed the gas pedal to the floor. "They'd have to catch me first."

They made the drive back to Alpha in under an hour. Trey and Vince headed down to the compound where the team was already congregated in the main room. Weapons littered every inch of flat surface and winterized camo gear was draped over every chair. Half the team had already dressed for a stroll through the tundra.

"What the hell's going on?" Trey barked. "Where's Elle? And my mom?"

"Trey?" His mother's head slowly poked up from the couch. Chase was next to her, urging her to lie back down, though she batted his hands away and stood up anyway. "I'm not as fragile as I look, young man. I swear, all of this hoopla over me, when I'm not the one everyone should be worried about."

Trey made it to his mom in four strides. He touched the forming bump on her forehead and winced when she let out a little hiss.

"Will you stop fussing?" Sophie pushed his hands away. "You need to get your asses out there and get Elle back."

"What happened?" Everything was starting to make painful fucking sense. His mom there. Elle not. And his team armed to the nines.

"Elle came to the youth center. I don't think she even realized where she'd pulled over, the poor thing. Lord, she was in such a state." Sophie, as abrupt as always, drilled her son with a harsh glare. "And after you get her back from that man, you and I are going to talk about how you treat the woman you're in love with. That poor girl could barely see the nose on her face she was crying so damn hard."

A stabbing guilt pierced through Trey's chest. He'd been abrasive and stubborn, and too hurt by her lack of in faith in him to see what was actually happening. He guided his mom back to the couch and gently pushed her down onto the cushion.

"We'll have whatever talk you want," he promised, "but you need to tell me what happened."

"We were talking outside of the youth center when that man came skulking up. I didn't recognize him, but Elle did." Sophie absently rubbed the knot on her head.

"Sophie verified that Cummings is Winters, or that Winters is Cummings," Charlie said from her laptop. "You know what the bloody hell I'm talking about. Not only did he recognize you from one of your run-ins, but he had every intention of using Sophie to get to you."

"That's right." Trey's mother stood up again, her hands latching onto his arms. "But I think he overheard me sticking my nose in your love life, and now Elle's the one that's in danger. This is my fault. Mine and my big mouth's."

"It's not your fault. It's mine. And I'm going to do something about it." Trey firmly detached himself from his mom and started loading up on weapons. "Charlie, you need to get me the coordinates on that phone. And right the fuck now."

"I already have the coordinates, but I'm not giving them to you," Charlie announced.

Trey's temper exploded. "What the fuck do you mean, you're not giving them to me?"

Vince implanted himself between Trey and Charlie, who was standing there, not backing down in the least.

"She means that she's not going to give you the fucking coordinates so you can go off on a tangent and get yourself fucking killed," Vince clarified, his voice too goddamned steady. "Think, man."

"I *am* fucking thinking!" Trey boomed. "I'm thinking about all the different things that bastard could be doing to Elle. You weren't stationed overseas with that sick fuck. He's twisted, and I highly doubt getting blown to fucking bits has straightened him out any. Move or I'll move you myself."

"If you underestimate Winters and go off half-cocked, he's going to use that to his advantage."

"He's right, Trey," Rafe interjected. "And he could be fucking anywhere. What are you going to do? Comb every square inch of this mountain? And what if he took her out of the area?"

"He didn't." Charlie brought an image up on the television screen—a map of their mountain.

"Is this what I think it is?" Logan asked.

"It's the GPS in Elle's phone, and it's definitely on her because it's moving," Charlie clarified.

Trey squinted. "It looks like it's following the old reserve road. Why the fuck would he be taking her *up* the damn mountain? There's nothing there except the old operations building."

Vince looked thoughtful. "You mean the one the Army used as a makeshift bunker for field exercises? That place is a shithole waiting to fall the hell down."

"It's a shithole with only so many entrances and exits— easy for him to keep tabs on, especially if he's by himself," Trey admitted. "Smart fucking bastard."

"But by the time he sees us, it's going to be too late for him. He'll be a sitting duck."

What Trey was about to say felt like razorblades slicing up his throat. "I don't think he's really worried about escape. He just wants a little payback."

* * *

The bitter breeze whipped against Elle's face, but she couldn't feel it. She hadn't felt much of anything since Winters had dragged her from the car an hour ago. Her single layer of socks and bare hands were no match for the freezing temperature.

"Stop dragging your fucking feet." Winters gave her a rough shove from behind.

Elle stumbled and grabbed on to the nearest tree. Bark

ripped into her bare palms, making her wince. Okay, *that* she felt. And what little moonlight squeaked through the trees showcased the trail of blood coating her palms.

"You better hope to God that Sophie's okay because I'd hate to be you if she isn't." Elle wiped the blood on her jeans. Her stomach somersaulted as her brain replayed the image of Trey's mom stepping between Winters and her—and then dropping to the ground. "Actually, I'd hate to be you either way. Trey's going to be pissed."

"Good. That's exactly what I want."

"Spoken like a man who hasn't seen him in commando mode. If you think he's going to let you walk away after having threatened his mother like that, then you're delusional."

"I know he's not going to let me walk away, because I have something even more fucking precious to him than that old broad." Winters jabbed his rifle into the center of her back, where she no doubt had a bruise forming from his incessant poking. "I got *you*. And please, keep dragging your feet through the snow. Maybe we'll get lucky and the incoming storm won't wipe out our tracks and your lover boy will get to us that much faster."

Shit. That was exactly what she'd been doing.

Elle needed to fire up her synapses and do *something* that didn't involve Trey—and probably the rest of the team—walking into a trap. Because it wasn't a matter of *if* he'd find her, but *when*.

For once, Elle was thankful Winters was behind her, because it gave her the opportunity to think—and assess. They reached the next steep incline, slick with newly fallen snow, and climbed. It was a little dicey and more than a little physically draining, but where there was an up, there had to be a down…

Elle waited until they reached the crest of the hill and did

a quick scan of the bottom—no large boulders and no menacing trees with trunks thicker than her wrist. Considering
she had no idea where they were headed or if they were almost there, she needed to act fast.

Elle faked a stumble. She whipped her arm out to knock
Winters' rifle to the side, and then she let gravity roll her
down the mountain. Rocks dug into her back and branches
tugged at her hair. She tucked her arms against her body and
protected her head from the worst of it. From somewhere
above, Winters cursed.

At the bottom, something slammed against her forehead,
bringing her to an abrupt stop. Stars swirled across her vision for a moment.

"Damn it," Elle cursed.

"Don't you fucking move a muscle!" Winters started
skidding his way down.

Elle scrambled to a standing position and took off as fast
as her numb feet would go. She ran—and when each breath
felt like a newly frozen brick in her chest, she ran a little
harder. It felt like a lifetime had passed when she realized
Winters was no longer behind her.

Elle paused and listened for a solid three minutes, hearing nothing except the heavy pants of her own breathing.
Avoiding tracks was impossible, but she took her time,
careful to keep as much to the rocky areas as possible,
until she found a thick patch of drooping evergreens. She
tucked herself against the base of the center-most tree—
and waited.

Elle battled against droopy eyelids. Her fuzzy brain
knew that sleep right now was not her friend...but it was a
fight she'd lost, she realized some time later as she startled
awake.

At the soft crunch of snow, Elle froze. The footfall was

too heavy to be a rabbit, not quite big enough for a bear—
which, she hoped, were all sleeping peacefully in their dens.

That left only one other possibility.

Sitting straighter, Elle squinted through the foliage and
saw Dean Winters closing the distance between them like he
had all the time in the world.

"I know you're here, Miss Monroe," Winters's voice
echoed through the trees. "There's really no point in pro-
longing the inevitable. Come with me now and we'll get you
warm...save all those little piggies from falling off. You
have to be getting awfully worried about frostbite by now."

Elle stayed still, her eyes locked on him through the
shrubbery.

"I'm going to take a wild guess," he added, "and say that
you've stopped shivering. You're a smart woman, Elle. You
know it's not going to be long before your body starts shutting down, letting the hypothermia take over. And there's
one hell of a storm about to blow in. You and I both know
your chances of surviving out here are about a million from
a miracle."

Crunch. Step. Crunch. Winters moved closer to her position, almost like he really did know where she was hiding.
To move or stay? Elle questioned in her head. If he got too
close, there'd be no way she could make a break for it. If she
moved, where the hell would she go?

Winters turned in her direction. From less than six feet
away, he pointed his rifle—at her.

"I've found you," he announced in a singsong voice, and
cocked his gun. "I'd rather do this whole bait thing with you
breathing—it gives me a bit more leverage with Hanson. But
I'm not averse to maiming a little bit. If you want to keep
all your original beautiful parts, sweetheart, I'd suggest you
come out right the fuck now."

Elle didn't have a choice. Her legs had long since stopped obeying commands. She'd be barely able to stumble, let alone run.

"You're trying my patience, Miss Monroe," Winters warned.

Elle spewed an entire roster of obscenities as she crawled from her hidey-hole. "I can't wait for Trey to find you. You're so going to get what you deserve."

"When he finds us, so is he."

CHAPTER TWENTY-EIGHT

Trey and the team followed Elle's GPS signal to the eastern part of the mountain, where the wildlife far surpassed any two-legged population. No one lived nearby for miles, as the area was not easy to get to on foot, much less on four wheels. It was why the Army Reserves had chosen this area for their field drills.

Trey kept his night vision binoculars focused on the single-level building where Cummings, or whatever the fuck he called himself now, decided to use the dilapidated barracks for his showdown.

Rafe knelt down at his side. "You realize this is a trap, right? There's no way he wouldn't have gotten rid of Elle's cell unless he was planning on using it to lure us here. He's playing fucking games."

"Then I'll play." And Trey was going to win, making sure the bastard got locked up in Leavenworth for the rest of his miserable life.

Yeah, not only was he going to play Cummings's fucked-up game, but he'd ring his bell and then make the bastard choke on it for putting Elle's life in danger. Her son-of-a-bitch father had put her on Black Dunes' radar, but she was in that goddamned barrack because of *him*.

As if he'd gotten a read on his rising anger, Rafe's hand landed on his shoulder in a firm squeeze.

"Head on straight, man," Rafe encouraged in a low murmur. "Trust me. I know what you're feeling right now, but you're not going to do her any good by going in there stupid."

Trey swallowed the nervous fury clogging his throat and tried to do just that, but this was a hell of a lot more than the most important operation of his life...this was his fucking heart. "I can't lose her when I just found her, man."

"You're not going to lose her. Stone?" Rafe questioned their team leader through the comm-link.

"We're in left flanking position now," Stone stated.

"On right flank now, too," Logan announced. "Vince?"

"Almost finished with the final touches on our distraction and then I'm joining Callahan. T–minus ten minutes to fireworks..." Vince started the countdown until Trey could finally *do* something.

"Charlie," Trey added. "How close are we on getting eyes inside that fucking matchstick building?"

"I'll have it in five..." Charlie's voice came online. "Four. Three. Two. Ah...gotcha, you bloody bastard."

A weaponized Charlie was a dangerous Charlie. But put a computer in the woman's hands and she was fucking lethal. Stationed at the base of the previous decline, she directed a heat-scanning drone over their heads like a toy airplane on 'roids.

"Looks like we're the only ones he invited to the party," Charlie verified. "There are two heat signatures inside the building, and we're the only ones outside of it. But that doesn't mean—"

"That he doesn't have the place rigged like a fucking funhouse," Rafe finished her thought.

"He doesn't." Trey knew he was right. "His whole point in taking Elle is to see me suffer, right? He can't enjoy the show if he ends it before I even step through the door."

Even though it made sense, it didn't mean they weren't going to watch their asses. Like they'd done a million times before in the field, the team divvied up and approached the large shack from all sides. Rafe and Trey stayed low, reaching their position toward the rear—right beneath what looked to be a bathroom window.

"Found a way in on our side," Trey murmured.

"Us, too," Logan announced. "Vince and I got a window here that looks like it leads to a storage room."

"Tread lightly. Whoever gets in position first gets a snake cam turned on that main room. Charlie, you let us know if anything changes in Cummings's position."

"Got it," Charlie agreed.

Bursting through doors and breaking in windows was one sure way to give Cummings a heads-up. They needed to be quiet. Trey and Rafe worked in silence to remove the windowpane from their side of the barrack. It was ridiculously easy, the wood frame practically disintegrating in their hands as they lowered it to the ground

"After you, my lady," Rafe quipped. He linked his fingers and gave Trey a boot up, and once they cleared the window, Trey turned and hoisted Rafe's two-hundred-pound ass up the side of the building. The move was quick and efficient, and didn't cause a damn bit of noise.

"T–minus five." Vince updated everyone on the countdown.

Trey carefully tested each floorboard before applying the

full brunt of his weight. Ten fucking feet felt like ten fucking yards, but he reached the door and slid to his stomach.

"I'm getting eyes now," Trey murmured.

Rafe was already passing him the snake cam. He shimmied it through the gap beneath the door. Snowlike fuzz filled the handheld screen while he worked it into position—and then voila. The damn thing flickered to life.

Four walls and an empty room large enough to have slept at least twenty soldiers didn't come as any shock. What did was the small cot shoved into a corner and a small living area halfheartedly constructed off to the side. Evidently the bastard had been hiding under their noses for some time.

Trey swung the camera to the left.

A burst of white fury nearly made the damn thing shatter in his hands.

Tied to a chair in the center of the room, Elle looked half unconscious, her chin dipping down to her chest. The vid-screen didn't need to be in color for him to identify the blotch of darkness above her right temple.

Blood.

The fucking bastard had drawn blood.

"Easy," Rafe warned.

"Fuck easy. I'm going to kill him." Trey was going to reach up and pull Cummings's dick out through his ass for having laid so much as a finger on Elle.

"We got an extra set of eyes pointing west," Logan interrupted. "Good thing we have a distraction, because one step out of either of our rooms puts us right into the bastard's line of sight."

Vince muttered, "T–minus three, kids."

Trey shifted closer to the door.

"What the fuck do you think you're doing?" Rafe grunted softly.

"Keep an eye on Cummings," Trey said, passing the cam over. "I need to see her with my own fucking eyes, not through this damn screen."

Rafe cursed but remained focused on the video feed while Trey pushed the door open just wide enough to notice that the snake-cam hadn't caught the worst of Elle's injuries.

Along with the bloody knot on her head, her face was covered in cuts and scratches. Blood soaked through her jeans, damn near looking like fucking handprints. And her bottom lip was busted open. She looked like she'd survived nine rounds with a heavyweight boxer.

Not only was Trey going to rip off Cummings's balls and shove them up his ass, but he'd shove them so high they'd get caught on his fucking tonsils.

* * *

Someone must've hammered an ice pick into Elle's fore-head. And her chest. And her back. There wasn't a single part of her body that didn't hurt. She fought against the heavy weight of her eyelids and when she finally won the battle, the room spun. She grabbed for the nearest stable surface and found she didn't have to go far—because rope tied her to it.

Sitting in the middle of an empty room, her wrists and an-kles bound to the chair beneath her, Elle focused on taking a deep breath and gagged on the urine-scented air.

"You're finally up." Winters lounged back in a nearby chair, looking like a man without a care in the world.

"This is the best you could do as far as accommoda-tions?" Elle croaked, her throat dry.

"Best I could do in this Bumblefucklandia. You're lucky to be here after that little stunt you pulled. Actually, I'm a bit surprised you woke up at all. That's a nasty bump on your head."

Elle didn't need to shine a penlight in her eyes to know she had a concussion, a real one this time because it took her a few moments to remember what he was talking about. "You almost sound like you care."

"Not in the least. You're just a more effective commodity if you actually have a life to threaten. If you're dead by the time Hanson gets here, he's got nothing to lose."

Elle's head pounded as she tried to follow along. "I thought my father hired you to make it look like I was being threatened. So what does this all have to do with Trey?"

Winters' chair clunked to the ground. He stood, stretching his lanky body. "Everything. Little did I know when I took your father's measly little job that it would practically hand-deliver the man who destroyed my fucking life. I'm not the kind of man to let an opportunity pass me by. I took advantage of it—which is why I took you. Nothing fucks with a man's head more than threatening the woman he loves."

"Then I suggest you go find her," Elle said harshly, "because she's sure as hell not here."

The words sliced Elle apart from the inside. The truth was, she didn't know how Trey felt. Given how their last conversation had ended, she couldn't imagine it was a fraction more than toleration.

"Don't sell yourself short, Miss Monroe," Winters jested. "There isn't a doubt in my mind that he's going to come for you, and when he does, I'll be waiting."

"To do what, exactly?"

"To fuck over his life like he fucked over mine." Winters only spared her an occasional glance as he started pacing. "He couldn't mind his own goddamned business—couldn't just avert his eyes and play fucking dumb. No. He had to suck the asses of the higher-ups and invade my desert, ruining everything I'd had in place for fucking months. Suddenly, no one wanted to chance having an American Delta team on their fucking asses—not even for military-grade weapons."

"So he put a kink in your arms-trafficking plans—how horrible of him," Elle said sarcastically.

"He blew them the fuck up—with me inside!"

Winters grabbed a mug off the table and hurled it. Elle flinched, but the glass rocketed by her ear, missing by inches, and shattered against the wall. The quick move saved her another blow to the head, but sent a bolt of pain through her midsection.

Winters no longer paid attention to her as he ranted and raved. Elle breathed through the throb in her head and caught movement from the corner of her eye. She squinted, trying to focus on the wisp of a snake slithering beneath one of the back doors.

No, not a snake.

A *camera*—one of the compact kinds she'd seen used in the movies.

The black, coiled length twisted toward her like some little Cyclops, and then the door opened—just barely. Elle blinked. And then she blinked again. Either her concussion came with hallucinations or Trey's green eyes stared at her from across the room.

He pressed a finger to his lips and then he vanished back behind the door.

"Can I get a drink?" she asked suddenly. She'd rather not be tied and completely helpless when all hell broke loose.

Winters came to an abrupt stop, looking at her as if he'd forgotten she was there. "What?"

"A drink. Please." Elle cleared her throat, emphasizing a wince, and prepared herself for a no.

"No fucking games," Winters warned.

"No games. Like there's anywhere for me to go, or like I'd get very far if I even tried."

Winters cut her ties and handed her a bottle of water... and then not only did hell break loose, it shattered. Multiple doors crashed open, and Alpha descended into the room in a mad rush of barked orders and chaos.

Winters hauled her off her chair. He used her as a shield, beveling his gun against her sore torso.

"Let her go, Cummings," Trey demanded, aiming his assault rifle at Winters.

"So you made the connection, huh?" Winters laughed bitterly. "Took you fucking long enough. And here I thought you were semi-intelligent, Hanson, but you keep proving me wrong. Not only did it take you so fucking long to figure out, but you left your woman all alone and defenseless and shit."

"In case you didn't notice the six guns aimed at your fucking head, she's not alone. You wanted me here, and I'm here." Trey slowly skirted the perimeter of the room, never once taking his eyes off Winters. "Let Elle go, and then I'll send everyone away. It'll be you and me."

"Trey, no," Elle murmured.

"You may be stupid, but I'm not." Winters shook his head frantically. "The second I let your little girlfriend go, it'll be all over."

"This is going to come to an end sooner or later. Wouldn't you rather do it in a way that doesn't have your carcass peppered with bullets?"

"You already fucked my life, so what the hell do I care? As long as I take you with me, I'm good."

Behind her, Winters's weight shifted. His grip on her

shoulder released enough for her to register the swing of his aim—toward Trey.

"Watch out!" Elle leapt forward in the hopes of knocking Trey out of the way.

A loud bang reverberated through the rickety cabin. The floor shook and the walls creaked. Elle slammed into Trey's rock-hard chest. His arms wrapped around her, and his body cushioned their fall to the floor.

A hefty mixture of concern and anger pulled his mouth into a tight line. "Goddamn it, Elle! What the hell were you thinking?"

"Please tell me you're okay." Her hands shook as she skated her palms across his chest looking for holes . . . and stopped when her fingers brushed a warm wetness. "Oh, God. You're shot."

She pulled her hand away and inspected her red-painted fingers. Panic had her struggling for each breath. Trey stared at her hand and then into her eyes. Elle blinked, battling against the funhouse spin of her head—then came the crushing weight on her chest.

"Elle." Trey gently reversed their positions, and then her name fell from his lips a second time, but it sounded different. More muffled. Further away. Despite their faces being only inches apart, things starting going blurry.

And darker.

"Elle!" Trey's shout barely sounded like a whisper.

So dark.

CHAPTER TWENTY-NINE

Fire licked up Elle's arm, making her groan... and then her groan made her groan. Someone must've forced her to swallow a bucket of rusty nails, because that's what it felt like when she coerced her tongue to move. *And fire*. Someone had set the rusty nails on fire and then stabbed her shoulder with a pitchfork... while an elephant sat on her chest.

Elle hissed as a bright light seared its way into the deep recesses of her corneas.

"About time you joined the land of the conscious," came a familiar voice. "You really are a sucky hostess, love... sleeping while you have visitors and all. No wonder you became a nurse instead of a society wife."

"Charlie." Elle grinned groggily and winced when her dry lips protested the movement. "Damn it. I don't think there's a part of me that isn't hurting right now."

"Hurting means you're alive and, trust me, it was a little hairy there for a while." Charlie's voice was stern, but she leaned over, gently squeezing Elle's hand. "Be thankful that it's a rare occasion and I'm here by myself, and not with a half dozen broody, overwhelming apes."

Here. Elle blinked and tried to figure out where *here* was.

Sterile white walls surrounded her. A cardiac monitor beeped steadily on her right. And the tubes. One arm bore an intravenous line infusing red blood cells, while a second line was running clear fluids.

"When did I get to a hospital? And what the hell happened?" asked Elle.

Charlie snorted on a humorless chuckle. "We tend to take people to hospitals when a bullet nearly shreds a main artery. And not that I don't applaud what you tried to do, but let's remember that you're not bulletproof, okay?"

Images from the cabin slowly started coming back—the shouting, the moving, the loud bang of the gun going off. *Trey!*

Elle's heart shuttled up to her throat, making the monitor next to her go ape-crazy. "Trey! Is he okay? Oh, God. And Sophie?"

Charlie cringed at the monitor and gave her fingers a soothing squeeze. "Calm down. You're going to make that thing explode. Sophie's fine. Trey's fine—if you call being a raging basket-case fine. Rafe was about ten seconds away from raiding the hospital's narc box and injecting him with a severe dose of Chill the Hell Out."

Charlie waited a beat and added, "And just so you know, he's been here every second since they brought you in. The guys finally convinced him to go wash the literal stink off his skin. I'm surprised the smell of him didn't wake you up."

Elle attempted to sit up and, holy craptastic pain, that was a big mistake. She grabbed her shoulder and inspected the heavy-duty bandage beneath the starchy hospital gown. "How long have I been here?"

"Forty-eight hours. We airvac'd you off the mountain, and they rushed you into surgery the second the helo touched down. You've been out ever since. Hell, you were intubated until this morning, but you kept trying to *buck the vent*—as they called it. Basically, they said it was you telling them to take the bloody tube out of your throat and let you do your own thing. Stubborn even when in a medical-induced coma."

"And what about Winters?"

"Rotting in the local jail and waiting for a military transport. Turns out not only is it illegal to steal and sell American military weapons, but faking your death and going AWOL from the United States Army isn't exactly an acceptable practice either."

A throat-clear turned both Elle's and Charlie's attention to the white-haired older man standing in the doorway. He was dressed in a lab coat and wore a stethoscope around his neck. "Good afternoon, Miss Monroe. I'm Dr. Foster."

He stepped into the room and pulled up her patient chart from the computer attached to the wall. "I'm the surgeon who performed your procedure two days ago. For the extent of your injuries, you're making a tremendous amount of progress. Is it okay if I speak frankly about your condition in front of your friend?"

Elle offered Charlie a small smile and a wink. "Of course. She's family."

Dr. Foster's attention bounced back and forth between the two of them: Charlie's pink hair to Elle's blonde; Charlie's snarky grin to Elle's seemingly innocent smile. They were both petite, but that's where the similarities ended. Yet Elle meant every word. Everyone at Alpha was her family.

"You heard the lady." Charlie's brown eyes shone with a suspicious mist as she cleared her throat. "We're family. Continue."

"You're a very lucky young woman, Miss Monroe," Dr. Foster continued. "You suffered a pretty severe concussion on top of the gunshot—a wound, I might add, that had it been a half inch to the right, would've destroyed your pulmonary artery. When I say you're a lucky woman, I mean it. You and your baby both must have a guardian angel looking out for you."

Elle knew it had nothing to do with luck and everything to do with Trey—and Charlie and the guys. She gave Charlie's hand another squeeze—and froze. Not only had *she* gone still, but Charlie had too. Eyes wide, the other woman stared at Elle, as Elle stared at the doctor.

"Wait. You said '*baby*'? I'm sorry, doctor, but I think you must've looked at the wrong patient chart. I'm not pregnant. I can't *get* pregnant."

Dr. Foster clicked through a series of multimedia files and turned the computer for her to see...

A sonogram...

With her name on it...

And a small, lima bean–shaped mass in a sea of black.

"H-how?" She gaped at the doctor and clutched Charlie's hand until the other woman winced. "I don't understand. How is this possible? It shouldn't *be* possible."

"When they brought you in, the hospital had your previous medical records faxed to us, and I have to admit, it did make us take a little pause. The injuries you sustained in your car accident were definitely severe."

"Leaving me only one ovary that wasn't capable of producing eggs," Elle clarified to the doctor.

"I know what the reports said—which is why after we made certain that everything was okay both with you and the baby, our OB/GYN looked into things a little more. We were in agreement that, at the time of your diagnosis, your body most likely *wasn't* able to produce viable eggs. But as the body healed, enough regeneration must have transpired to make the improbable possible."

Dr. Foster clicked a button and a black-and-white image printed—which he placed in her shaking hand. "Everything looks right on track for a healthy five-week embryo. Congratulations."

Elle couldn't move. Or speak.

A baby.

A tiny, barely-a-month-ago-conceived baby.

* * *

Trey stormed down the hospital corridor like a raging tsunami, hell-bent on getting to Elle's room ASAP. Go shower, they said. Go eat something, they said. He hadn't been able to deal with the constant nagging anymore and had finally given in, and what the fuck happened?

She woke up—*and he wasn't there.*

Trey reached her room and pushed the door open with a flourish—and stalled. Elle lay asleep on her side, golden hair fanned across the pillow and hands tucked beneath one cheek—which definitely had more color since he'd left. The heavy weight on his chest lightened the tiniest bit.

Careful not to wake her, he sat in the chair next to her bed and gently stroked his knuckles over her newly warmed skin.

Four tours overseas. Countless black op missions. Years with Alpha. And Trey had never felt fear as intense as he had while Elle bled out in his arms—except for when the nurses had wheeled her out of his sight and all he'd had left of her was the blood soaking his shirt.

No way was he letting her walk, run, or wheel her little self away from him again. Ever. He loved her—straight down to the fundamentals of his DNA. Losing her in any way would be to lose his heart, body, soul. His very fucking existence.

Soft fingers skimmed the top of his hand. "Trey?"

Eyes half-mast and heavy with sleep, she peered up at him through long lashes.

"Hey there, sweetness." He brushed his knuckles over her cheek again. "I'm here."

"You're okay? And your mom's really okay?"

"Everyone's fine...except you."

"I'm okay."

He shot her a loving glare and pointedly glanced from the heart monitors to the IV lines to the bag of blood still infusing into her traumatized body. "Try convincing someone who didn't watch you pass out from blood loss."

Her sleepy grin widened. "Well, I didn't say I was ready to go climbing any mountains just yet. Or hills. And I may want to take it easy on speed bumps for a while."

"I think you're going to be taking it easy on *everything* for a while."

"Doctor's orders or yours?" Elle teased.

"Both." He scrubbed his hand over his face and took a deep breath. "Goddamn, Elle. You scared the ever-lovin' shit out of me. What the hell were you thinking, jumping in front of Cummings that way?"

"That I didn't want to lose you," she confessed in a whisper.

Her honesty floored him and doused him in a flash of hope. For two fucking days, he'd replayed their last conversation, and for those same two days, he'd tortured himself about what would happen when she woke. With the way he spoke to her, she had every right to tell him to go fuck himself.

Trey eased her chin up, gently redirecting her focus to his eyes. "That goes both ways, sweetness."

Careful not to bump her IV, he threaded his fingers through hers and stared at their interlocked hands. Her once smooth, creamy skin had nicks and bruises, a sign of what she'd been through the last few days—because of him.

"There's so much that I want to say to you that I don't know where to start." Trey swallowed the lump of fear in his throat. "But I guess I'll begin with telling you that I'm sorry. Christ, I know that sounds really fucking lame, considering you almost died, but I am. You wouldn't even be lying here right now if it weren't for me."

Elle squeezed his fingers. "What are you talking about?"

"I'm talking about the entire situation with Cummings." Thinking about the bastard rotting in jail, Trey got pissed all over again. "If it weren't for me, you never would've been put into this position."

"You're not responsible for the actions of others, Trey. Winters made his own choices. *He* put me in that situation, not you." She gave his fingers a firmer squeeze when he started shaking his head. "It wasn't you."

"I wasn't the one who kidnapped you, but you were put in that situation because of how I feel about you." Trey took a deep, shaky breath. "Which brings me to the second thing I want to talk about…actually, it's more of a warning than anything. And it's that I'm not going to let you push me away—no matter how hard you shove. I'm here. With you. For good. For the rest of our lives."

"That's…a really long time," Elle commented softly.

"Damn straight it is." Trey dug into his pants pocket until his big, clumsy fingers found what he was looking for. He pulled the ring out, feeling like he was going to throw up as her eyes registered the emerald she'd admired at Charming Treasures.

"What are you doing?" she asked, breathless.

"Let me finish, baby, please." He cleared his throat and, hell, got direct and to the point. "I want you in my life, Elle. And more importantly, I want you to *be* my life. I know you have worries, and I get it. I do. But I'm going to make it my life's goal to prove to you that as long as we have one another, *nothing* else matters. It's *you* that controls my heart, body, and soul. I love you—so goddamned much. I'm *in* love with you—so goddamned deep. Marry me. Make me the luckiest bastard in the world."

"But what about chil—"

He cupped her cheek and rubbed a stray tear away with his thumb. "No buts. I love *you*. I want a life and future with *you*. I'm happy as long as I have *you*."

Elle's tears started dropping too fast for him to catch them. It scared the living hell out of him. He was two seconds away from getting the nurse, thinking she was in pain, when she graced him with a watery smile. "Do you really mean that?"

"Sweetness, I've never meant anything more."

He waited for her answer.

And waited.

Goddamn, he couldn't fucking breathe. He released a nervous chuckle. "So are going to accept my ring or are you going to leave me hanging?"

Elle giggled. The soft sound was a symphony to Trey's ears. "I want to give you something first."

* * *

Elle pulled out a grainy black-and-white photo from beneath her pillow and handed it to Trey with a trembling hand. Then she waited and watched for any sign that he knew what he was holding. His brows stayed furrowed in concentration as he stared down at the sonogram.

"Dr. Foster was here a bit ago," she explained. "He assured me that the surgery went as planned and that our baby and I are doing great."

He looked up from the photo, his mouth hanging open a bit—shell-shocked—a feeling she knew well. "Our baby?"

He didn't say anything else. Just as she started getting worried, Trey cupped her face and kissed her. It was barely a brushing of mouths, yet the fiercest and most emotional one they'd shared to date. Elle gripped the back of his neck and groaned out her displeasure when he gently pulled away. He leaned his forehead on hers and, from this close, there was no disguising the hope and love lighting up his eyes. "Seriously?"

Elle nodded, unable to say the words.

"Oh, baby." He kissed her again before gently placing his palm on her flat stomach. "And baby."

The gesture brought fresh tears to Elle's eyes. "It's still so early…"

He rubbed his thumb absently against her belly button but never took his eyes off her face. "Being part of us, there's no way she's not a fighter. She's already defeating the odds."

"She?" Elle gave him a watery smile. "You want a girl?"

"Hell, yeah, I do. Blonde and blue-eyed and tough like her mother. Though you realize that dating will have to be put off until she's thirty. Maybe forty."

"Wow. You're really looking into the future, aren't you?"

"I am. I love you, Elle. So much." He took her hand and held the beautiful emerald ring between his fingers. "Now that you gave me one incredible gift, I'm going to be a greedy bastard and demand you give me the best one yet."

"Demand?" Elle teased coyly. "I don't do demands, Mr.

Hanson. But I do happen to do happily-ever-afters with the man I love."

It was Elle's turn to pull his mouth to hers, and she kissed him until her cardiac monitor started beeping in protest. "I love you, Trey Michael Hanson. Former Delta operative. Son. Brother. Soon-to-be-father—and husband."

"So is that a yes?" Trey murmured against her lips.

"Yes!" Elle laughed.

No doubt her face was a red, blotchy mess, but she didn't care. Trey had swaggered into her life as a one-night stand—and then he refused to go. Not only did he help her rediscover herself, but her strengths, too. And her dreams. And her fears. And the realization that love really could break through all obstacles.

Elle pulled him into a kiss that left her cardiac monitor screaming in protest.

"I'd say, 'Get a room,' but you already have one." Vince's voice broke up a heated kiss. The SEAL's teasing was cut off by a loud grunt and a curse. "Christ, woman, watch where you're aiming that pointy elbow."

"I did, and it landed perfectly. Can't you see they're having a bloody beautiful moment? You're lucky I only aimed for your stomach," Charlie growled.

Trey and Elle chuckled as they relinquished each other's mouths to see the entire team—plus Sophie Hanson—standing just inside the doorway. And then everyone rushed inside, offering hugs and kisses, and shedding more than a few tears. Somehow, Trey fought his way back to Elle's side and she just knew—that's how they'd always walk through life.

Side by side.

EPILOGUE

Lebanon County, Pennsylvania
Six Months Later

Trey scanned the area, growing more impatient by the second. Failure was not an option. No fucking way. Not this time. Not ever. "It's got to be here."

"It is." Vince nodded to the buzzing freezer chest in front of him. "Right the hell there, man. Grab it and let's go. Bea's looking at me like she's trying to make my clothes disappear with her mind."

The all-night clerk at the Grab-N-Go, who had to be pushing ninety, waggled her eyebrows and red-tipped fingers in their direction.

"Christ, man. Hurry the fuck up," Vince muttered.

He nudged Trey away, probably glad to have something to focus on other than Bea's sex-me-up stare, and plopped a gallon of ice cream into Trey's hands. "It says right there that it's chocolate damn chip. Take it, pay, and let's get the hell out of here."

"This is the one with extra chips. They made Elle sick the last time she had it."

"So get her the damn cookie dough."

"Raw dough isn't good for pregnant women."

Vince looked ready to strangle someone, and no doubt Trey was high on the list. It didn't matter. His woman wanted chocolate chip ice cream and he was getting chocolate chip ice cream—and the right fucking one.

Vince cast a wary glance at Bea, who was now strategically shifting her top to maximize her cleavage.

Trey finally found the right brand buried beneath all the others. He grabbed two and paid, making quick tracks back to the compound. The second the elevator doors slid open, the plastic bag was yanked out of his hand.

"You're welcome, sweetness," Trey teased. He ogled the sight of Elle's curvy backside scampering back to the kitchen. "You should probably know that Vince had to give Bea a mental lap dance for those two half-gallons."

"Thanks, Vince," Elle called out as she eagerly pulled away the freshness seal.

"Yeah, thanks, Navy." Charlie pulled a potato chip from Vince's hand and popped it into her mouth before gagging and grabbing a nearby paper towel "Ew. Yuck. What the hell bloody flavor is that?"

"Salt and vinegar." Vince glowered, but didn't stop Charlie from swiping his soda and taking a huge gulp. "And root beer."

"Why the bloody hell would you get salt and vinegar chips and root beer?"

"Because I thought you'd keep your grubby hands off them," Vince retorted.

Elle turned to Trey, grinning. "Aren't they so cute when they get like this, baby? It makes me think back to all that sexual dancing around we did, and it gets me a little misty-eyed."

Vince and Charlie stopped arguing.

"Sexual dancing?" Charlie eyes widened. "Hell, no. There's nothing sexual or dance-like about Navy and me."

"That's damn fucking right," Vince agreed with a nod. "Violence maybe. Maybe a bruise-inducing sparring match. But definitely no fucking dancing."

"You know what? That sparring match sounds good." Charlie grabbed Vince's bag of chips and drinks and headed in the direction of the gym. "Let's go, Navy. Winner gets the junk food."

"It's my fucking junk food!" Vince bellowed, but followed.

Trey chuckled as his friends disappeared. "You did that on purpose, didn't you?" he asked.

Elle grinned mischievously, a spoonful of ice cream already perched at her lips. "A pregnant lady's got the right to enjoy her ice cream without listening to them bicker. Besides, I didn't say anything that wasn't true. They'd both be happier if they finally admitted what all the rest of us realized a million years ago."

Trey slipped his arms around Elle's waist and palmed the gently swelling curve of her stomach. "You're one dangerous woman, sweetness."

She popped the spoon into her mouth and hummed. "But less so now that I have my chocolate chip fix."

"When you're done, can I have my fix? And just so we're on the same page, it involves you naked and screaming my name." Trey nipped her ear and enjoyed the feel of the corresponding shiver.

"Too bad we can't have our fixes at the same time."

Trey didn't need to see the grin on her face to know it was a challenge. "Hold your bowl tight."

He scooped her up into his arms and started stalking toward their room.

"Oh my God. You're going to break your back!" Elle squealed. "What are you doing?"

"Combining our two fixes—among other things."

Hard-nosed Charlotte Sparks's last obstacle to becoming an operative is a trial mission—and six-and-a half-foot Alpha Security member Vincent Franklin. But when the op calls for them to pretend to be engaged, the heated action soon gets very real...

Please see the next page for a preview of *Hard Justice*.

CHAPTER TWO

*T*hump-thump. *Wack.* *Thump-thump.* *Wack.* Someone wailed hard on a sparring bag, the sound reverberating through Alpha Security's corridor as if it was on the overhead communication system. The closer to the gym Vince got, the louder the low grunts became. Logan and Trey, two of his Alpha teammates, hovered outside the door, which left a handful of possibilities as to the owner of the serious aggression.

"Why are you two girls hiding out here in the hall?" Vince smacked Logan on the back, and peeked into the training room.

Since joining Alpha Security a year ago, Vince had been having this particular wet dream every damn night, but his imagination hadn't a damn thing on the reality.

Filling out a sports tank to perfection, the snug fabric hugging the ample curves of her breasts like a fucking glove, Charlie Sparks bounced on the balls of her feet in a hypnotic to-and-fro movement. A little blue jewel winked at him from her belly button as she pivoted her hips and turned her torso into a punch. And, as always happened when he laid eyes on the feisty Brit, his cock stirred to life.

Frowning, Vince watched the way she attacked the sparring bag as if it had just insulted her mother, and she showed no signs of slowing down, despite the dewy glow sliding over her skin. "How long has she been at this?"

"An hour." Trey sounded just as displeased as he felt, offhandedly nodding toward the left. "And before that it was about thirty minutes of Scooter time—give or take."

Vince glanced over to the Scooter, the life-sized dummy they kept on hand for weapons training, and winced at the half dozen throwing knives sticking out of his neck. And his chest. And his groin, exactly where his dick would be fucking shish kabobbed if he'd been human.

Logan's gaze tracked the way Charlie drilled fist after fist into the sparring bag and added, "And she was in Stone's office earlier. Five minutes after coming out, she was castrating Scooter."

"Door opened or closed?" asked Vince.

"Closed. For half-a-fucking-hour."

Fuck. Nothing good ever came out of being summoned to the boss's office. A former SEAL like himself, Sean Stone prided himself on keeping things within the unit as even as possible. Having a conversation with the man in his office, much less behind closed doors wasn't exactly the norm.

An hour and a half of aggression plus some Stone time and it brought her within a handful of minutes of when she'd disappeared with Preppy. Evidently something hadn't gone the way she'd expected.

"Did either of you ask her what happened?" asked Vince.

The guys looked at him as if he'd sprouted a dick in the middle of his forehead, but it was Trey who spoke. "Does it look like we have a fucking death wish? Jesus. I have a kid on the way, one I'd like to see grow up and raise alongside my future wife. No way am I sticking my head anywhere near the lion's mouth."

"She's five-foot-nothing."

Logan shook his head, chuckling low. "Dude. You've been on the team for a while now and it's like you haven't learned a damn thing. Charlie makes some four-star generals look like domesticated pussycats."

He was inclined to agree. Though petite with that too-damn-hot English accent, Charlie was no wilting flower. He'd been on the receiving end of her sharp wit more times than he cared to count, not to mention her roundhouse. But that wasn't where her edge stopped.

Wearing a tight tank that ended above her navel, the most exquisite inkwork he'd seen in a damn long time wrapped around her right torso and slid beneath the band of her yoga pants. The understated beauty of rich brown tree limbs and pink cherry blossoms was as gorgeous as it was fitting. And if he wasn't afraid of receiving a debilitating kick to his groin, he'd ask for a head-to-toe glimpse of the entire damn thing.

Thinking about where that tattoo ended, and whatever else might lie beneath, Vince's cock went from half-mast to full salute. He adjusted his pants and forced himself to concentrate more on Charlie's body mechanics than the body itself.

"You're overextending your arm on the punch." He stepped into the gym, completely aware of the fact his friends had high-tailed it in the opposite direction the second he opened his mouth.

Chickenshits.

"I don't recall asking for your bloody advice, Navy." She didn't even look in his direction as she drilled another series of punches into the bag, no doubt envisioning his face float-ing in front of her.

"The friendly thing to do would be to say, 'Thank you, Vincent. You saved me from having my arm in a sling for four weeks.'"

"If you want friendly, go upstairs." Charlie nodded above them where Alpha Security's cover business, the bar Alpha, was in full midnight swing. "I'm sure there's a blonde or brunette or redhead looking to be the next member in the Navy Boy fan club."

Thwack. Kick.

Hell, she was right. He could go up to the bar and, within five minutes, have a willing companion for the night. Once upon a time, he would've done just that and the fleeting sexual release would've easily smoothed away the constant edge that always hovered beneath the surface. Now it just left him cold...and craving the woman in front of him even more—which is probably why he'd been as celibate as a fucking monk for the last six goddamned months.

Vince took position behind the sparring bag and held it in place, knowing he was living dangerously but not giving a shit. "You almost sounded a little jealous there, English. Careful, or I may start thinking you actually care."

As expected, her brown eyes narrowed. She kicked pre-cariously close to his right hand. "There's absolutely nothing to be jealous about. I could get a bad dye job and fake boobs if I wanted, but I don't want to fly around like a deflated bal-loon if something sharp pokes me in the chest."

At the mention of her chest, his eyes dropped to her cleavage. Hell, he couldn't help it. He was a fucking man, and the two secured globes were fucking perfect. Unfortu-nately, she noticed his shifted attention.

Charlie twisted her torso, winding up for another roundhouse, but this time didn't pull back. Before he registered her aim, the top of her shoe connected with his ear, making it ring like a goddamn church bell.

Vince released the bag with a growl. "Jesus Christ, woman. You're a fucking nuisance."

Hands on her curvy hips, she stepped into his space, the top of her head barely hitting his chin. Mighty Mouse with a bad attitude. "Oh, please. You're a big bad SEAL and you can't take a little tap?"

"You want to turn this into a hand-to-hand sparring match, *my little English muffin*? Fine with me."

She ducked his frontal assault and spun, her foot impacting two inches above his knee. The damn thing gave out and gave her the upper hand for about five seconds. Vince took his time, blocking each of her moves while he waited for the one that would let him gain back the advantage. When her eyes shifted left, he spun right. Now behind her, he pinned his forearm across her collarbone and anchored her back against his chest.

"Are you done yet?" His lips brushed over the shell of her ear. Every internal alarm he had went ape-shit, including the one between his legs that was rock hard and nestled perfectly against the small of her back.

Charlie stilled for about two seconds, her backside moving into a slight sway. And hell if she didn't do it again, the second time pulling a low groan from his throat. His grip lightened to step away, but it was too late. Two small hands yanked down his arm and a set of teeth bit into the flesh of his hand.

Vince released her on a howl.

"Yep. I'm about done now." Charlie ignored his colorful curses and swayed her ass over to her water bottle.

"Vince." Stone stood just off the mat, arms folded across

his chest. And fuck, his boss didn't look thrilled. "I need you in the meeting room. Now."

Vince nodded, not having any clue how much of the show the former SEAL had seen.

"And Charlie"—Stone slid his gaze her way—"I want your ass in there in another ten."

Charlie wiggled her fingers at Vince as he turned to follow their boss deeper into the underground labyrinth that was Alpha Security headquarters. They had not only a training room, but a shooting range, offices, and a meeting room that made the Pentagon look half-assed.

And all of it built into the Blue Ridge Mountain. To the outside world, Vince and his team were business owners and bouncers that had taken over the running of a much-loved neighborhood bar. To a select few topside, they were the men who got shit done when the government's hands were metaphorically—or logistically—tied.

The meeting room was empty when they got there. "You want a bag of ice for that hand?"

"Maybe a fucking tetanus shot." Vince glared at his boss's smirk. "Look, about what happened in the training room, I—"

"This isn't about the training room, although it does involve Charlie."

Fuck-and-him. Stone wasn't an easy guy to read—at all. But his silence spoke a thousand fucking words. "What about her?"

"I've offered her a chance to take a primary assignment in a case."

Vince narrowed his gaze on his boss. "English has been champing at the bit to take on more field assignments, so I know there's a lot more to it than that. What aren't you saying?"

"A lot." Stone's face was grim. "Starting with the fact that it's a DHS case."

"Department of Homeland Security?" Vince's eyes widened. That sure as hell wasn't what he'd expected to come out of Stone's mouth. "What the hell kind of case are you giving Charlie that involves DHS?"

"Kidnapping with possible human-trafficking links from a ring based out of Miami. Possible corruption *within* the DHS ranks."

"Shit."

"Of the deepest and foulest kind." Stone nodded.

Vince's gut tugged. Something didn't quite feel...right. "Wait. Then why the fuck do you want to bring English into this as a primary? You think she can track them down electronically?"

"That would be fucking nice, but no. It's a bit more complicated than that."

The clearing of a throat had both men turning. Charlie stood in the doorway of what she and Penny had dubbed the Room of Testosterone. Her brown eyes shifted to him before traveling back to Stone. "What's Navy doing here?"

"I told you that if you decide to do this, that you'd have a partner." Stone nodded toward Vince. "Franklin's yours."

Charlie's calculating gaze slid his way before returning to their boss. "No way in bloody hell."

"I told you before, Charlie, that if it isn't with one of ours, it doesn't happen. There's no fucking way I'm letting you go back on the inside without someone we can trust standing next to you."

"What about Logan?"

"Already scheduled for another detail, and since we don't know how long this one's going to take, I can't chance sending him out."

"Chase?"

"With him. And I'm not sending Trey out knowing that his mind would be back here on Elle and the baby. Franklin's your second. You can either accept it and sit down to hear the rest or I can call DHS right now and tell them it's a no-go. Your choice."

Her trying to pass him over in favor of one of the other guys chafed him raw. He might be one of the newest to Alpha, but that didn't mean he was a fucking rookie. In his years of service, he'd seen and done things that would give a person's nightmares nightmares. Fuck, he still woke up most nights in a goddamned cold sweat.

Charlie sat down two chairs away from Vince, refusing to meet his gaze. He didn't even know exactly what the assignment entailed, but he was suddenly hell-bent on making sure he was there for its duration, whether the little British bombshell liked it or not.

"Charlie was approached tonight by a DHS agent looking for a new angle into one of their cases. They're about two steps away from writing it off and calling it a loss," Stone addressed Vince.

It took him a moment to register what his boss was saying and to connect the dots together—toward Preppy Boy. Vince shifted his attention to Charlie. "That's who that guy was at the bar? The dipshit with the fucking chinos?"

Charlie barely gave him a nod.

Vince turned to his boss. "Okay...next question. Why the fuck are they approaching English? That kid was barely out of diapers; there's no way in fucking hell he's high enough on the DHS food chain to know about Alpha."

"They didn't approach Alpha Security; they approached Charlie because they believe she's the inside they've been lacking. *I'm* making it an Alpha Security issue. I contacted our department liaison and told him that *if* she decides to go through with it, it will be us taking point. Actually, taking the fuck over. Color me surprised when he actually looked relieved."

Stone leaned his ass on the edge of the table, his gaze bouncing between them. "I want to make sure I make one thing clear...neither one of you are under any obligations to do this. DHS can take care of their own housekeeping issues. Dennison's going to give you both the rundown and if you don't like it, we end the call and it's over. The end."

As if perfectly timed, the video-comm beeped with an incoming call. Stone flipped on the secure feed, the screen pulling up a slightly disheveled older man, somewhere in his mid-sixties, who looked like he'd just come off a bender— or a stakeout.

"Agent Dennison." Stone nodded toward the DHS agent, the two men obviously having met before.

"Stone. What were the fucking chances that our last play before I called your ass actually ended up being one and the same? I can't tell you how much easier we're all breathing around here."

"I know you meant for that to be a compliment, Rich, but really what it sounded like was that you were willing to put a civilian life at risk before you finally called someone who could maybe get the job done." Stone glowered at the man through the video-comm. "Luck had it that the civilian your man approached happens to be one of mine. And since she is such, her and her partner here have the veto power on this little operation of yours. If they don't like what you have to say, they don't have to do it."

Agent Dennison's friendly demeanor instantly vanished, replaced by a growing scowl. "You realize this clusterfuck is growing to astronomical proportions, right?"

"I do. And I also know that you've suffered some casualties along the way, and I'm sorry about that, but I'm not going to put my operatives on an assignment that they're not one-hundred-percent on board with." Stone gestured to Charlie and Vince. "These are the two you need to convince, and if either of them isn't up for it, then it doesn't happen."

"This isn't a fucking game."

"Damn right it's fucking not," Stone snarled, uncharacteristically losing his temper. He turned toward Vince. "You have questions? Ask him. And don't feel like you have to sugarcoat things for his fragile disposition, because these are your asses on the line."

There wasn't much Vince wouldn't take on. Despite his having the SEALs years ago, the love of a challenge was still engrained in his DNA. But since they'd obviously—somehow—lumped Charlie into this, he was going to make sure it wasn't a fucking Hail Mary play.

Vince didn't bother holding back. "What happened to the agents you've already sent on the inside?"

Dennison's discomfort put Vince on edge as he waited for an answer.

The DHS agent finally spoke. "The suspected front-runners of the trafficking ring are a big deal here in South Florida. Big name. Big crime. Big scare factor... and it's not all buzz. And unfortunately, they're not very trusting individuals. In their line of work, they can't afford to be. Anyone we send on the inside to gather intel gets under their scrutiny and ultimately, gets ferreted out."

Way to dodge the fucking question.

"What. Happened. To. Your. Agents," Vince repeated.

Dennison shifted in his seat, looking like he'd rather swallow rusty nails than say the words aloud. "As best we know, their covers were compromised."

"As best you know...and you can't ask them?" Vince definitely didn't get the warm and fucking fuzzies.

"No. One's in critical condition. One's missing. And one..."

"One what?"

"We've had an agent that's been deep undercover for years."

"And what? You lost him or her too?"

"Shortened version?" Dennison looked like he was about to hurl. "We don't know if he's been compromised and is fighting to maintain his cover, or if he's..."

"Joined the other side," Stone finished for the agent. "Basically, they don't know where his loyalties really belong and considering anyone else they send on the inside doesn't come out the same way, hopes aren't high for a happy reunion."

"So bring your agent in and question his sorry ass," Vince suggested matter-of-factly.

Dennison let out a huff. "If we do that, we can kiss any chance of finding those missing girls, good-bye. Whether our agent is in on the ring, or if he's still maintaining his cover, we'd put the entire damn thing at risk. If we oust him, they'll shut down and move operations. We don't have time to send in someone new. It takes too long for them to gain trust, if they get it at all. We need someone who has it automatically, someone who can feel out where our agent's loyalties lie, and to help find information on the trafficking ring."

Dennison's attention slid to Charlie. *What the actual fuck?*

Arms folded across her chest, Charlie simply glared back at the agent as if she had the power to hurtle javelin spears through the video comm.

"We know this isn't an ideal situation, Miss Sparks," Dennison began, cut off by Charlie's snort.

"You *know*?" she asked, her voice low and deceptively calm. "Do you also know that I vowed never to step foot in that bloody city again? *Ever*? If you think my sudden return isn't going to be suspect, you're delusional."

"We think that not only is your return not going to be questioned, but it's going to be celebrated. Our sources tell us that Arturo's sick—terminal cancer. He's riding out his final days, claiming to be cleaning shop and shutting down."

Vince finally saw a flicker of emotion cross over her face. It was there and gone too quickly for him to decipher what it was. "But you don't believe him," she stated.

Dennison snorted. "A bastard like Arturo doesn't one day wake up and decide an overabundance of power isn't for him—cancer or not. I'm more likely to believe that he's expanded his criminal forte into human trafficking than that he's turning his holdings into legit businesses."

Agent Dennison looked fucking constipated as he glared at them through the video screen. "You don't look as though you agree, Miss Sparks. I was led to believe that you've never condoned his lifestyle—that it was the reason you left."

Charlie looked like she wanted a turn to reach through the screen and throttle the DHS agent. "Why I left Miami is none of your bloody business. I'm just trying to figure out why a man on his deathbed would be looking to expand his criminal reach when he's not going to be around to enjoy it. And it's not like he has a viable heir to the throne. It doesn't make sense."

"That's why we need someone on the inside, Miss Sparks. For years, you were his shining jewel. If anyone could slide back into the life without question, it's you. If our sources are correct, and Arturo is the mastermind behind this trafficking ring, you could very well be holding the lives of these innocent girls in your hands."

Guilt trips were a low blow and, despite the fact Charlie wasn't the type to be guilted into doing something she didn't want to do, the woman had a soft spot for doing the right thing when innocents were involved.

Dots slowly began to connect in Vince's mind.

Miami. Crime. Arturo.

A grim, colorful picture started forming in Vince's head. He hoped he was fucking wrong. "Are you talking about Arturo-fucking-Franconi? You want us to infiltrate the community and gain intelligence on one of the country's deadliest fucking mob heads? Why the hell do you think English would be safer going on the inside than anyone else?"

Agent Dennison stared him dead in the eye. "Because Miss Sparks happens to be his niece."

ABOUT THE AUTHOR

April Hunt blames her incurable chocolate addiction on growing up in rural Pennsylvania, way too close to America's chocolate capital, Hershey. She now lives in Virginia with her college sweetheart husband, two young children, and a cat who thinks she's a human-dog hybrid. On those rare occasions she's not donning the cape of her children's personal chauffeur, April's either planning, plotting, or writing about her next alpha hero and the woman he never knew he needed, but now can't live without.

You can learn more at:
AprilHuntBooks.com
Twitter @AprilHuntBooks
Facebook.com

Fall in Love with Forever Romance

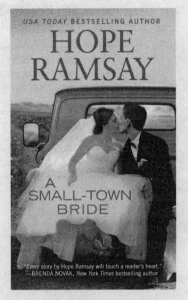

A SMALL-TOWN BRIDE
By Hope Ramsay

Amy Lyndon is tired of being "the poor little rich girl" of Shenandoah Falls. In her prominent family, she's the *ordinary* one—no Ivy League education and no powerful career. But when her father tries to marry her off, she finally has to stand up for herself, despite the consequences. Cut off from the family fortune, her first challenge is to find a job. And she's vowed to never rely on another man ever again, no matter how hot or how handsome.

Fall in Love with Forever Romance

HOLDING FIRE
By April Hunt

Alpha Security operative Trey Hanson is ready to settle down. When he meets a gorgeous blonde in a bar, and the connection between them is off the charts, he thinks he's finally found the one. But after their night together ends in a hail of gunfire and she disappears in the chaos, Trey's reasons for tracking her down are personal...until he learns she's his next assignment. Fans of Rebecca Zanetti and Julie Ann Walker will love the newest romantic suspense novel from April Hunt!

THE HIGHLAND DUKE
By Amy Jarecki

Fans of *Outlander* will love this sweeping Scottish epic from award-winning author Amy Jarecki. When Akira Ayres finds a brawny Scot with a musket ball in his thigh, the healer will do whatever it takes to save his life...even fleeing with him across the Highlands. Geordie knows if Akira discovers his true identity, both their lives will be jeopardized. The only way to protect the lass is to keep her by his side. But the longer he's with her, the harder it becomes to imagine letting her go...

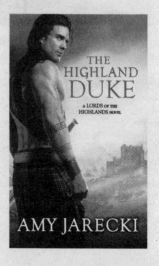

Fall in Love with Forever Romance

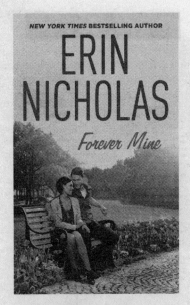

FOREVER MINE
By Erin Nicholas

The newest book in *New York Times* bestselling author Erin Nicholas's Opposites Attract series!

Maya Goodwin doesn't believe in holding back. Ever. As a cop, she never hesitated to throw herself into harm's way to save someone. As a doctor, Alex Nolan knows all too well that risks can have deadly consequences. So Maya—daring and spontaneous—is the exact opposite of who he's looking for. But he can't resist exploring their sizzling attraction, even though falling for Maya might just be way too hazardous for his heart.

mance

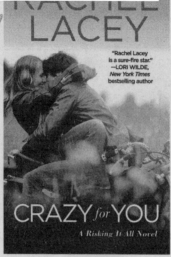

RACHEL
LACEY

"Rachel Lacey
is a sure-fire star."
—LORI WILDE,
New York Times
bestselling author

CRAZY *for* YOU

A Risking It All Novel

CRAZY FOR YOU
By Rachel Lacey

Emma Rush can't remember a time when she didn't have a thing for Ryan Blake. The small town's resident bad boy is just so freakin' hot—with tattoos, a motorcycle, and enough rough-around-the-edges sexiness to melt all her self-control. Now that Emma's over being a "good girl," she needs a little help being naughty...and Ryan is the perfect place to start.